Heartstrings
in
B-flat Minor

Heartstrings
in
B-flat Minor

SCOTT JOHNSON

HEARTSTRINGS IN B-FLAT MINOR

iUniverse books may be ordered through booksellers or by contacting:

iUniverse
1663 Liberty Drive
Bloomington, IN 47403
www.iuniverse.com
1-800-Authors (1-800-288-4677)

ISBN: 978-1-5320-2484-9 (sc)
ISBN: 978-1-5320-2486-3 (hc)
ISBN: 978-1-5320-2485-6 (e)

Library of Congress Control Number: 2017910498

Print information available on the last page.

iUniverse rev. date: 07/17/2017

JJ,
to this day, I turn around looking, and you're not there

Contents

Prologue

You think you know someone. It could be a sibling you've known since birth—yours or theirs—or the BFF would-be sibling you never had or anybody else. Take your pick; it really doesn't matter. Then think again.

Remember that a lost soul, deep down, retains the essence you thought you knew. So either love the person back from the ledge or protect yourself in a deadly clinch. Neither way comes easy.

Know that cautionary tales spring from life. Listen. Learn.

Chapter 1

MAKEUP IS US

An overwhelming presence of snow puts a hard edge to the Windy City where a lone CTA bus crawls south with caution on Sheridan past Belmont's dead traffic lights malfunctioning in the cold. Otherwise desolate, this major thoroughfare is devoid of morning rush hour traffic. Eerily, it's as though half the city's residents have called in sick to work—or at least half of those lucky enough to have jobs from which to be absent. Visible through the frost-encrusted windows of the southbound bus are the faint silhouettes of four passengers inside. One of them is a stylish black man in his midforties, Sterling Jackson, though for introductory purposes he prefers Dr. Sterling Jackson.

Sterling's fine suit and topcoat attest to the apparent heights he's reached from humble Cabrini-Green origins. Sometimes he still rides the bus since he has never mentally recovered from a childhood car accident and doesn't drive. Bound for Lincoln Park, Sterling is making his first foray from his spacious Lake Shore Drive condo since the blizzard hit. Tropical images of where he'd rather be are tempered by his having to wear insulated gloves inside the bus, thanks to a broken heater. Stuck here with numb toes, he is unimpressed that this ghost town of a city, the city that allegedly works, seems unable to do better than just cope with its present situation.

Shut down, he thinks. *How like my own circumstances.* Financial woes, as with the city, have Sterling edgy. The fact is, since adolescence, he often has worried about where his next buck will come from. Earning a living seemed like an insurmountable task. It still often does, notwithstanding all his apparent success. Expenses rise; clients come and go; prospecting never ends. How to start and restart, where and when? "Same old," he mutters, reflecting on the constant need for money.

Despite his well-hidden self-doubt, Sterling has managed over the years to earn a pretty healthy, if occasionally streaky, living, all on the edge of the law. When he has prospered, it mostly has been thanks to the kindness of ladies who became lovers and then investors of a sort, though not always in that order. No matter how brilliant or esteemed these ladies may have been in their daily walks of life, all have been plain suckers in Sterling's conniving eyes. He figures the need to find enough such suckers matches the monetary production pressures put upon any number of legitimate businesspeople.

Another day, turn another dollar, he mentally coaches himself, not forgetting for a second that he's down to one main meal ticket. *And that one's getting shaky.* Keeping those dollars trickling in is the goal behind Sterling's bus ride through an arctic twilight zone. He closes his eyes, shutting out from sight the surrounding snowpack. However, two annoying cell phone conversations from behind require that he bring on a full meditative state to block them from his consciousness. Through his self-hypnosis, even the mammoth vehicle's metallic grunts and frozen groans soon fade away.

Flashes of Jamaica cross his mind, taking him back willfully to where and when he first learned self-hypnosis. It was there and then he'd also learned stealthy techniques for hypnotizing others. The memories warm him against the layers of cold inside the unheated bus. "Those were the days," he recalls, smiling wanly behind closed eyes.

Farther down Sheridan, past Diversey in a tiny Lincoln Park condo with a bedroom view of the lake, a weary traveler has just returned home. Sheryl Taylor battles jet lag, unsuccessfully attempting sleep. A product of Chicago's white-bread North Shore, she moved to the city after college and has never looked back. City life has been more in keeping with her globe-trotting career and a need to be handy to either airport. A head-turning blonde, fortyish being the new thirty, Sheryl is only hours removed from having touched down at O'Hare—thankfully so, after having safely shepherded her tour group out of Tahrir Square's protest pandemonium.

"I'm a hero!" she laughs aloud to herself, yawning as daylight fights the blinds.

She feels a state of semisleep possibly coming on, and this experienced traveler believes the mind never really sleeps anyway, so at times like this, a person should make sure to rest the body. Meditatively secure now that she is back in her own familiar bed, Sheryl finds her restless mind returning to Frankfurt, where she connected to her homebound flight two days ago after a hair-raising flight out of Cairo.

Frankfurt, a bustling minimetropolis, is a major hub for European travelers that long has been the scene of carefree tours for Sheryl. It also was where as a young student at Goethe University she cut her teeth on travel and adventure. She had only one compressed summer semester there, but she fondly recalls diving headlong into life beyond the Midwest, deftly handling long days including studies in a language other than English.

In Frankfurt, she also discovered firsthand the thrill of mingling with foreign men so different from any she'd ever known, men far removed from her undeniably sheltered world. The mere sight of some of these young men, many of them dark-skinned students from favored backgrounds around the globe, like hers, flushed her fair face and fluttered her heart. "Those were the days," she recalls, wanly smiling, eyes closed.

Her innermost thoughts center on dearest Ilkin Kahn, of Istanbul. "If only we could have …" She fantasizes about overcoming the obstacle of being worlds apart. Abruptly flipping the off switch on Ilkin, Sheryl turns her concerns to the actual man in her life, hoping he's as anxious to see her as she is to see him. After wondering whether he's gotten her texts since she touched down at O'Hare, she briefly worries he might be in trouble, or in a hospital. But she quickly ditches such concerns given that she's been home only a matter of hours; there's no need to be so anxious over their reunion, even if absence may have made her heart grow fonder. "Quit acting like a schoolgirl," she lazily reminds herself, happy just to be alive. "Get some sleep. He'll pop up."

Nights in lockdown at the Egyptian hotel remain fresh in her head, easily pushing thoughts of any man to the periphery. There were enough close calls in Cairo to last anyone's lifetime. There were highs and lows and moods and fears beyond imagination, yet it wasn't even her first wild experience in Cairo. She is determined it will be her last. *No more Egypt! And there might be some others added to that list too.*

Maybe survival comes with a warning. It's gotten too crazy everywhere to remain active in the international field, she decides. Perhaps it's time to step behind the scenes, take up that desk the boss has offered. She can do local tours on the side—live at a slower pace and not out of a suitcase, at least for a while. "I have to sort all this out," she pledges. She also desperately needs to turn around shaky personal finances that didn't autocorrect while she was in Egypt. Rolling over to count sheep, she mutters, "I can never get ahead."

∽❧∽

Outside, blocks away on the incoming bus, Sterling remains transfixed on his bouncing seat. Mentally, he's way beyond Jamaica by now, having drifted back to even earlier times right here in Chicagoland—which, despite current evidence to the contrary, does have its share of warm sunny days. He's basking in such days now, north-suburban days, when he and the target of today's unannounced visit-to-come first met. *Life was so much easier then*, he tells himself. *Anyone would agree.*

Today's target is Sheryl. Despite Sterling's need to spin her more yarns about continued court delays in lawsuits against his beleaguered but promising company, in which she has money, he can't help but admire how she must have trooped through this most harrowing expedition of her touring career. She's been all over the news the last few hours, with testimonials pouring in from tourists she helped survive and escape Cairo. *I'll play it worshipful*, he decides, strategizing.

∽❧∽

For her part, Sheryl, were she not counting sheep, also easily could be reliving those long-ago early days with Sterling. Occasionally, during bouts of insomnia, her thoughts do slip way back to those very days. Such thoughts always trigger others, including musings over all the what-could-have-beens and sighs over the ones that got away during all these years tied up with, and invested in, Sterling. Other memories too painful to entertain right now fight for attention, but she staves off tears and pushes them aside. "It has to work in the end, Lord, but soon," she prays randomly but fervently.

Counting sheep isn't working, as expected. Insomnia takes hold, and her thoughts drift to how she and Sterling met. "My God, Y2K seems like a lifetime ago." Back then, having just done her junior collegiate year abroad, Sheryl had a lifetime of hope ahead of her.

∽❧∽

Looking for a little pocket money and a chance to flesh out her résumé, Sheryl has taken a summer job at a packaging plant not far from her suburban home. A pampered North Shore girl, she finds the factory's whir of machinery quaint. Overwhelmingly naive she is, especially for someone who already has traveled widely.

Makeup Is Us has an employee roster top-heavy with females, especially during peak production in the summer season, with inventories to build for the approaching holidays. Hence, every summer, the cosmetics company's plant teems with young coeds working through school breaks. A few lucky college guys who have stumbled upon the idea also work there, surrounded by young women.

One rainy day after work, Sheryl makes for the company's parking lot under cover of an umbrella. Crossing the street near a bus stop, she spots one of those lucky college guys just missing a bus. At this point to her, he's just a familiar face around the plant. He ducks into the bus stop shelter, becoming its sole occupant. Sheryl reaches the bus stop and leans inside. "Need a ride?"

"Hey," he responds, seemingly caught off guard. "That's tempting, but I can't impose. Thanks for the offer, though. Very cool."

"What's your hang-up with my offer?"

"It'd be a long ride. I couldn't put you out like that."

"You've already said that. Try something new. I'll give you one last chance." She smiles. "Want a ride?"

He looks for a bus coming in the rain and sees none. "Guess I'd be a fool to turn down that offer."

Lightning cracks nearby, and thunder rumbles in the distance. The rain picks up its intensity. Sheryl grabs the young man by the forearm and pulls him under her umbrella. "Let's get to the car! This umbrella has a steel shaft!"

They run to the lot, splashing all the way to Sheryl's vintage Renault Dauphine. She opens the front passenger door for her coworker, shielding him with the umbrella as he gets inside. By the time she's dashed around to the driver's door, he's figured out how to unlock the foreign contraption. She jumps into the tiny interior as another bolt of lightning strikes.

"Holy moly," she yells, "that was too close for comfort!"

He laughs. "Yeah, but where'd you come up with this car?"

"You like it? Let's just say I'm grateful for the transportation—and that it's a long story." She starts the balky engine. It sounds like an eggbeater. "Which way?" she asks.

"Take a left out of the lot."

She throws the stick into first and heads for the street entrance. The eggbeater revs as she sloppily shifts into second to pull out into traffic. Then it really winds up as she times her shift into third to just get them through an intersection on the yellow. At forty-five miles per hour, the engine sounds pushed to its limits.

"What about hitting fourth gear, girl?"

"It only has three—this is as good as it gets!"

"You're kidding. They allow this on the roads?"

"No restrictions," she intones with a chuckle.

They putter along through a railroad underpass with water splashing as high as the roof. A bus passing in the opposite direction throws up a wall of water for them to pierce. Water forces its way past Sheryl's vent window, which she cracked open earlier to help the defroster clear the interior's humidity. Everything is wet, including them.

"Man," says her passenger, showing genuine signs of nervousness. "I might've been wiser to wait for the damn bus."

"What're you so nervous about?"

He hesitates before answering. "I was in a bad wreck as a kid. My parents were killed. The other driver too. And it was all Dad's fault. I watched as the whole thing developed. So I'm not only a bad passenger, but I have no desire to ever drive, either."

Sheryl takes her eyes off the road, locking them for a moment with her passenger's. "I'm so sorry," she says with empathy that makes him flush. "You poor thing."

"Hey, I'm not complaining," he says. "Just is what it is."

Sheryl refocuses on traffic and the treacherous conditions.

"But thanks," he adds.

She senses his embarrassment and keeps looking down the road. "Well, anyway … I can understand how my driving might make you nervous. Sometimes it makes me nervous. From now on, I'll be keeping my hands at ten and two and my eyes dead-ahead where they belong."

"Sounds good by me."

It dawns on her that they still don't know each other's names. "So I'm Sheryl. Sheryl Taylor."

"Sterling, Sterling Jackson. Where do you call home?"

"Hubbard Woods. I'm back with my folks for the summer."

"Oh, I see—Hubbard Woods. How nice for y'all. I suppose you went to New Trier."

"Good guess, but wrong—try Shoreline Country Day School."

"Of course," he chuckles. "I should've known."

"It's not so hoity-toity as you'd think."

"Sure … right."

"Well," she laughs in acquiescence, "at least in our minds it wasn't, sort of—but of course, we all were rebels in our own minds, like kids anywhere. What did we know?"

"Makes sense," he agrees.

"Where'd you graduate?"

"Ever hear of Cermak High?"

"Sounds kind of vaguely familiar, I think."

"Let's just say it's no country day school. They sometimes serve bullets with lunch."

"How educational for you, I'm sure," she deadpans, not knowing what else to say. The Edens Expressway entrance ramp looms ahead.

"Do you take this thing on expressways?" he asks.

"It'll take us wherever we need to go," she assures him.

"Then let's go for it, I guess," he says not so assuredly.

Sheryl floors it as they head down the ramp toward already-building rush-hour traffic. The little engine winds up, and sweat beads up on Sterling's forehead as they watch for an opening into the highway's flow. A spot magically does materialize between two semitrailer trucks. She guides the Renault into the leading semi's slipstream, essentially drafting behind it. Sterling's white-knuckle posture betrays his apparent fear, and he exhales in relief.

"Nothing to it," she beams from behind the wheel. "Where next?"

Sterling turns around for a peek at the semi bearing down on them. Not exactly enjoying the view or the ride, he answers, "Armitage and Western, more or less. I'm staying with my cousins for the summer in a two-flat my uncle owns."

She smiles. "One big happy family!"

"Ah, yeah, that's us. Especially with my sister and her kid living in the other flat."

"How nice!"

"If you say so."

At the Kennedy Expressway junction, traffic grinds to a halt. The reversible lanes flow north this time of day, offering no help. There's no choice but to gut out the bumper-to-bumper madness that creeps into all commuters' heads. They inch along herky-jerky in first gear.

Sterling snipes, "This is more your car's speed."

"Very funny."

The skies open up more than ever, spitting little balls of hail that ricochet off the Renault like a barrage of pebbles against a Quonset hut. Water begins to leak through Sterling's door seals. Despite being a bundle of exposed raw nerves, he can't help but laugh.

He teases, "I didn't know there was a wrong side of the tracks in Hubbard Woods, but that has to be the answer for this car being in your possession!"

"You can start walking anytime, big shot."

The downpour continues. "Any other day, I just might've done that."

Bogged-down traffic provides plenty of chitchat time for them to get to know each other. Finally, nearing Addison, a reason for the jam, additional to the rain, becomes apparent. Up ahead, a wrecked car is blocking the two right lanes, and a tow truck is maneuvering to hook it. Traffic funnels down even more to one lane on the left shoulder.

Sheryl gripes, "Every time I come down this way, there's some wreck or other."

Sterling counters, "Every time I come down this way, I'm heading home."

She blushes with embarrassment. "Hey, you know I didn't mean anything by that."

"Of course not," Sterling sarcastically replies.

They see a parked squad car on the opposite shoulder, rooftop lights flashing. A cop at the wheel is dealing with the wreck's troubled driver, who sits in the backseat, head bowed. All commuters creep along even slower now around the wreck site, single-file. Finally, the Renault reaches the other side of the accident. Sheryl directs her attention down the road, letting the clutch slip while shifting less than smoothly. Lanes open up quickly to normal, and she hits the gas.

Sterling looks faint. "Lord, save us," he prays aloud.

Once they are past the mess, it's relatively clear sailing, except for the relentless deluge still pounding the car. Sheryl is glad that they're past the accident but anxious to leave the expressway. They continue along with the pace of traffic to Armitage, finally exiting and turning west toward Western.

Sheryl thinks the aging retail, residential, and industrial mix looks as foreign as anyplace abroad. She's never been here before, and being in a French car only heightens her sense of being on an imaginary foreign adventure somewhere. Unrelenting rain accentuates the oddness of her afternoon and how it has strayed from usual routines. She normally would have long since been home by now. For sure, she'll have to cook up a story for her mom and dad whenever she does get home. With all the heavy storm activity, Sheryl realizes that her mom even could be worrying right now.

"We're getting close," Sterling warns, interrupting her trance.

She snaps to attention. "Oh, great!"

"Yeah, we're almost there—a couple more blocks. Look for Oakley and take a left."

Minutes later, they're double-parked in front of a run-down two-flat in a neighborhood showing early signs of revival.

"Not exactly Hubbard Woods, eh?" says Sterling.

Sheryl gives him a cheery smile. "What's the difference? Home is where the heart is, right?"

"You're good, girl. Never at a loss for words."

"Hey, I mean it. We're all at home in God's kingdom, anyway; that's how I look at it."

"You've hit the nail on the head."

Sheryl feels instantly flushed, paranoid over having brought religious metaphors into the conversation so early in their friendship.

But Sterling continues the line of conversation. "So ... about that God's kingdom stuff, I mean ... that's how I've always felt too."

"Really?"

"Really. But I was too shy ever to mention God stuff to anyone before."

"You, shy? Come on now. I'm not that naive."

Unflinchingly, he looks into her blue-gray eyes, and with a fortuitous rumble of biblical-style thunder in the background, he says softly, "Honestly, that's how I feel. We're all in this together, under God's direction, if only we will listen. If we don't listen, well, that's trouble."

"That's sweet, Sterling. How nice to meet a man who's not embarrassed to say so."

"The pleasure is all mine, girl. Anyway, Sheryl, I can't believe you've hauled me all this way home. Otherwise, I'd still be on the train, hoping to be on time to catch my next bus."

"Well," laughs Sheryl, "we couldn't have had all that, right?"

"That's for sure. With all this rain, who knows when I might've gotten home? Meeting you has been a real blessing," he says sincerely.

"Let's call it a dual blessing, for both of us." With her mind on getting home and an eye on the mirror for any car coming up, Sheryl adds, "I'll be seeing you around the plant then, Sterling."

"That'll be nice, Sheryl."

A neighbor's car approaches in search of parking.

With one foot outside, Sterling asks, "Are you clear on how to get home from here?"

"No problem. I'll just retrace my tracks. Nice to have met you."

"Same here. Drive careful," he advises, exiting to the leafy cover of an old oak tree.

Sheryl waves and then lurches forward in first, fantasizing about introducing her family to Sterling someday. Images from *Guess Who's Coming to Dinner* flash through her mind. She laughs aloud to the pounding wipers' beat. What a good time she's been having. However, by Western and Armitage, rush hour in the rain brings her back to her senses: standstill.

Chapter 2

UNCLE AUSTIN

Weeks pass at work with Sheryl and Sterling crossing paths only as called for in the course of their jobs. Makeup Is Us romances are discouraged to little avail, but for the sake of propriety, they don't act overly familiar. However, the titillating excitement factor of their secret friendship is undeniable, and it helps them pass the days. Unbeknownst to Sheryl, though, Sterling has similar games going, at different stages of play, with a number of her seasonal coworkers.

One Friday in the teeming lunchroom, they find themselves eating together at a table alone. While exchanging opening pleasantries, each casually scans for potential eavesdroppers. Thanks to clanking dishes in the cafeteria line and the general racket of the crowd, they feel detached amid it all, on their own little island. Dylan serenades them, piped in over speakers.

Sterling offers, "Hard to believe summer's already half over. After our little drive through the monsoon, I'd have thought we might've spent more time together by now."

"Same here—how's your summer going outside of this place?"

"Not bad. How about you?"

"I've been busy, but lately I'm getting nervous about returning to school."

"Why? It's not like you'll be a freshman and a stranger in a strange land."

"Ah, but you're wrong, sort of. I'm no freshman, true, but I just did my junior year in Frankfort, and I feel like I'll be starting all over—like a stranger in a strange land."

"Hey, you didn't tell me about doing last year abroad. That must've been wild."

"I don't know about wild, but it was the experience of my lifetime, for sure. Now, though, it already seems like ages ago and like I'm back to square one."

An air horn sounds to mark the end of lunch. Time to go back to work. Sterling gripes, "Damn, who can eat that fast?"

As they slowly gather up their garbage, Sterling suggests, "Listen, I have an errand to run in Evanston tomorrow. I'm taking the L and will be done around two. Want to meet up when I'm done and hang out awhile?"

"Sure," she quickly confirms. "Sounds cool."

The next day, the two meet at Fountain Square in downtown Evanston. It is a bright and sunny afternoon, and they walk the lakefront at Dawes Park before retrieving Sheryl's Renault to wander northward through Northwestern's campus to historic Grosse Point Lighthouse. Finally, they end up at the awe-inspiring Baha'i Temple overlooking Wilmette Harbor.

Following a pathway dotted with tourists around the nine-sided temple, one of only seven such temples around the world, they drop out of the crowd at a bench overlooking a reflecting pool. Surrounding them is one of nine replicating gardens that fan out from the temple's nine identical wall faces. The westernmost wall hints of pink in the late-afternoon sun angle.

"Isn't this gorgeous?" Sheryl chirps with enthusiasm.

"Unreal. I had no idea this place existed."

"We call it the Orange Squeezer."

"I can see it. But it's like a postcard from the Middle East. Have you been inside?"

"Yes, and it's as beautiful inside as it is outside. You'd be hard-pressed to find anything comparable, anywhere."

"Do they have tours?"

"Of course—and a full gift shop too."

"Is the temple open to outsiders for worship?"

"Yes, again, and they also give introductory talks on Sundays. It'd be worth your while to check it out. I'll come back with you tomorrow, if you want."

"My, you really are a fount of knowledge—a tour guide in the making!"

"You're getting to know me already."

What Sterling, young con artist on the rise from the projects, already is getting to know is that Sheryl seems to have an interest in religion on top of her drive for academic and career achievements. Basking in the sun, he thanks God for his having hit such a mother lode of potential with her as a possible mark. He can't help but excitedly think of the numerous times Uncle Austin, his mentor and a career confidence man, has stressed the value of preying upon highly religious women.

"It's their unsuspecting nature," Austin has often preached, "and an unnatural desire to turn around troubled souls that make for perfect conditions of gullibility." This combination of traits, according to Austin, makes it easy to get a foot in the door and earn their trust while also making it easy to regain them to your side if true motives are discovered: a win-win, Sterling concludes. It was also Austin's suggestion that Sterling take the Makeup Is Us summer gig, for which Austin pulled strings to get his protégé the job.

I'll be eternally grateful, Sterling silently pledges to the absent Uncle Austin. Austin's overall idea sees the packaging plant as a perfect recruiting site for future marks for his enterprising nephew. There he can line them up, some short-term, some for the long haul, still others as possible time-release reconnection projects in the future. At this stage with Sheryl, she could be any one of the three, or nothing, but signs are promising. It's all about prospecting.

Returning to the moment, Sterling asks, "How do you feel about some of the various religions of the world, like the Baha'i faith?"

"All legitimate faiths that have their basis in God and His goodness are wonderful. Essentially, they all stress the advancement of His most basic principle, the Golden Rule."

Sterling nods in apparent admiration. "That's easy to absorb." Momentarily, he forgets that this discussion started out as a tactic of his. Looking at Sheryl in the bright sunlight at this magnificent temple of worship, he's overcome with an unfamiliar rush of holy thoughts and admiration, all for her. He fears becoming diverted from his game plan. "I hope you don't mind if I say you look beautiful here, inside and out."

Sheryl flushes. "Say away."

He strikes out on a follow-up remark, taken aback by his romantic feelings for Sheryl.

"Care to step into my Father's temple?" she asks him.

"Of course." He melts, and thinking Lord knows what, Sterling reaches for her hand. She takes it. He's surprised at his racing heartbeat as they ascend the temple stairs. *Man, there's something different about how I feel for this mark*, he thinks as he opens the door for her. He's recognizing conflicting romantic emotions he was warned of while being tutored on how to fleece unsuspecting, moneyed, young north-suburban women. *Uncle Austin would not be pleased*, he thinks.

Way across Chicagoland, a black Sedan DeVille pulls up to park in front of the Bucktown two-flat on Oakley. Its lone occupant is the driver, Austin Jones, a tall black man in his early fifties who still thinks of himself as the all-American hotshot basketball player he once was. A slight hitch in his gait betrays a long-ago injury that sent him to the bench for good, no degree in hand. He goes to the lower flat entrance and lets himself inside with his own key.

Austin takes over the dining room table playing solitaire. Through partially drawn drapery, he spots some French tin can of a car slowing to double-park in front of his property. With one eye on his cards and the other outside, he sees his nephew, Sterling, embrace a blonde woman at the wheel and hop outside full of energy. As the pair talk through the open window, Austin observes that the blonde is young and beautiful.

"That's my boy," Austin beams to the empty room as the car pulls away.

The front door opens, and Sterling walks in smiling. "Hey, Uncle Austin. I see you got the Caddy all cleaned up. Big deal going on tonight?"

"Could be. You know me—always something going on. What about you, nephew? Who's the mark in the tin can out there?"

Sterling laughs at the car reference. "Yeah, that car's a piece of work, huh? You should take a ride in it, for laughs."

Austin chuckles. "Not for laughs or money would you ever find me in such a thing. I sure hope the path that plunked you into its seat is paved with gold."

"Is Hubbard Woods gold enough?"

Austin bestows a look of approval on his favorite nephew. "Yes, that sounds plenty fine enough to me. Is she a summer job acquaintance?"

"Absolutely, but I'm thinking of her as kind of a future draft choice. There are a couple others ahead of her in the priming process."

"Well, that may be all well and good, but you make sure to touch her up this summer for some small sum—understand me? Just to set precedent for those future plans you mention. Plant a seed. You can't let these sorts of things go to chance."

"I hear you, Uncle."

"You know what I'm talking about—gotta set the hook. Then you play the line a little."

"Makes perfect sense. Don't worry, I'll do it."

"That's the spirit. I'm keepin' the faith." Austin lays down a few cards, thinking something seems different about the way his nephew is talking about this girl, like maybe he's holding back on something about Hubbard Woods gold. "Have a seat, son," he suggests.

Sterling takes a seat at the table.

Austin looks up from his cards and drills him with a stare that's honed and confident from having looked down its share of gun barrels. "You wouldn't be holding back on me about that blonde now, would you, boy?"

"Holding back? Like what, Uncle? She's just another mark in the making. Don't forget—it's you who's always taught me to evaluate my marks like cards in my hands and to play them out according to their merits. That's all I'm doing."

"Don't be talking like no teacher's pet to me, Sterling. If there's something else about her, like you think you've found true romance with her or some such nonsense, spit it out."

"Hey, she's a doll, I'll admit, totally undeserving of being conned like she's gonna be. But you have to understand just how right you were about that plant job being a breeding ground of golden suburban marks for me. Hell, it's all I can do to juggle them without everyone starting to compare notes."

Austin grins and shakes his head in approval. "I always knew you had it in you, Sterling. Too bad I can't say the same about my own pitiful spawn. That sister of mine had twice the spunk of your aunt Esther."

"Thanks, Uncle."

Austin's face saddens. "I still get choked up thinking about that fool father of yours and how he wasted the both of them there in the streets—nearly taking you with them." Austin lays down his cards and wipes away a tear. "Losing a sibling, boy—that's something you never really get over. You worry about your kids night and day, but somehow you never stop to worry about your own brothers and sisters. I've lost three and can't believe it to this day."

Sterling hates it when his hero gets all soft like this, something Austin does only in front of him. Although Sterling is grateful for the closeness this signals, he can't stand the urge it engenders within him to cry too. His eyes well up, but he fights off tears just at the brink. Talking, he figures, will help stem the flow. "Uncle, I wish I could've known them better, all of them—my parents, my aunties, and my other uncle. Thank God you were there to catch me."

"Amen, and I remain here for you today, son." Austin breathes deeply, picks up his cards, and resumes playing as though there were no emotional break. In a strong voice he assures his nephew, "That's what family's all about, Sterling. Now, where are those two boys of mine this fine Saturday?"

"I wish I knew, Uncle. They don't check in with me."

Chapter 3

No Rest for the Weary

In the present day, the frigid bus still creaks along Sheridan through overwhelming cold and snow. Sterling opens his eyes. Echoes of talks with Uncle Austin warm him even as the sight of the surrounding snowpack returns. The annoying cell conversations also return behind him.

Even still, Sterling's concentration is strong as he thinks of his cousins, now long dead from street violence, and of their pop, Uncle Austin, who finally ran out of luck with a stroke. The idea of being the last of the line hits Sterling. He wonders why he's never thought of that. *More pressure*, he thinks with an inward laugh, *just what I need*.

The southbound bus abruptly halts. Bitter surroundings fully bring him back to reality, priority one being money troubles that plague him like tinnitus. Yet worse for the moment, the driver reports a transmission problem. Exasperated, the wheelman claims another bus is en route to pick up everyone and take them along their way.

"Wonderful," grumbles Sterling.

Allegedly, the replacement will arrive soon and hopefully with a working heater, says the driver.

"Sure—don't bet on that!" exclaims a guy in back.

The other passengers groan similar expressions of irritation with the CTA. Sterling weighs his options, which include getting off the bus and hoofing it a few blocks. Normally, that would be his no-brainer solution. However, howling wind gusts and swirling snow offer good arguments for staying inside the freezing bus. At least it breaks the wind.

What am I doing here? wonders Sterling, as anyone would on a day like this. He silently curses Uncle Austin for having led him into a life of crime. Mulling over a career of shady escapades, Sterling inaudibly declares, "Sometimes, I wish good old Uncle Austin had steered me into a different line of work, something to count on—with benefits and a salary."

Then again, he misses Uncle Austin so much now that he's dead and gone. *And if anybody could have helped with my current headaches, it would have been him … Well, maybe, maybe not. These aren't exactly ordinary, garden-variety troubles. And the recession hasn't helped any, either.*

A possible path to Sterling's salvation is Sheryl, now just several long city blocks away. She's come through before when least expected. He hopes for the best once again. Getting antsy, he considers walking. But the bus rocks on its suspension in wind gusts convincing enough for him to vote yes to waiting for the rescue bus. Sterling tries to relax as Uncle Austin always preached. *Anyway,* he figures, *she's a zombie stew right about now due to jet lag.* But that is not a bad thing for his purposes. It is just as he would want it, just as he has planned.

Sheryl sits at a folding table in her building's laundry room, no makeup, sorting through accumulated mail as three washers whir with her loads. She's thinking how lucky she is to have gotten in five hours of uninterrupted sleep on the plane. An ability to sleep on planes has been a saving grace throughout her career, although after all she went through in Cairo and now with everything that's pending back home, it's a wonder she slept at all.

Somehow, for the moment, Sheryl finds laundry-room noises more relaxing than the quiet stillness of her own apartment. It's a trade-off, with sad vibes of solitude seeming eternal upstairs versus facing up to tasks at hand down in the dungeon. Doing something productive has her blood pumping at least. Besides, she couldn't find anything to wear. "Have to face that laundry challenge," she said earlier, finally succumbing despite a low energy level.

Laundry, though, is not her sole challenge. Far tougher crises remain to be solved, all financial in nature. She can't help thinking of how not so long ago her condo was paid off, and she had money in the bank, owned a healthy IRA, and was totally debt-free. Not so anymore. Staying put in the laundry room allows her to multitask, sifting through piles of mail without zipping up and down the elevator to push along her laundry. As feared, the pile of mail reveals bill after bill, dunning notice upon dunning notice. Nearly every envelope opened details something from her desperate state of financial affairs. "There will be a solution, right?" she whispers. All she can do is hope and pray.

However, if Sterling doesn't come up with most of what he owes her soon, she worries about becoming a street person by spring. She stares ahead blankly, dropping another overdue credit card statement onto the folding table. Sheryl tries pinpointing the exact root of her troubles, the perhaps benign start of it all. "When was it?" She strains her brain, on the brink of breaking down from exhaustion and stress. "How did this all begin, Lord?" The question "how?" echoes over and over again in her skull.

No relief. Her headache is building. Self-interrogation triggers memories of the summer at the Makeup Is Us plant, her one and only blue-collar experience. "Happier days they were," she recalls, glorifying the boring job and exciting summer fling that came with it. "Very happy, right?" She sighs. "Weren't they? Or was I fooling myself with Sterling from the start?" More sighs.

Maybe not for the first time, she sees the pivotal day that ultimately led to her pile of bills on the folding table; it was toward that particular summer's end. She recalls the events like a grainy movie projected on the backside of her forehead.

Sheryl observes Sterling jogging across the parking lot to catch up with her after work. He has missed his bus and needs a ride to the Edison Park train station. It's not particularly out of the way for Sheryl, so no problem. Driving along, they make small talk about going back to their respective schools soon.

At the station, Sheryl senses that Sterling has more substantive things to say. "Something on your mind?" she asks once parked at the curb.

Seeming embarrassed, he replies, "There is. But it's kind of hard to talk about."

"What's wrong?" she asks, full of concern.

"It's one of my cousins. He was arrested last night. Naturally, if my uncle finds out, there will be big trouble—and my cousin already deals with nothing but trouble in his life every day."

"Sorry to hear. What happened?"

"He got busted for pot while hanging out with some chumps, a bunch of fools. What's worse is he's got his girlfriend in a family way. My uncle would slap him silly if he knew."

Sheryl's brow furrows with alarm over issues she has little experience with, personally or within her circle of friends. She imagines that a cold jail cell is trouble enough for anyone. The unwanted pregnancy presents an even colder thought because of cold solutions now widely available. "Aside from being empathetic, what are you supposed to do?" she asks.

"Don't know. Gotta get him out on bail first. Not an easy chore since I just paid out my summer earnings on tuition and room and board. This couldn't have come at a worse time."

"Any relatives you can turn to in confidence?"

"Can't turn to my aunt in confidence on anything. She's a junkie, sorry to say."

"Sorry to hear, Sterling. What can I do to help?"

"I can't ask for what's needed, Sheryl, because it boils down to money. And I follow Shakespeare's advice: 'neither a borrower nor a lender be.' I have to find a solution on my own."

"Admirable, but how much would it take to bail out your cousin?"

Sterling hangs his head in apparent shame. "If it weren't for this fix I'm in, believe me, I wouldn't even be having this conversation with you. But … it'll take five hundred dollars to get him out of jail. I really only need two hundred, though, since his brother has coughed up three hundred."

"I can handle that, Sterling," Sheryl says with compassion. "No problem, honestly—and no need to pay me back until you are able to without a strain."

"Wow, Sheryl … I … I can't thank you enough."

"No need to say anything. I'm happy to help." She retrieves her checkbook from her purse. "How should I make it out?"

"Cash would be best. Cops don't take third-party checks. I'll find a currency exchange."

As she starts writing the check, Sterling clears his throat. "Um, Sheryl, this next part is really hard, but as long as I've crossed the line, could I ask another favor?"

"I guess so," she tentatively counters. "Why not?"

"Well, this'll cross some boundaries with you. But I'm asking for my cousin, not me."

On guard and getting the picture, she asks, "And just how can I additionally help him?"

"Well, as I said, he got his girlfriend in a family way, and aside from them not wanting their parents to know, there's the fact that having a baby now pretty much would mess up any chance for either one of them to have any kind of future."

Sheryl stops with the check. Sterling sees her disgust.

Quickly, he backtracks. "I knew that'd be one step too far, Sheryl—and believe me, I fully understand. Please, forget I asked, really."

"That's kind of hard to do, Sterling. You asked—you, a future doctor, talking about taking a life, like there's nothing to it."

"Uh, well, we're talking about an embryo, Sheryl. Who's to say it would go full-term anyway, with my cousin's girlfriend not having any money for prenatal care?"

Sheryl puts down her checkbook, fully disgusted. "This new direction of our conversation has me feeling very uncomfortable, Sterling."

"Like I said, I understand. Seriously, please forget the whole thing. I'm disgusted with myself for having asked. Just was feeling family pressure for my cuz."

"I don't mind helping with bail—really, Sterling—but I can't be a party to abortion."

"I'm backed up against a wall. My cousins are like brothers to me. We have each others' backs; we're family. Nobody asked me. I just thought I'd run it past you."

A downtown train arrives and leaves without Sterling as he remains in the Dauphine. Sheryl watches the train disappear and wishes she were somewhere else. Then she mulls the situation over as Sterling hangs his head in apparent humiliation.

Taking a deep breath and exhaling slowly, she regains control of her emotions. "Just for the sake of discussion, what's the going rate for such a disgusting deed?"

Sterling mutters, "Three hundred dollars."

"Three hundred?" she repeats with a blend of surprise and revulsion. Sadly, she snaps, "Only three hundred dollars to snuff out a life before it barely even begins?"

Sterling nods.

Sheryl gazes outside at passersby, thinking of how they'd all started out as embryos, every one. *Whether wanted or not*, her psyche declares. Abruptly, she hears herself say, "All right, Sterling, I'll tell you what—let's say the full five hundred dollars to cover bail comes from me. Then you guys take that three hundred your other cousin has for his brother and put it to whatever sordid use is needed." She clams up as quickly as she made the offer.

Sterling stutters, "Sheryl … I, uh …"

But she raises a hand to silence him and then quickly writes the check to cash for $500. She tears it from her checkbook and hands it over to Sterling. "I think you'd better get on your way now, Sterling."

Opening the door, he says, "Sheryl, I feel horrible about this whole deal. But thank you. I can't believe I hit you up for something like this—all on my cousin's account."

"For me, he's nowhere to be seen, Sterling. This one is on you. Take responsibility for your own actions before trying to lay the blame on somebody else. I have to go."

Sheryl pulls away fast and just as quickly releases an endless stream of tears. She can't see where she's going and wipes madly at her eyes with her stick-shift hand, as the eggbeater engine winds up noisily, nearing the redline for second gear. Sobs escalate, but then she slowly gains control of the tears. Finally, she remembers to hit third gear. "Get me out of here" is all she can think. She knows she needs to pull herself together for her expected arrival back home.

The memories are strong for Sheryl still as she sits at her laundry room's folding table, mail strewn about, eyes locked in a blank stare across the noisy room. Sadly, she sighs at memory lane's flashback. She begins to hyperventilate, her head moving in unison with her breathing pattern. Silently, she cries out, *Oh, Lord, was that really the beginning of the end for me? A party to a crime in heaven all those years ago?*

Therapeutically, she sways her body to the same beat as her breathing. Somebody walks past the open door, which catches the corner of Sheryl's eye. She worries that someone peeked into the laundry room, and she can only pray that her seat at the table, in a ninety-degree angle to the door, shielded her frantic state of mind from the unknown witness. However, the pull of paranoia is strong, and she doubts she went unnoticed. Either way, the close call snaps her out of her trancelike condition. *For now, anyway*, she cynically thinks. *I really do need some sleep.*

A bell rings on one of her washers, announcing completion of the final spin cycle. Sheryl sees that her other two wash machines also are motionless. She moves most of the wet laundry to a couple large dryers, sorting out a few delicate things to hang-dry upstairs in her apartment.

"That'll make it look real third-world," she jokes with herself. Her living conditions back home seem substandard in comparison to the luxury hotels with full service on the road.

As she returns to the table to wait out the dryers, her mind jumps all over the globe, back and forth in time and space. Good times, bad times, all left behind to the past. Yet there's no escaping the fact that lately she often has been returning home to overwhelmingly bleak personal circumstances. Her tiny but beloved apartment has become a refuge.

Somewhat maniacally, she chuckles, "Nothing like home sweet home."

Chapter 4

LOOK OUT BELOW!

Snow still swirls along Sheridan Road, though in a more gentle dusting pattern since the wind off Lake Michigan has decelerated from howling to tolerable gusts. The replacement bus stops at Diversey, and Sterling and the other three passengers board it. From outside, they remain barely visible behind frosted-over windows, this being another cold, creaking public shuttle.

When the doors open at his stop, Sterling steps down to the crusted sidewalks. Shivering at a "Don't Walk" signal, he watches the remaining passengers get hauled deeper into Lincoln Park. Then he jaywalks across a deserted Sheridan Road before the next green light appears.

At Sheryl's condominium building, Sterling enters the foyer in his snow-covered topcoat. Donald, the doorman, waves hello from his seat on the other side of the lobby doors. Sterling smiles in appreciation of the recognition as he brushes snow from his coat and vigorously stomps his shoes to clear them of the white stuff. Once he's done, Donald buzzes him into the tastefully decorated lobby.

"Well, hello, Dr. Jackson," Donald greets him. "How do you like this weather, sir?"

Sterling opens his topcoat and silk scarf to better show off his fine suit. "Are you kidding, Donald? This winter stuff gets tougher to handle each and every year. I swear, next year, it's off to Miami for me. How about you—you like this stuff?"

Donald rises to his feet in deference to Dr. Jackson. "Oh, really, I don't mind it so much anymore."

"Oh really?" kids Sterling.

"Well, sitting inside here where it's nice and toasty—instead of being out walking that old beat in all kinds of weather—it really isn't so bad, you know what I mean?"

"I do."

"Heck, I've seen worse than this anyway."

"And when would that have been?"

Donald thinks it over and chuckles. "Well, now that you put it to me, I can't really say."

"That's what I thought," kids Sterling. "Anyway, is Ms. Taylor in the house?"

"Yes. In fact, I think she might still be in the laundry room. If you want to check it out, go right ahead."

"Thanks, Donald. You're a real mensch, my man."

Donald chuckles. "Well, thank you, sir. I could say the same for you. And that laundry room should be just the place to warm you right up."

"That's what I need all right, Donald. Take care."

"You too, Dr. Jackson."

Sterling smiles gratuitously, and the doorman retakes his seat.

Sterling turns on his heel, his frozen-stiff shoes clicking on the shiny faux marble floor as he crosses the lobby. Reaching a hallway, he enters a narrow corridor that ultimately leads to the building's garbage room and outside back door. But first, at an open doorway, he finds Sheryl with her back to the door, folding laundry. A granny's grocery pull cart stands half-stuffed with folded clothes.

As though she has eyes in the back of her head to spot an intruder, Sheryl spins around to identify the figure in the doorway. She breaks into tears at the sight of Sterling. He wastes no time in rushing to her side.

"Oh, baby," he says, taking her in his arms. "What's the matter, dear?"

"A lot is the matter, dear."

"We'll figure it out. Allow yourself to decompress. You've been through a lot."

Still in his arms, Sheryl self-consciously pulls at her tangled hair. "I must look wild and ancient," she suggests.

"You look wonderful, as always—anytime, anyplace, year in, year out."

"Right, if you say so. I'm so mindless from lack of sleep, I'll believe anything."

He strokes her hair smooth and kisses her. She kisses him back. Soon, he pauses kissing to speak. "That must have been some experience for you, all that insanity on the streets."

"I'll never go back, that's for sure, not to Cairo."

"You deserve combat pay."

Suddenly angry, she pushes him away. "Isn't that just like you? Always money on your mind! And it's usually my money you're thinking about."

"What are you talking about? I was joking."

"That may be, but I can't help it if it triggered things that aren't so funny to me. Thanks to you," she says, picking up some bills and sticking them in his face, "I'm ruined, bankrupt!"

"Come on, you can't be serious. Who else takes care of you like me?"

"You've got to be kidding me, Sterling!"

"You exaggerate, dear, and you know it."

"Oh, is that so?"

"Yeah, that's so. What are a few bills that got forgotten while you were abroad? We all have bills that slip through the cracks now and then."

"Oh, that's a good one coming from you." She angrily tosses the bills back onto the pile on the table. "Let's talk about your bills—as long as you're bringing up the 'we all' thing. I have them memorized by now, and I don't recall letting them fall into any cracks!"

Sterling backs up to the door, quickly scans the hall for witnesses, and sees none. "This is true, my dear—you've been a wonder through all my legal woes. But honestly, good news is right around the corner, and your long-held patience is about to pay off."

"What, like I haven't heard this before?"

"Honestly, my lawyers just gave me some very promising details."

Sheryl, sniffling and looking fatigued, drops her combative air and wipes away her tears. "Don't be playing games with me, Sterling. I can't take it anymore and don't deserve it. Never did. All your excuses and promises have turned my life into a perpetual nightmare."

"I promise, baby," he assures with zeal. "Let's get you upstairs and cleaned up. Then we'll go celebrate your homecoming and windfall days ahead."

His finishing smile finally melts her resistance. She cracks a little one of her own. "Oh, why not?" she agrees. "It's a cinch I wouldn't be able to sleep."

A dryer's bell rings. They dispense with the repartee, examining each other in silence for a few moments. Simultaneously, they lean in for another kiss. Sterling ultimately breaks their embrace to make a big show of folding her laundry as she watches.

He exclaims, "Hey, that was some performance you put on at the airport! Saw it on the news at breakfast. Quite the media star, I'd say."

She chuckles. "Maybe somebody will come along and offer me big bucks for the real stories behind my Egyptian adventure. With any luck, there might even be something left over after knocking off a few bills."

"Right, that'd be nice," he remarks, not biting on the reference to debts.

"Yes," she mumbles melancholically.

"So," he counters, "I was figuring you'd be famished by about now."

She appears ready to pick up the pace. "Well, it just so happens I am! But it has to be American cuisine! Any problem with that, good doctor?"

"Your wish, as they say, dear, is my command."

"Good. Obviously, I need a little time to get ready."

"Of course."

"All of this is such a surprise. I had no idea you were coming."

"Surprises are the best, right?" Done folding, he finishes packing her granny cart and leads the way to the hallway.

Sheryl takes a last look for anything possibly left behind in the laundry room and then tags along after Sterling. "Cool your heels here a bit," she says as they reach the lobby. "I'll get ready as fast as possible."

Sterling stammers, "I, uh, really would prefer to wait in your living room. I can't help but remember a certain other time I waited down here for you—and all that soon happened that day."

"Don't be silly! That was a once-in-a-lifetime thing. Believe me, it won't happen again, ever. Besides, there's no way you're coming upstairs. My place is a mess. I haven't had a chance yet to tidy up anything."

"Come on," he counters, "as if I haven't been up there before, even after trips."

"Sorry, Sterling. I'm not budging. It's not negotiable."

"Okay, but try and make it snappy."

"Don't make me laugh. Settle in with a good magazine, dear, and consider yourself lucky I've already finished my laundry. See you soon!"

She exits to a bank of elevators, where one doorway opens for her right away.

❧

Back in her apartment inside a tiny bathroom, Sheryl feels like she's still overseas—or more to the point, on a cruise ship, considering her bathroom's constricted space. Stripped down and ready to shower, she first fiddles with a half-clogged showerhead to produce an erratic stream of water. "Third-world," she grumbles.

Soon she's done showering away any remnants of the road. She clears steam from the middle of the mirror with a corner of her bath towel. Overwhelming sadness stares back at her. Or is it weariness, or both? "Look at you," she unhappily mutters.

Thoughts of Sterling down in the lobby don't do much good at first. However, while the mirror fogs up again and she towels off, she allows herself to start thinking that perhaps better days finally really are just ahead, and she hurriedly leaves the steamy bathroom to find something to wear.

Fifteen minutes later, Sheryl enters the elevator wearing a great parka. As the elevator descends to the ground floor, Sheryl primps in a wall mirror, thankfully alone, and tries to get pumped up for Sterling's alleged news. She recalls having walked this plank before. It seems like she's always having to pump it up, one way or another, as with various on-the-job challenges overseas, often working alone in crowds—and thankful for crowds within which to hide her sorrows. "There's no crowd here," she laments to the empty elevator.

She has nobody with whom to commiserate about sorrows from always living on the run, about being unable to establish more than fleeting relationships with men of any quality, while always being mindful that the one man who is most consistently in her life, whether at the forefront or in the background, has been the source of much sorrow. Said sorrow, undeniably, always greets her upon her return home. Yet this same man, undeniably, has been the source of many pleasures. "So it is with men," she rationalizes.

The elevator slows to a stop at the ground floor. When the doors open, she shudders. For a moment, she can't step forward. She contemplates reversing course and going back upstairs. With a mental sigh, she presses onward. *Anyway*, she further rationalizes, *I'm starving.*

Sheryl and Sterling leave her building, bundled against the cold. The wind at last has died down, as has the snowfall, but it's still a wintry mess. They blaze a trail with exhalation puffs reminiscent of a locomotive's pulsating exhaust, trudging west on Diversey for the American Cuisine Grill a block away. "I'm ready for a big steak," declares Sheryl between puffs of air.

A sudden wind gust off the nearby great lake hits their backs, spinning them around in their tracks. Sheryl's mouth takes in a blast of freezing air that numbs her lips even while exhilarating her brain. Instantly, her daydreaming thoughts turn elsewhere, sans Sterling.

New Zealand's Kawarau Bridge: in her mind, she's there. It is September, early spring on this side of the planet. Sheryl stands midway out on the sturdy, century-old bridge a short drive northeast of Queenstown. She braces against an Antarctic blast of frigid air hitting her dead-on.

Involuntarily, she gulps cold fresh air into her already light-headed system. Pleasantly dizzy and tripping on the oxygen injection, she leisurely scans her surroundings and is reminded of why she so loves this little bitty land down under. The mixture of lush flora and rocky terrain with a river running through it is stunning, especially given her suspended viewpoint. *It has everything!* is all she can think, busy as her mind already is.

Mentally, she's blocking out her tour group of Texas Tech newbie grads. They boisterously surround her on the bridge, whooping it up in preparation for bungee jumping. Ignoring the racket, Sheryl fantasizes about immigrating here, knowing that anywhere she goes in this compact land of extremes, there are plenty of sights and weather zones at which to marvel. Landscapes range widely, from pristine beaches to alpine ranges to tropical forests. Strange mixtures of fauna, both native and introduced, are to be found everywhere, and despite spring's occasional Antarctic wind gusts, Sheryl is covered liberally with sunscreen since most of the country annually basks in over two thousand hours of sunshine.

All this and bungee jumping too! she jokes with herself, not entirely thrilled over some pressures from her tour group to go ahead and take a jump with them.

"Don't be chicken!" they shout every so often.

Sheryl, now thirty and at the top of her game, smiles and nods but remains steadfast against taking a leap with her younger charges. However, she can't ignore the attention draped on her by Troy, a muscular cowboy type. While taking in the scenery and verifying that she has a poncho in her purse—since rain pops up here anytime, sun or not—she notices Troy checking her out as he talks football with pals. She applies extra sunscreen to her face and throat partly to tease him.

Be smart, she counsels herself. Involvement with anyone in her groups, whether paying customers or fellow workers, has proven disastrous in the past. There's no denying it. She shouldn't even try.

A masculine voice calls out, "Hey, Sheryl," in a pleasant drawl that ends her near-trancelike drift from reality. Troy approaches.

Could be trouble, she thinks.

"When are you going to jump?" he asks. "I'll go if you go."

"That second part, I'd like to see, Troy. I hear you're chicken."

"Then jump! I'll be next in line."

They watch one of his classmates, Rachel, a normally upbeat redhead, stand at the brink, terrified. She sneaks a peek way below. Raucous razzing from travel mates convinces her that the time to jump is now, and she launches herself. Sheryl, from a short distance, holds her breath as she watches Rachel plummet, screaming, till the bungee cord tightens. Rachel hits the river and submerges halfway below the surface, only to be sprung from the drink as the cord recoils. Her lively audience howls in support.

"Well, Sheryl," persists Troy, "you next?"

"Why don't you go next and I'll think about it?"

"Shoot, it's ladies first where I come from. Don't worry, though—if you take the plunge, I'll be coming fast, right behind you, honest." He chuckles at his double entendre, pleasantly winking in case she missed it.

"Troy! What would your mother say?" kids Sheryl.

"Come on, Sheryl," begs Troy. "If it would make it any easier for you, we can jump tandem. It'd be my pleasure."

"I'll bet. But if I'm jumping, it'll be a solo act."

"Hey, understood!"

"Well, that's a big if—because I've managed to avoid bungee bouncing many times and can't say I regret it."

Sheryl has sidestepped the call to jump during half a dozen trips here. Pressure has been mounting, though, since there's always a Troy in the crowd egging her on. And admittedly, she figures, in the rapidly growing world of extreme-adventure vacations, it's inevitable that sooner or later she will end up jumping. After all, as soon as tomorrow, she'll again be facing the same pressures. The Texans, mixing bungee jumping with white-water rafting in a weeklong thrill quest, have another jump in mind: the Nevis High Wire, over three times as high as here. She thinks, *I'd be better off to get it over with here and now.*

Troy interjects into her thoughts, "Listen, Sheryl, the truth is, the guys have been giving me grief about not jumping. And now that Rachel's jumped, there'll be no hearing the end of it if I don't. You could be my inspiration here, Sheryl."

Sheryl figures he appears sincere. She looks below, again thinking how inevitable it is that sooner or later she'll have to do a bungee jump. Sheryl also knows, from tour-prep research, that Kawarau has a spotless safety record. Thinking now that there could be no better place for her bungee debut, she makes a snap decision. "Why not?" she enthusiastically barks.

"That a girl!" shouts Troy. "You won't regret it, Sheryl."

"Well, we'll see about that," she offers, still less than sure.

They march to the Bungydome, a splashy high-tech visitor center, to buy tickets. The Kawarau Bridge Bungy is the birthplace of commercial bungee jumping. It offers a forty-three-meter vertical drop to the Kawarau River below. Daredevils have their choice of jumping solo or in tandem. Then there's the triple-edged question of whether to bob just short of the river at the end of the drop, kiss the Kawarau, or be plunged into it. The ticket booth menu seems limitless.

"Decisions, decisions," mutters Troy as they read the options.

"Oh, get wet," suggests Sheryl. "Why not? Even if just a little."

"You got it. I'll match you. Is that what you're doing?"

"I think I'll take a full plunge, as long as I'm doing it."

Troy looks at her with surprise. "Oh, okay then, that's me too!"

They watch another tourist contemplating whether to jump. He stands on a turntable synchronized with 130 video monitors that all together give him a virtual taste of the real thing. The high-tech demo prompts a return of hesitations about jumping in the first place, both for Sheryl and especially for Troy, whose face turns ashen-white.

Bordering on false bravado, Sheryl browbeats him a little. "Come on, Troy, be a man. Lead the way."

"Right, right," he mumbles, apparently unfazed by the insult. With that, Troy snaps up a ticket for the full dunk.

Sheryl considers reneging entirely. Nervous, self-conscious, and unable to go for broke, she ends up opting for just kissing the river. Minutes later, they are at the launch pad.

"Get on with it, Troy!" some cowboy shouts from behind.

A strapping male attendant whose blasé attitude says he's heard it all, excuse-wise, has had enough of this and mechanically helps Troy into waist and ankle harnesses. Troy sucks it up.

"Are we going for style points?" Troy asks, challenging Sheryl.

The largely Texan audience howls, "Hell, yeah!"

Sheryl doesn't back down. "Sure! Like I said, lead the way, Troy. Show me how it's done."

Troy steps to the brink. Naturally, he hesitates a final time. Sheryl waits rigidly behind him. Suddenly, she panics as scenes from her unfinished life rapidly play out in her mind, freaking her out to no end. Could this be a sign about this escapade being a needless death march after all? She inwardly battles. *Now or never!* she thinks. Yet her life flashes before her eyes. In the middle of a rabid crowd, she fights inner fears that these flashes are previews of a bad ending if she takes the leap.

She figures that Troy also must be freaking out. "Get it on, Troy!" someone shouts as the razzing continues from behind.

With self-preservation in mind, Sheryl encourages Troy to resist peer pressure. "Don't do it for them, Troy—really. There's no shame in calling it off."

He takes a deep breath to calm himself. "No way, girl. I'm taking the plunge," he insists.

He actually looks ready for this. The crowd quiets in an unexpected show of compassion and respect as he makes the sign of the cross. Inhaling deeply to pump up his inner strength, he suddenly springs horizontally away from the tower. "Yahoo!" Troy hollers out, Texas-style.

His echoing bellow leaves an audio trail that bounces back and forth across canyon walls as he descends rapidly toward the river below. Sheryl watches him plummet, her focus finally detached from the passing scenes from her life. Within seconds, Troy disappears into the river, convincing her that something bad awaits if she goes through with this. However, as his tether pulls back up and Troy springs back out of the river, she breathes a sigh of relief.

"He did it!" a former heckler admits.

"With a lot less fuss than you!" remarks another.

Troy's fellow alumni cheer him wildly from above as a motorized rescue dinghy rushes toward him, having been docked at the landing of a long staircase to the top of the canyon wall. Troy, for his part, bobs up and down at the end of his rope, speechless. The dinghy driver frees him from the harness and rushes him dockside, where he regains his equilibrium and waves happily to the admiring bridge crowd way overhead.

On the bridge, cheers for antlike Troy below fade. Razzing returns, this time directed at Sheryl. "Don't let that chickenshit show you up, Sheryl!" shouts the same lout who moments earlier was taunting Troy.

So much for respect or compassion, thinks Sheryl.

"Yeah!" yells a brassy female member of the Texas troupe. "After all, you're our fearless leader! You can do it, right?"

Sheryl somehow manages to hide from everyone what feels to her like wide-eyed terror—everyone, that is, but the attendant sizing her up for her fitting. He can see her outright fear.

"Don't listen to them," he advises. "Hundreds back off every year. But if you go for it, believe me, you'll be fine."

"I'm fine now," she assures him. "Don't worry, I'm ready."

"Okay."

Once Sheryl's ankles are shackled together with padded straps, panic returns to hit her hard. As the attendant double-checks her waist harness and its extending straps around her thighs, she realizes there's nothing left for her to do except go for it, especially after her own prejump instructions for Troy. She promised, and he's due return on that trust.

The attendant motions for quiet, and the audience hushes.

Sheryl thinks of God being always at her side. All fear of jumping immediately leaves her. Ankles tethered, she bunny-hops to the platform's edge and launches herself into a freefall. Her mind freed from fear, she lives totally in the exhilaration of the moment. She smiles at a bird in flight and nose-dives to kiss the river. "Whoa!" she exclaims breathlessly when she reaches the water.

Rebounding into a bobbing action, she thinks about how some people say suicide jumpers die of fright before bottoming out; surely this has to be a similar feeling right to the end, but nobody dies of fright in bungee jumping. Common sense, though, rebuts that there's no comparison between bungee and suicide jumping.

In any event, with the deed done, she's anxious for the pickup boat to grab her so that she can get back up to the bridge for more. "That was exhilarating!" she exclaims to the rescue team as they pull her up.

Once she is reunited on the span above with Troy, who likewise exudes exhilaration, he says he'll cover the cost if she'll jump with him. She's game. They take a plunge together to the standing ovation of all the Texas Tech tourists.

Their tandem leap leads to a night of camaraderie on the town. Troy is impressed that Sheryl's a teetotaler like the women in his family back home on the range. They dance up a storm, working themselves into a lather at a humid club away from the rest of the hard-drinking tour.

Conversation breaks on the dance floor reveal surprisingly numerous areas of common feelings and interests. They keep dancing and talking as the night rambles on. By the wee hours, they feel heightened romantic vibrations possible only between strangers in a strange land.

Chapter 5

AMERICAN CUISINE

On a snow-packed Chicago sidewalk in the present day, Sheryl winds down from a windblown tornadic spin next to Sterling, who is doing the same. They catch each other in their frozen tracks, laughing, eyes locked, as they steady themselves against the next arctic wind gusts off Lake Michigan. Speechless and out of breath, they exchange stiff smiles that hurt their frozen faces. Regaining confidence, they resume their trek up Diversey toward the American Cuisine Grill.

Soon a revolving door to the nearly empty restaurant delivers Sheryl Taylor and Dr. Sterling Jackson to an aging maître d' waiting for more diners to materialize. They have been here often, but not lately.

The maître d' springs to life at the sight of them. "Ah, my friends!" he exclaims, fawning over their arrival at the starving eatery. "Welcome back. It's been too long since we've had the pleasure of your company."

"Seems like forever," confirms Sheryl.

"I assume you've been off to an exotic land, leading a life others only imagine."

"Yes, but it's one trip I'm trying to forget about—and fast."

"What? Why? Where was this? I've never heard such talk from you."

"Let's just say there was way too much excitement, and not of the fun variety."

"Enough said," says the maître d', shifting gears. "Now, where would you like to sit?"

Sterling glances at the many open tables. "Make it your finest table," he quips, "away from the maddening crowd."

"You got it," the maître d' responds with a broad smile. Picking up two menus, he looks to Sheryl. "One of our good old-fashioned American meals will help you forget all about whatever spoiled your trip, I'm sure."

"That's exactly what I had in mind."

"Thank you, so much. Right this way please." He leads them across the main floor, past two couples dining with apparent enjoyment, to a quiet table around a corner where the only other visible tables are empty. It's as though Sheryl and Sterling will be eating in their own private dining room. "Does this work for you?" asks the maître d'.

"You've outdone yourself once again," Sterling assures him.

Sterling and Sheryl shed their coats. As they settle into chairs, the maître d' supplies them with menus and returns to his station. A busboy brings water and rolls and butter and disappears.

"Nosy old man," Sterling snarls, glancing in the direction of the maître d'. "Always fishing for something."

"What are you talking about? He's nice and totally genuine." She takes a roll, passes Sterling the basket, and butters up her bread.

Sterling also goes for the rolls. Slowly, he concedes, "Okay, maybe you're right. But I was just reacting to his being intrusive with you right after you'd said let's please get off the subject."

"I know, but that was a reflex reaction anyone might've had. He backed off right away."

"Anyway, my bad. I'm just feeling protective of you after your rough trip."

"No worries. I understand."

"I, uh, need to hit the men's room—it was a long wait in the lobby."

"It was, was it? Try Cairo under siege for a week or so if you wanna talk long wait."

"Touché, but I gotta go. When I get back, I'll get into the lawyers' news."

"It better be good news this time, and real good, because I'm at my rope's end."

Without a smile, he assures her, "It's good." He gives her a gentle peck on the cheek before leaving.

Alone with her thoughts, Sheryl glances out the window. Her snowbound neighborhood triggers sympathy shivers for a passing couple walking east into the teeth of another arctic blast. Brushing aside a stray thought of Troy and the Kawarau Bridge, she grapples with the idea that it's been only days since she was embroiled in the chaos that is the new Egypt. She further reminisces about how only weeks before that, the various riots somehow had seemed far away, nameless others' problems. Her tour groups had come and gone like clockwork, with her happily headquartered in the lap of luxury. *Life was good*, she thinks without thought, quickly adding, *or so it seemed.*

Life generally has been good whenever she's been away from home. Her number finally came up, though, in Cairo. She can't believe how quickly the Tahrir Square riots became her own ongoing nightmare. She thanks God for having been so lucky—surely blessed—to have escaped. *Lucky?* She inwardly laughs hard enough to raise a smile on her face. *Lucky to get back to all this?* Thinking of debts, she concludes, *I must be joking.*

Overcome by anxiety, she uses her menu as a privacy screen while fears of ruination breed paranoia that says everyone sees her fears as clear as day. From experience, she's confident that if she can avoid eyes for just a short spell, she'll be okay. To ward off the familiar symptoms she considers borderline insanity, Sheryl force-feeds herself businesslike thoughts of how the Egyptian trip had been her first lengthy assignment of any sort in nearly a year. Suddenly more relaxed, she basks in recognition of how her overall skills were still going strong.

She realizes she flawlessly handled drastically altered arrangements in Cairo. *Yeah!* her inner core says encouragingly. All had started normally enough, with her staying long-term in one resort, repeating the same tour several times over for a few weeks for the continuous arrivals and departures of the various tour groups that her boss, Thomas Kearns, sent her way. Every last individual in each and every tour had the usual tedious needs of unprepared tourists, and she handled them all—including when all went to hell during her last group's tour with the arrival of what would become known as the Arab Spring. Peeking over the top of her menu, she silently asks, *That's proof I'm all right, right?*

Most impressive in her own self-congratulatory opinion was her effortless ability to shift from one language to another; she had not gone rusty. Even still, suddenly frantic, she wonders how ready she really is for the next couple trips Kearns has lined up for her: Hawaii and Turkey. They seem right around the corner, and Cairo will take some time to leave behind. Meanwhile, she's feeling pretty gun-shy about going anywhere.

But wow, Sheryl suddenly realizes, *it's been sixteen years since my first Magic Pigment Hawaiian tour. Darn! Where's that broach they gave me last year for fifteen years' service? I'd better be wearing it this year!* She figures it must be around the apartment somewhere, but where? Beyond contrasting thoughts about Hawaii, she frets over the one-week turnaround from her return to the mainland till her departure for Turkey. This is just the sort of stuff that contributed to her having insisted on shorter, more widely spaced tours over this last year. After all, as her fellow tour directors seem to get younger every year, living out of a suitcase for Sheryl isn't always so glamorous anymore. Thoughts about what to do persist over both workplace and financial arenas.

She is startled back to reality, nearly letting the menu slip from her hands, upon seeing Sterling returning from the men's room. "So," he asks while taking his seat, "what looks good?" Picking up his menu, he seems not to notice that Sheryl's hands are slightly shaking as she holds hers.

"Oh, the usual—same old menu."

As Sterling catches up on the menu, Sheryl privately flashes to how her laying off long trips for a while had been, on the surface, a result of her volunteer duties feeding the homeless through church. In reality, all that church stuff was only half the story. As usual with her life, there was the other half, the secret half, the half involving Sterling. It's this half, she quickly concludes, that now leaves her feeling helpless, drained of all self-respect and funds, and maybe even soon to become homeless, in need of a free meal herself. She asks God, *How did I ever let him get this stranglehold on me? Sometimes I can't even think for myself anymore—when I'm home, anyway.*

Sterling, unaware of her private conversation with the Lord, asks, "Still thinking steak? I think I'm thinking red meat too."

"I may not have a clue about anything else, but I know I want a rib eye. I'm starving."

Their waiter comes. They tell him to make it two, medium rare. Both choose soup over salad, an easy choice this time of year. Once they are alone again at the secluded table, the conversation finally gets around to brass tacks.

"All right," Sheryl says, starting the ball rolling with a cynic's intonation, "what's the latest from your crack team of lawyers?"

"Geez, woman, how can I tell you anything with that kind of attitude? Are you going to give me an open mind?"

She forces a derisive smile. "Of course. I'll do my best."

"Thank you," he says with a theatrical bow of his head in mock appreciation. "So anyway, we go before the judge again Monday. He's already pretty much agreed that some of my corporate funds will be unlocked for personal expenses."

"Wow, big surprise."

"What do you mean by that?"

She snickers. "I'm just saying—funny how after all these years your lawyers suddenly get a brainstorm about trying to unlock some dollars for that."

"Hey, I can't help it if there were other issues they had to handle first. It's all a methodical process—total bullshit, but they're working within the system."

"The system. How all-inclusive for you. How handy. In any case, I can't help but worry that the truth is you've been ripping me off for years."

"If that's what you want to think."

"It's what it is, as far as I can see. You've drained my funds dry. I used to be flush with the world—owned my condo outright." Sterling tries interjecting, but Sheryl won't allow it. "Truth hurts," she continues, "right? I know it hurts me!"

"So be it, my dear, if you say so. But redemption's coming, you'll see—the verdict and money's all coming to pass, like I've said all along. Just in the nick of time too."

"You mean just in time to save my condo, right?"

"Of course that's what I mean," he assures her with a false ring. "Monday will be a huge step toward getting us both out of hock."

"Well, I hope you mean ladies first on that pledge."

"Naturally. Don't worry about that. But also don't forget that the noose tightens more every day on my own mortgage too."

"Which puts me at the end of the line, I'm sure."

"No, baby, we're in this together, and better days are just ahead."

Their soup arrives, and the server promises that their steaks will be up shortly.

"Good news," chirps Sheryl. "I'm starving!" She dives into her soup.

❧

As Sheryl begins eating, pausing between spoonfuls to recount her battles to obtain scarce airline tickets out of Cairo, Sterling's mind wanders deeply into his shared past with her. Although he gives the appearance of listening attentively to her story, inwardly he finds himself recalling how he drifted back into her life six years after their Makeup Is Us days. He walked back into her life handing over the $500 he had owed her all those years. Now, with a minor touch of retroactive guilt, he remembers how Sheryl thought the money was bail for his cousin. The truth was that it purchased an abortion for one of Sheryl's summer coworkers who had allowed Sterling to get too frisky. Smugly, he thinks, *Yes, for sure those were the good old days.* Thinking about the wide-eyed, long-legged beauty he'd put in a family way leads him to wonder whatever happened to her.

Sheryl, apparently thinking she has Sterling's full attention, excitedly recounts, "Finally, my main ticket broker came through for me!"

Sterling nods with a smile at her storytelling and says admiringly, "You're amazing with all your connections around the world." He maintains sharp eye contact to convey that he's captivated by her strength and heroism, even while daydreaming of the other girl.

Sheryl is obviously pumped up in the glory of recounting this most hair-raising of her many adventures. She humbly declares, "I prefer to think my deliverance from evil was more a demonstration of God's protection than any earthly connections of mine."

"There's no doubt, my dear," he finds himself saying. "No doubt about it. How else can we explain it?"

As Sheryl moves on with her saga, Sterling smiles and heads back to dreamland and that first reunion with Sheryl. It was then he crafted the backstory for what would become his lifelong cover for his career as a criminal. He recollects with pride how from the start with Sheryl, it was easy passing himself off as a doctor, Dr. Sterling Jackson, gynecologist. *How perfect!* thinks the professional ladies' man with an inward chuckle. He can't help an impulsive smile, which Sheryl seemingly takes as interest in her exciting tale of escape from Egypt.

The waiter approaches with their steaks. Sheryl smacks her lips at the sight of the juicy rib eyes. "I knew I was hungry, but I had no idea I was this hungry." She already has a mouthful before Sterling picks up a fork.

As he slices off a chunk of his own juicy red meat, Sterling is happy about having gotten her off talk of money woes. *Home free*, he figures, *for now anyway*, though he knows time will tell more truly.

Chapter 6

KTC

American Cuisine's ladies' lounge is vacant as Sheryl enters and heads for a sink. Taking a high-tech toothpick from a pack in her purse, she loosens a chunk of meat from between two molars. Recalling the very recent eating of scraps under siege back in Cairo, she still can't believe that she is not only home but also already wary of Sterling after having missed him so much. *Nothing new there!* she grouses to herself.

Looking at her face in the mirror, she notices a tired trace of aging and thinks back to her first steak dinner with Sterling, when both were still young. The fancy dinner was in celebration of events stemming from his having resurfaced in her life earlier that same day, six years out from Makeup Is Us.

Sheryl is a rising-star tour director at Kearns Travel Company—or KTC, as its brochures tout. She is fluent in three languages and passable in three others, and the references who helped her land this great gig all raved about how she has been everywhere and is cool under fire. KTC specializes in packaged tours of the States and trips abroad, for groups both large and small. Whether alumni adventure travel or sales-incentive conventions, KTC has something for everyone. Housed in a midrise complex near O'Hare, the company is apt to be running up to a dozen tours concurrently, from lazy river cruises up the Danube to treks along the Great Wall. The tropics, of course, also are popular.

Thomas Kearns rules with a soft touch from his corner office, where the panoramic view appropriately enough captures a never-ending string

Sheryl tucks the money back into the envelope and slips it into a desk drawer. "Well, I give you credit for knuckling down and continuing to hit the books."

"Believe me—I surprised myself by getting through it. Wasn't easy."

"I'm all for education, but by the time I had my BA in hand, I was ready to spread my wings and fly away." Sheryl checks her watch, mindful of needing to return to Kearns's office.

Sterling notices her time-check. "So I should let you get back to work. How about dinner soon? It'd be great to catch up when there's more time to talk."

"Sure, why not? But I leave for Jamaica in a couple days."

"Jamaica? Man, I love it down there."

"You've been there?"

"Many times. It's like home sweet home."

"Interesting," she replies, wheels turning in her head.

"My mother's side came up from Jamaica in the forties, after the war. We used to vacation there when I was a kid. Loved it! But the trips ended after that car wreck. Everything ended."

"Listen," says Sheryl, getting up, "hang loose here while I finish up a meeting with my boss. Shouldn't take long. Maybe we can squeeze in a little dinner after work, as long as you've come this far in your quest." She gives him her first genuine smile since finding him in the waiting area.

"Cool, that works. Say no more."

Sheryl heads for Kearns's office, surprised to be glad that Sterling suddenly is back in her life. *Medical school does tend to take over peoples' lives*, she thinks, excusing his long absence. Suddenly, it seems like only days instead of years since she swore to walk away if she ever saw him again. She tells herself that his reappearance is divine providence. What better way to solve Kearns's problem than to present him with someone who happens to be intimately familiar with the island and who also is in need of work and available immediately? And in the process, she can up her solution-solving reputation at work.

Outside Kearns's office, Sheryl pauses for thought. *Think fast*, she orders herself, as doubts about the wisdom of accepting Sterling back with open arms quickly surface, undercutting her confidence. *This could be a mistake!* Entering Kearns's office as he hangs up the phone looking frustrated, she wrestles with the nagging, negative thought pattern that cautions her: *what if Sterling lets me down?*

Despite this authoritative voice of warning reverberating inside her head, once Kearns informs her that he's had no luck in finding her an assistant, Sheryl finds herself suggesting he consider an old acquaintance of hers for the job. The fact that this acquaintance sits in her office with family ties to the island is all Kearns needs to hear.

"Send him in for an interview!" he says.

"Maybe we can resolve your headache right here and now," responds Sheryl buoyantly.

"You do vouch for the guy, right?"

Forgetting all reservations about the proposal, she blurts out, "Of course!" A tingling rush of excitement overtakes inner doubts, and she's convinced this is a good idea. Plus, hey, she needs an assistant, right? She suddenly remembers local sources for Jamaican residents trained in the hospitality business—the island is loaded with temps. *Whatever*, she rationalizes. *This is a trusted acquaintance. And he's overqualified!*

She rushes back to her office with the news.

❧

Shock and joy hit Sterling when he hears of the possibility that he will be on a plane to Jamaica with Sheryl in two days. Uncle Austin will be proud, he thinks, of how quickly he's been able to reconnect with the North Shore mark he set up six years ago. Jamaica or not, Sheryl's back in the fold. He has a good inner laugh. *And what could be nicer than Jamaica? Great gig!*

The interview goes well, with Sterling bluffing his way through it with general observations of Jamaica gleaned from a long-ago slideshow of one of Uncle Austin's trips. Kearns, in a pickle with little time to request other references from the applicant, relies solely upon Sterling's word and Sheryl's recommendation. Proceeding quickly, he offers Sterling the job.

An hour later, Sheryl and Sterling celebrate their sudden unforeseen circumstances over a candlelit steak dinner at the clubby Rose Hill Restaurant near her office. Sheryl treats, diluting her unexpected supply of hundred-dollar bills in the envelope from Sterling.

Two days later, they, along with a large contingency of Fighting Illini alumni, take off on a charter flight to Jamaica. Nothing in Sheryl's life ever again will be quite the same.

Chapter 7

JA Dreamin', Mon

Time passes leisurely on the northern coast of Jamaica, although for tourists the chartered shuttle-bus rides out of Sangster International Airport can be a little hairy. From Montego Bay to Ocho Rios, a nearly shoulderless roadway runs through hilly scrub-jungle forest, and when the road is not twisting in lowlands, it is on blacktop ribbons rimming the sea. Despite many tense white knuckles aboard, a calming sense of getting-away-from-it-all-adventure permeates the shuttle cabins.

One such shuttle deposits Sheryl's Fighting Illini group at the No Worries Beach Resort. No Worries is a laidback all-inclusive resort with a large private beach just outside Ocho Rios. Lushly landscaped, the sprawling property will be Sheryl's headquarters for a string of KTC tours as Kearns rotates new groups in and out from Chicago.

Sterling is her administrative assistant, a rare spreading of the workload for Sheryl that comes with good timing. She's worn out from a series of round-trips to the Far East and in need of rest. For a change, she feels pleasantly anchored somewhere. The resort soon starts to feel like home.

One fine day, Sheryl and Sterling walk the No Worries beach together, barefoot but on duty in matching shorts and KTC golf shirts. People all around them are either baking in the sun or cavorting about in the ocean. No worries fill the air.

Sheryl says, "This is the life, wouldn't you say?"

"Can't be beat," Sterling confirms. "We're lucky a couple of those bookings fell through. It's more than ever like a paid vacation!"

"Yeah, it was fun from the start, but this is over the top."

"Yeah, mon," Sterling lazily agrees.

"Too bad for Kearns, though," reflects Sheryl. "This is tough on his budget. I'm sure he's not thrilled about our little vacations."

"We're lucky; he's not—it all evens out," quips Sterling.

"Well, right now it all seems pretty stacked in our favor."

"Nothing wrong with that, especially for you. Think of how you're always away at iconic vacation spots, but never on vacation. That must be tough, watching everyone else kick back and soak up the experience while you're working."

"Oh, I think that kind of stuff often. Believe me."

"So you've earned these weeks off."

"Speaking of which, I can't wait till next week."

The following week, Sterling begins talking with Sheryl about a future together. Heat, humidity, and fun in the sun over successive weeks have melted her common sense. She has lost track of her reservations about his character, first brought on years ago by his pitch for bail money and matter-of-fact talk of abortions. Yet she finds herself imagining them in a long-term relationship. Camouflaging the character questions about Sterling could be the fact that Jamaica, this time more than any previous trip here that Sheryl can recall, relaxes her to the core.

On a secluded stretch of the No Worries beach, the two stroll at sunset. They walk completely alone as the sun dips closer to a wet turquoise horizon. Sterling gently pulls up the reins on their walk beneath a coconut palm and tests his luck beyond talk. As he presses in on their first kiss, Sheryl goes limp in his arms, pretty much ready for love. This doesn't surprise her.

When they come up for air, he asks, "Your first?"

"First what?" she laughs. "First kiss? You kidding me?"

"First with a black man."

"So what if it is? Opportunity has to knock sometime. In any case, for sure it's not your first kiss with a white girl."

He softly chuckles. "Maybe so."

"Well, big shot," she chuckles back, close to his face, "maybe the case is you're not exactly my first man of color either, in the broad spectrum of things. So there."

"Touché."

Entwined in each other's arms, they exchange the curiously locked-in glances of new lovers on the brink. Slowly but surely, they return to their passionate business at hand, which isn't talking. They adroitly buckle their knees in unison, settling down in the sand without ever breaking their embrace. Evening falls upon them. A full moon replaces the sun.

Mesmerized by the flow of moments, they lose track of time in the moonlight, becoming steamy bodies clinging together in the humid night air. Sheryl, partially disrobed but still a virgin after several close calls with Ilkin, feels worldly beyond her imagination. Exhilarated, she feels her heart thump beat-for-beat with Sterling's. With a lump in her throat, she chokes back words; anything she might say seems inadequate for the moment. She wonders, *Could this be love?*

So passes spring into early summer, by which time, more often than not, they sleep together in her room; they have come close to the real deal sexually, but with her always pulling back at the last moment. Fifteen years of Sunday-school training keep her from slipping over the brink.

☙

During their time together in Jamaica, Sterling has found himself captivated by Sheryl's smile and energy. He dreams of ditching a life of crime in favor of life on the square. *People do it all the time*, he tries persuading himself.

But going-straight delusions subside, and he begins to recover his priorities, despite remaining captivated by her smile. That smile, however, loses a little more of its power over him each night, during forced solo marches to his own quarters in the 4:00 a.m. hour. He doesn't much like these overnight hikes and lets her know it, but he complies with her wishes.

There comes a night, though—another brightly moonlit one at that—when he determines that all her pulling back must come to an end. This night, under their favorite coconut palm on that secluded beach with memories of their first kiss, Sterling hatches a plan to break through Sheryl's moat of virginal defense. As they recline together on a sand dune admiring countless constellations, his thoughts are on a zipped-up bag stashed in the breast pocket of his No Worries beach shirt. It holds a finely rolled spliff of primo Jamaican ganja.

Sheryl, unaware, sighs, "Another perfect night."

"That it is, my dear. Couldn't be finer … well, maybe." He leaves her hanging with a devilish look on his face.

"Maybe what?"

"Oh, nothing," he chuckles. "Forget it—nothing, really."

She screws up her nose to make a funny face, feigning frustration. "Come on, what could make it finer than this?"

"Well, this is Jamaica, you know."

"What do you mean?" Apparently, she doesn't know.

"You know, 'when in Rome' and all that stuff. You're the world traveler—you know what I mean. Like how this is Jamaica, mon. Know what I mean?"

"No, mon, I don't know what you mean. Tell me."

"I remember your talking about having tried a little drink now and then during your college days back in Germany. You said it was just kind of the thing to do in Germany, you know, a little beer, maybe a shot of schnapps—experimentation in keeping with your surroundings."

"What, you want to have a drink? Go ahead. I won't mind or make any judgments. People drink around me all the time. But I'm not in college anymore. It's out of my system."

"Cool, but that's not it—kind of close, but no cigar."

There is a moment of silence as they both look up to the brilliant night sky.

"Okay," remarks Sheryl, "I get it, Sterling—you're talking about pot."

He laughs. "Well, yeah. We're kind of in the motherland of pot. And this ganja they have down here … well, suffice to say it's way beyond whatever floated around your campus."

"I'm not totally ignorant, you know. I've heard the stories."

"Have you also heard it's a religion down here? There's a whole movement revolving around it—Rastafarianism."

"So I've heard—the Rastas, mon." She laughs, and he joins her.

"Right," confirms Sterling, "and I know from our first real date how interested you are in all religions. Heck, you took me on a tour of the Baha'i Temple, remember?"

"Oh, I see where this is headed. Of course I remember. So I don't suppose you happen to have some of this religious pot—or ganja—handy by any chance, do you?"

"Well," says Sterling smoothly, "it just so happens I do. Wanna give it a try?"

Sheryl smiles tightly and looks out over the ocean, catching the faint lights of a distant vessel making passage through the night. Sterling gives her space as she weighs the pros and cons of compromising her lifelong convictions regarding sobriety. For her it's no little thing.

She rationalizes aloud, "True, I've sipped a drink or two on larks and suffered no lasting ill effects, at least as far as I know. So one could say maybe this just is a chance to explore something similar that'd be of no real harm."

"That's it, you got it," Sterling insists, glad to hear her upbeat tone.

But she wavers, countering, "Or would it be more along the lines of the tree of knowledge of good and evil, bound to bring nothing but trouble?"

"You got me there, Sheryl. Really, maybe each person's answer is totally unique. So it boils down to what do you think?"

"Oh, what the heck! Why not? Like you say, when in Rome, eh?"

"That's the spirit!" Sterling grins mischievously. "Okay, so let's give it a go together. I have to admit, I'm not too experienced at this either."

"Oh, right," Sheryl cynically replies, "I'm sure of that."

Sterling reaches inside his shirt pocket for the bagged spliff. It's an expertly rolled conical cigarette, considerably wider at one end than the other.

"If you're such a rookie, where'd you get it?" asks Sheryl.

Sterling spins a tale about a tourist recently having foisted a bag of ganja upon him at the No Worries beach. "And no," he chuckles, "don't worry—he wasn't with a KTC tour!"

"He better not have been."

"Rest easy, girl. He was just some random tourist."

"Why did he approach you?"

"Who knows? He'd bought more than was needed for his vacation, was heading home, and didn't want it to go to waste." Sterling opens the bag and extracts the pungent joint.

Sheryl winces at its odorous kick. "Man, that's some stinky stuff," she remarks.

He chuckles. "You're telling me. But listen, even though I haven't smoked more than just a few joints in my life, nothing compares to this stuff. And that tourist—man, he was like a pro at rolling a Jamaican spliff. The shape is unlike any joint I've ever seen."

"He rolled it for you?"

"He rolled a bunch for his group's last binge and gave me this leftover one as a starter—plus a baggie with the rest of the buds and some rolling papers. It's all stashed safely back in my room, triple-bagged to keep the smell in check." He produces a lighter and lights up the large end as Sheryl watches in amazement.

She admits, "I'm thinking of numerous other times I've passed on such opportunities."

Between a couple starter puffs, Sterling says, "That all was to save it for here and now with me, bathed in the incredible ambience of a Jamaican beach on a night like this."

"Little did I know."

Sterling coughs on his third puff. Instead of being annoyed at the cough, he's quite amused, even as the hack repeats itself a couple more times. Shaking it off, he draws a long, smooth drag on the glowing spliff, and after gagging nasally, he holds his breath to retain the smoke. He silently holds out the spliff, passing the torch to Sheryl. She hesitates to take the joint from his outstretched hand and looks confused. Sterling continues to hold his breath, screws up his eyes at her, and waves the spliff in front of her face.

Sheryl takes the spliff and stares at it from stem to burning stern.

Sterling exhales. Feeling dizzy, he lies back in seeming slow motion against the sand, staring up at coconuts. "Wow. I'm telling you, babe, this is awesome stuff."

"Babe?" she echoes with humor. "That's a first." She seems to like the term of endearment and takes a very cautious puff, letting it out faster than she drew it inside.

"That's it?" he teases. "You can do better than that!"

"We'll see." This time she takes a purposefully slow drag.

"That a girl!" exclaims an encouraging Sterling.

She exhales and then repeats another long, deliberate inhalation. Her deep puff produces a slight hiccup of a cough, which she stifles through pursed lips and oral recoil just as she saw Sterling do. She toughs it out and holds her breath. He, in turn, gets excited watching her antics and light-headedly takes back the spliff as it dangles from her hand. Their eyes connect as he tokes.

Sheryl, exhaling again, breathlessly observes, "Wow is right." Appearing dizzy, she adds, "This sure must be good stuff."

"That's putting it mildly," Sterling concurs, which cracks up the both of them.

"Strangely," she adds, "I'm finding the aroma is becoming familiar, more tolerable," and this cracks them up even more. Everything is funny as they look about the beach under moonlight from heaven above.

They get halfway through the spliff before Sterling stubs it out in the sand. "That's about enough for me," he admits.

"I guess I'm okay because I wouldn't know any better."

"Well said."

Snickering, they sit back together under the coconut tree to take in the night's sights and sounds. Gentle wave action lulls them into total repose. Before long, they are kissing.

Privately, Sterling thinks, *How well is this working?*

The answer becomes plain as their passion grows. Sheryl suggests, "Why don't we go back to my room?"

"Indeed, why don't we? Let's go."

Sterling congratulates himself for bringing her down this road.

Once back in Sheryl's room, Sterling sticks true to his action plan for the night; for the first time, he avoids the forced 4:00 a.m. march back to his own digs. Neither looks at the clock as she succumbs to his penetration quest. It leaves her wanting more.

"Freeze this moment forever," she says dreamily as they cool off under a sheet.

∽૭ᖾ

The next morning brings a change of heart. Sheryl awakens with wracking guilt over having given it all away, compounded by fears from realizing they took no pregnancy precautions during their lovemaking, or any kind of precautions at all, not that she keeps anything handy or that he even bothered to bring up the subject.

Sterling's snoring brings her focus to him next to her in bed, an unfamiliar sight with the sun breaking in through her blinds. *Oh well*, she thinks as she guiltily reflects upon the night, *here's the new reality. Done deal, virginity gone—no time for regrets.*

She stretches out against her pillow, eyes locked on the whirling ceiling fan, and a sudden joy comes over her, joy that now, she guesses, she is finally a full-fledged woman. Abruptly, she realizes that some buzz remains from that ganja, and she quietly giggles. A myriad of thoughts flash through her head, darting here and there from throughout her lifetime. These thoughts settle quickly into a rhythmic montage of images from the previous night.

"Wow," she exclaims, waking Sterling.

"What?" he mumbles, stirring and reaching out with an arm to pull her close.

"Nothing, dear," she gently answers, with no desire to arouse him further. Preferring solitude with her thoughts, she coaxes, "Go back to sleep." Thankfully, he does.

When this day's overnight hours come around, though, Sheryl, having refused Sterling's early-evening pitch for a walk to their favorite coconut palm down the beach, insists on propriety again—or at least the appearance of it, since later that morning will be the start-up of another tour's arrival. She wants nothing of their cuddly No Worries togetherness getting back to Kearns.

Kearns is no prude, but he is known to highly frown on romantic entanglements among his employees. She fears career repercussions if he hears about her breach of company protocol—and with a part-timer at that. The thought also crosses her mind that Kearns, a native southerner, might have prejudicial thoughts about her being intimate with a black man. She has even angered herself for having such thoughts. *But you never know, right?* she thinks as she speculates on Kearns's stance about any of this.

This train of thought sparks soul-searching and examinations of her own dark corners of thought. She can't help but wonder what the general reception would be if she were openly in a mixed-race relationship. Further, what would it be like to have biracial children? *If ever there was a time for traditional taboos falling by the wayside,* she reasons, *it's now.* Yet her alter ego asks, *Correct?* for confirmation.

That's a question she has no time for now. All she knows, when push comes to shove, is that she feels herself falling hard for Sterling. This is real-life drama for her, him being her first full-fledged lover and all.

They continue growing closer both on the job and in the bedroom. The Jamaican spirit embodied in the resort's No Worries theme rules the days and the nights. Her one ganja experience seems to have altered her center of gravity for a considerable while.

One night she declares to Sterling, "I've never felt such a sense of calm," forgetting many other similar calms after Bible study classes elsewhere in time.

"Same here," he quickly agrees.

She takes him at his word in every topic of conversation. One topic suddenly brings up a new story of a business venture that Sterling is spearheading with his cousins. They're moving ahead with, he says, a long-planned clothing company—a can't-miss designer label with hot early reviews. The next thing she hears is him talking about a "ground-floor opportunity" that he can offer her—"if," he says, downplaying the pitch, "you were to be interested."

Sheryl was raised to be wary of schemers, so she strings him along for a few weeks on the investment talk with a polite show of interest as caution alarms ring in her head. Her wariness is not so much due to any mistrust of

Sterling, whom she's more drawn to every passing delightful day; his cousins' involvement is what concerns her most about the alleged opportunity. The topic remains in the background, though, as they direct tours while discreetly flirting with each other on the job.

As the final tour nears completion, Sheryl takes a call from Kearns. He's opening a second office in Florida and wonders if she'd be interested in managing the place. The surprise chance to move out of the field and into an office catches her flat-footed. It's a dream offer, or it certainly could be, because even this early in her career, she occasionally wonders how long she can continue living out of a suitcase. She's seen many older tour directors drag through their paces, barely able to hide their loss of love for the job. Still, that's them. They're old. Youth, for now, remains on her side, and overall, of course, she loves the travel. Nevertheless, she's savvy enough to give Kearns the upbeat vibe he needs to hear.

"That'd be amazing!" she replies. "Boss, I don't know what to say!" But she hedges her bet a bit and asks, "Can I just sleep on it till tomorrow?"

"Sure, I know it's out of the blue. But if I could ask, what are your concerns?"

"The part about pulling up my Chicago roots. It would be a life-altering move. I have to look at all the angles."

"I understand," he says empathetically, "but remember that being in the travel business sometimes means traveling to a new home base." That concept barely has sunk in with Sheryl when he adds, "Oh, I almost forgot the part about doubling your salary, plus bonuses on your staff's production—and an occasional choice tour gig of your pick to keep up on travel."

"Wow," she says, very pleasantly surprised.

They agree to talk at the same time tomorrow. Inwardly, though, Sheryl is already beginning to consider it a done deal. *Why not?* she reasons. *I'd be nuts to turn it down!*

However, at a seaside jerk chicken stand that afternoon, Sterling gives her pushback. "Now, I'm not saying the money and opportunity don't sound good, so don't get me wrong," he says, his tone striking her as disingenuous. "I just wonder if, in the long haul, it's really what you want to do—or ought to do."

Annoyed, she asks, "What's wrong about it?"

"For one thing, I can't be following you off to Florida."

"What?" she asks, that factor being far off her radar. Despite her hunger for love and her infatuation with him, she remains very much career-oriented, and opportunity is knocking.

"Well," he stammers, "maybe it's nothing to you, but with my clothing company taking off in Chicago, I ask, what about us? Or more to the point, is there even an 'us' in any way, shape, or form? So … that's what's wrong with Florida as far as I see things."

"Life's full of complications, Sterling," she replies, wondering how he has come to expect to have a say in her comings and goings. "If we're meant to be, we'll be. Everything's fine here in Jamaica, but we still barely know each other. This is my career we're talking about. So meanwhile," she says resolutely, "I'm giving this serious thought."

She digs into her jerk chicken basket at their tipsy table behind the shack, determined to enjoy both the chicken and the million-dollar view. Sterling follows suit. The blinding sun and calm waters become trance-inducing for them. Munching away and staring out to sea, every so often, as if on cue, they silently stare at each other. Each time, before long, their gazes return to the mesmerizing horizon.

Sheryl takes advantage of their prolonged break in conversation to reflect on how this is not the first time a man has tried persuading her away from career opportunities. Ilkin did much the same. With him, it became a polished and oft-repeated routine, often out of nowhere, just as she was thinking how wise he was to be keeping silent on the subject.

Ilkin would implore, "Come to Turkey! You never will have to work again"—even while admitting that she would be no more than just tolerated by certain factions of Turkish society.

Sure, that's going to work, Sheryl thought as she imagined walking ten paces behind Ilkin whenever out in public. But she was full of doubt about her decision because truly, she was deeply in love with Ilkin.

The conclusion of their relationship has troubled her ever since. Definitive answers didn't come in time then. Sheryl only can pray for them now. Maybe she has been too driven in her career at the expense of a love life. What to do? As she squints against the sun's reflection off the Caribbean, her pensive mood is derailed by Sterling, who abruptly breaks the silence.

"Tell Kearns you have complications from a side venture that tie you to Chicago. Say whatever you need to say to keep on working his tours and hope there will be no hard feelings. Emphasize that it's just that the timing is not so good for you right now."

"And what do I say when he asks about this side venture?"

"Just that you'd love to fill him in, but for now, it's all confidential. You'll let him in on it when the timing's right. What can he say?"

"That's not a worry for you. For me, saying the right thing is."

"Stalling him is the right thing, I guarantee it."

Sheryl verges on telling off Sterling for being presumptuous but instead retains her composure and says, "So tell me about this side venture."

Sterling proposes that she quit her full-time position at KTC and instead freelance travel gigs through Kearns and other tour packagers, all while maintaining a home base in Chicago, from where she will be an integral partner in his burgeoning clothing company. One day, they will be multimillionaires individually and a couple for life. "We could be doing Jamaica for long weekends or on a whim!"

"Sounds wonderful," Sheryl numbly reacts. "But realistically, what's the business plan? What are the odds?"

"We're perfectly placed to target the hot youth market, and our case studies all point to a massive success story. I'm telling you, it can't miss."

Sheryl laughs. "Sure, can't miss, guaranteed."

"Funny," he says, not amused.

Following chicken, they comb the beach and then get in a little sailing on a No Worries craft. Before long, it's time for another perfect seaside sunset.

"A fella could get used to this," professes Sterling, "meaning a lifetime of it with you."

She has forgotten the earlier acrimony and confesses, "At times like this, I can see it too."

As dusk falls, they fall into each other's arms. Later, under a bright night sky, they wander back to her room. Snug and cuddly in her bed, it's 4:00 a.m. before they know it—and time for Sterling to pack it in for his own room, about which he doesn't grouse.

The next day, Sheryl tells Kearns she's not able to pull up stakes right now. "The timing is just wrong for me, boss. I'm so sorry but so grateful for the offer."

"I understand, I guess, but I am surprised."

"For now, I … uh …" She fumbles as she tries to explain. "I just want to keep Chicago my home base."

"Understood," Kearns assures her. "So that's it. No problem."

"Can we leave the door open moving forward if Florida ever comes up again?"

"Of course! I'm glad you asked, really. The door's always open for you."

"Thanks!" She is hesitant to play the freelance card Sterling suggested, but she decides to try another angle for time off. "Meanwhile, JA Tours and Conferences has offered me a job through hurricane season. And I have to admit, I'm kind of in the mood to go native down here awhile longer. Would you mind? It'd be like a working sabbatical."

After a beat of silence, Kearns chuckles. "Do it while you're young. They're good people. I can get some freelancers to fill in the gaps for a while—but I will need to know after hurricane season if I can rely on you full-time again. Stay in touch, Sheryl."

Feeling like a heel, she simply says, "Thanks, Thomas."

JA Tours and Conferences, happy to have Sheryl on board, keeps her at No Worries as tour liaison director, basically the same job she's been doing, only now for JA Tours instead of KTC. They have many clients who love the hurricane season bargains. This is perfect for Sheryl because she can use the money and the continuing free digs. However, no openings exist for Sterling.

"Hey, that's fine by me," he tells Sheryl. "I really just feel like kicking back a bit. Hell, I thought I'd be stuck in a career I hated, doctoring in Indy. But no, here I am in Jamaica with you! What could be finer?"

"I hope you've put away a little for a rainy day."

"A little. But so much has happened so quickly, I could use a breather."

For now, No Worries allows Sterling to retain his KTC room at a reduced guest rate. He quickly grows to love his role of privileged guest with insider contacts. Over a few weeks' time, he continues filling Sheryl's head with financial and romantic fantasies, mixing business jargon with sweet talk and gentle nuzzles at the beach. Still, as with any guy, he talks himself into trouble one day, abruptly crying poor to the employed Sheryl.

"Man, I'm broke," Sterling declares as they walk their favorite stretch of beach.

She's unsympathetic. "What do you expect when you don't work? Get a job. And what about your hotshot company? Aren't there things you should be doing?"

"It's just getting off the ground," he retorts. "There's no money in it yet, as you know. And my cousins are on top of start-up logistics and interfacing with designers. It's all cool."

"How is it you trust those cousins of yours to oversee everything while you're down here all this time?" She's beginning to wonder if he's been trying to fleece her all along.

"Baby, listen—my cousins are more on the ball than you think. You've never met them, so don't judge them."

"What little I do know is all bad."

Sterling sighs sadly and shakes his head. "All you remember is a little trouble from when they were pretty much still kids—and street kids at that, growing up without all the little North Shore niceties you were lucky enough to have."

Sheryl is having none of this today. "How like you to say." Without another word, she makes an about-face and heads back to the resort, leaving him in the lurch at water's edge.

Settling into her lobby office, she's happy to get back to work. If it weren't for the steady flow of mellow guests turning over weekly and keeping her busy, she thinks Sterling would be getting on her nerves. "Think again," she mumbles. "He's on them already."

❧

Back at the beach, Sterling, in full recline on a dune, silently berates himself for his poor first stab at an initial financial deal with Sheryl. Yet through self-counseling he remains sure that there's plenty of time left in the current tour season to set his money hook in Sheryl. "I'll wiggle my way out of this corner," he tells himself with a laugh, on the brink of cockiness.

Sinking into the sand, Sterling soaks up the sun while entertaining stray thoughts of how nice Oak Street Beach back home is this time of year. He congratulates himself for having bullied Sheryl into blowing off Kearns's Florida pitch, keeping her based in Chicago, handy for Sterling. *Once this sweet Jamaican vacation ends*, he daydreams, *and we go back home, it'll be time soon for her to hit the road.* This will give Sterling time to cultivate additional marks.

That night, over a late dinner on a starlit patio, Sterling apologizes for having played both the race and I'm-broke cards. He sees that the solution is for him to get a job, he says. "You're totally right."

Sheryl says, "Hey, I like the sound of this."

Sterling milks his growing familiarity with the resort to get close to the hotel's manager, Ronny Walker. Walker is a young on-the-rise Jamaican who works for a Spanish-owned island chain of resorts. During lunch with Sterling on an oceanfront veranda one sparkling day, Walker also provides an interested sounding board for Sterling's self-aggrandizing tales.

"And that's how I got through med school," boasts Sterling.

"The world needs to look out for you," laughs Walker.

Sterling regales Walker with alleged tidbits of the bawdy lifestyle he indulged in during his Indianapolis internship. The good thing didn't last, though, thanks to the hospital's going bankrupt just as he'd started his residency there. He and all his playmates scattered to the wind.

"Which is how I find myself here, mon," he concludes, "a doctor without a hospital."

Walker theorizes, "I suppose the slow pace down here gets to you."

"On the contrary, my friend. Frankly, I can't say I'd ever go back if I could find proper employment right here in Jamaica."

Sterling is aware that the No Worries Resort and all the other hotels in his new friend's chain employ resident doctors, with room and board also provided. It isn't long before Walker comes to Sterling about an opening right here at No Worries. In addition to his being paid a steady income, his living accommodations will include an upgrade to a private bungalow at the far end of the beach.

Walker adds, "I'll just need a copy of your diploma and licensing from the States to get you registered here."

"Hey, no worries," chuckles Sterling, knowing his cousins can forge anything.

"This even could develop into a career move for you with the company."

"That would be a dream come true, my friend."

Within days, the paperwork arrives, and Sterling moves into his isolated beachfront bungalow. He also gets familiar with his consulting room in the lobby, opposite Sheryl's office. Now he will find out whether cramming self-schooled medical studies into his evenings the last couple years actually worked. Surprisingly, after just days on the job and a few extracted sea urchin quills to his credit, Sterling's confidence borders on cocksure. Now, as a high-status No Worries figure, he feels the skids are greased for his continued courting of Sheryl. However, in his clinic one evening after work, she shows that maybe she's not as easily impressed as he thought.

Sheryl wisecracks, "You sure worked fast on Walker. I'll give you that."

"How's that?" he innocently protests.

"How's about maybe that opening wouldn't have happened if you hadn't played your cards so perfectly? Walker gets a kick out of having you around, and you know it."

Sterling laughs, full of himself. "I don't know what you're talking about."

"Sure."

"Well, I have to say things did turn out nicely. I understand they transferred my predecessor elsewhere."

"Right, so at least he's not out of work."

"The game of life."

"I see—the game of life. I'll remember."

Sterling, meanwhile, is tripping out over his new Jamaican lifestyle. *Who would have predicted any of this a year ago?* He studies local history in his spare time.

Over rum and dinner one evening with Sheryl, who takes only a sip of her drink, he opines, "I think all American blacks should hold sacred everything about Jamaica." With a touch of sincerity, he adds, "There for the grace of God go any one of us—and it's just too bad for some of us that it's always barely one step ahead of poverty."

It's not often that Sterling gets on a soapbox about racial inequities. But when he does, he leans into threatening postures, spewing barbs against the world and anything white, over all past and continuing injustices. He rants such things now under his breath at their table.

Sheryl remarks, "That has to include me, no matter how romantic you try to be."

"Not true. Don't say that."

"Then what's with all the posturing? At least with me. I understand history."

Sterling denies posturing, adding that he doesn't appreciate her bringing up such subjects.

"I didn't bring up anything," she clarifies. "I'm reacting to your blanket racist charges."

"Oh, I can't win with you. We can't win with anybody."

"If I could erase that legacy for you, I would, but I can't."

As whenever these types of moments occur between them, it all stops as abruptly as it began. They drop the subject, enjoying their dinner and view—always a saving grace, the view.

Over ensuing weeks, assorted plans of larceny dance through Sterling's head regarding how best to fleece Sheryl. As they coast through their days working across the lobby from each other, filling their evening off-hours with island vibes and incredible sunsets, he senses that her sense of caution about him and his clothing business is growing lax. So he hopes.

One breezy beach night, he's determined, here and now, to see if she finally will take the bait. They exchange small talk awhile about how their days have gone. Sterling boasts of his first really busy day in the resort's infirmary. "Our resources may be small, but we delivered big today. All kinds of things coming in from the beach and pool—and nobody went off to dinner still bleeding."

"Sounds like Walker made a great hire, all right," ribs Sheryl.

Sterling laughs as a dozen simultaneous memories of the day pop up. This doctoring stuff gets pretty interesting. Smugly, he segues into his ground-floor opportunity rap. When he is done making his case, he asks, "How can you not see it? This brand is going global, and you can be an equal partner for only twenty grand! Twenty grand," he repeats derisively, as if it's chump change.

"Equal partner in what? I haven't seen a single sample."

"That's the view from the ground floor! As soon as our patent gets through the courts, we'll be sitting pretty with the coolest in-demand clothing line. The lawyers, though, are bleeding us dry. Truth is, we need a little money infusion to stay afloat."

"Ah, the truth, finally. Well, it sounds pretty risky to me."

"There's always some risk, of course, but not so much here. Believe me, I wouldn't steer you wrong." He chuckles. "Because, baby, there'd be hell to pay if I did! Right?" He drags a smile out of her.

"Well … how about giving me till the end of the year to see how I'm standing?"

Sterling can't hide his disappointment. "A lot could happen between now and then."

She holds firm. "We'll talk about it then," she promises.

"Just remember, it's ground floor now, but by then … who knows?"

"Oh, I'll remember, promise. But it's a chance I'll just have to take. We'll talk then."

"Till then, then," he says with a smile.

They change subjects and continue with their night, with dancing in the mix. This night sets a new pattern that repeats throughout the sultry summer; he briefly touches on his clothing company updates, to whet her appetite; she listens indulgently, sometimes wondering if he's maybe making sense. But always they go on to other things quickly, inextricably joined at the hip, so to speak, enjoying the exotic community together and building a wide range of local ties.

Sheryl almost forgets that the clothing company ground-floor opportunity still lurks in the background, despite Sterling's occasional business updates. The truth is she's learned to discreetly tune out whenever the subject is broached, without his being aware.

One afternoon while wandering about the Ocho Rios flea market, Sheryl entertains Sterling with tales of her travels. "So these KTC guys I worked with in Thailand just went totally bamboo. They left Kearns high and dry without warning—pretty much like I've done here."

"You figure he thinks you've gone bamboo?"

"I'm sure that's crossed his mind. But back then, the point of the story from my perspective was"—she chuckles fondly in recollection—"my workload tripled overnight."

"I'm sure you were up to it."

"Got me a promotion and a raise, actually."

Before summer's end, seemingly bona fide romantic feelings have gained a toehold in Sheryl's heart, entangling the two more than ever. Crazy in love, she thinks, they talk away deep into their many tender overnight hours, always pointing to a blissful future together. It isn't long before the inexperienced and totally ill-prepared Sheryl finds out she's pregnant.

"My God!" she exclaims on seeing the home-test results. "I can't believe it." She's freaked out and heavily conflicted over having turned into such a sinner almost overnight. Her actions of late suddenly seem so unseemly, especially after she takes the news to Sterling. He immediately talks of a quick abortion.

"What?" she protests.

"If there were any other way ..."

Already at wit's end, Sheryl now is doubly crushed to hear her lover talking so casually about such procedures. *How could he go there so fast if he really loves me?* she wonders. *Why be surprised, though?* she thinks as she recalls the way he dragged her into his cousin's abortion woes. Woebegone and secretly fearing that she would be shunned by North Shore society types if she were to bear Sterling's child, Sheryl acquiesces.

"It's the right thing," he tenderly assures her.

Sterling arranges what is pitched as a totally safe, quick, and easy operation, through some Rastafarian connections he's been cultivating. The trouble is, if they want to maintain confidentiality for Sheryl, the logical facility is twenty kilometers away. In Jamaica, that's like traveling to a distant country via sketchy roads. Their Jeep excursion up into the lush mountains brings a sense of adventure for Sterling, despite his fear of cars, but it's a huge guilt trip for Sheryl. She hates the dark path to which she has led herself. Bailing out of the procedure continually crosses her mind.

"I can't believe I'm doing this," she cries, bouncing in the backseat with Sterling.

"There's no other way," Sterling whispers, bouncing along with her.

Ultimately, they reach a ring of rural huts. The barnyard conditions of the so-called operating room into which she is herded are appalling. Totally ashamed, Sheryl manages to halt the course of their ghastly expedition.

"Dear," counters Sterling in one final effort, "I'll make sure they clean up the operating room, fast. I can understand how you feel."

Sheryl simply says, "No way do you understand."

Turning from a waiting team of two midwives, Sheryl ducks back outside the hut, expecting Sterling to follow fast. He does, along with their driver, and they leave.

"Lord, forgive me," Sheryl begs over and over again.

"You haven't done a thing yet, Sheryl. Don't worry."

She glances at him, blurting, "Yet? Like I did a thing with you to get here in the first place? All the rest, your only concern, well—that's all just too gruesome to even consider."

The most traumatic and also truly dangerous ride of Sheryl's life continues. Each bump in the road stimulates pain in her innards that she imagines is similar to the pain she's just dodged. Her idea of how the bloody crime scene would have looked turns her stomach. She wonders if she would've had any innards left after those midwives were done with her.

"Oh my God," she groans in despair, feeling totally sick.

"Stay strong," Sterling encouragingly suggests.

He puts an arm around her, attempting to provide comfort. It's all she can do to keep from puking on him. Up front, their driver concentrates on the unpaved downhill road through the jungle, unaware of the drama behind him. Sheryl, disgusted with herself, slumps from exhaustion.

"Stay strong," Sterling repeats, thinking he's soothing her, unaware that she harbors a strong desire to let loose venting venomous thoughts on him.

The Jeep keeps bounding downhill, occasionally beating back overgrown brush. "Just get us back alive," weeps Sheryl from a seated fetal position.

Back at No Worries, she feels more conflicted than ever. One moment she's convinced she never could have lived with herself after aborting her child. The next instant she wonders if she did the right thing in bailing out at the hut. Maybe the midwives were highly skilled and their facilities sufficiently clean, though scary-looking to anyone not from the Jamaica hills. The underlying thought behind every other thought is that her naive carelessness with Sterling now will shadow her forever, with or without him in her life. She's having his baby. She fully understands that it's too late now, and only the Lord knows how this will affect her career.

In coming days, work takes over for both Sheryl and Sterling. But Sterling has seen Sheryl's loss of faith in herself and figures it will play nicely into a series of mind-control games he has planned for her. Soon, if all goes according to his plan, she never will know what hit her, so to speak. He inwardly brims over with confidence, like any confidence man.

Sterling finds his status as an island doctor intoxicating, especially the aspect of getting days off, unlike Sheryl during a tour week or stretch of tour weeks. He gets covered by a doctor who rotates around the resort chain on a fill-in, where-needed basis. Most of his spare moments find him up in the hills, getting extracurricular schooling through the Rastafarians.

Since his comfy unemployment stretch, with Sheryl busy at work, Sterling has been pursuing long-ago advice from Uncle Austin—that if he ever has the chance, he should network with people who know the art of hypnotism. Here in Jamaica's hill country, he has found the tropical Obeah religious sect of hypnotism and mysticism. *Uncle Austin would approve*, he thinks proudly.

Now that he is employed, Sterling no longer can drift to twice-weekly meetings with a local high lord in the art of mind control, Snake Gibb, and Sheryl will soon face a final deadline for reconsidering the midwives. Today the stars align between his day off and Sheryl's busy schedule. With her glad to have him out of sight for the day, he heads for the hills.

Snake, tall and pushing sixty, remains vital with the physique of a much younger man. Salt-and-pepper dreadlocks and a calm intelligence command respect everywhere he goes. As in previous sessions with Sterling, Snake delves into intricacies of influencing another's thinking. "There's no reason, mon, ever to let anyone get the upper hand on you. You always must maintain the upper hand in every way."

"Teach me your ways," Sterling boldly implores.

"If you listen well, you will learn, my friend."

Snake grew up fearless in the Blue Mountains east of Kingston. He is the son of a respected town leader with roots to the Jamaican Maroons, runaway slaves who actually were let loose by their Spanish owners in 1655 as the British took over Jamaica. Generations of Gibbs, whose family name traces directly to a sugar plantation and slave owner, have practiced the ancient art of hypnotism. Snake also is a substitute father to his much younger and very beautiful kid sister, Miriam, who was conceived by their father, now long gone, when in his eighties.

"He became quite the rogue," Snake likes to quip, "after my mother died. Miriam's mother was the town beauty queen—and young, about like Miriam right now."

So it is that Sterling has a life quite separate from the one Sheryl thinks they share, complete with a different cast of characters. Sheryl's trusting nature and busy schedule have kept her too preoccupied in the past to worry about his lengthy disappearances. Now she would just as soon not be dwelling on him. Sterling is grateful for the ability to come and go as he pleases.

During all this coming and going, Sterling not only has become adept at hypnotism; he's obtained an introduction to Miriam. "My lucky day," he's fond of telling her. Miriam stands like a Brahman against other young women of the village. Just nineteen, her beauty already is legendary throughout the mountain range.

Snake is proud to have his new American friend, Sterling, hanging around and promising to open a medical facility in their village. "You have no idea what this will mean to our village," Snake said several weeks ago while giving thanks.

Like Sheryl, Snake has no idea that the alleged good doctor leads a double life. He believes Sterling is on a sabbatical from a Chicago teaching hospital and that he has turned it into a working vacation by helping out at No Worries. Understandably, Sterling is seen as a busy guy, with limited time to spend visiting the mountains. When he is around, Snake takes in Sterling's tall tales of valor, believing he has unlimited potential to bring good to their ramshackle mountain village.

Sterling, no different from any man, immediately was smitten with Miriam. Being away from her has been torture, worsened by her not having shown up yet today. Snake's lesson of the day for Sterling involves working to achieve inner peace. Sterling soon enters another dimension, where total recall replays any scene through self-hypnosis.

"Go with it," Snake coaches from the here and now.

In the world of trances, Sterling recalls getting the lay of the land of the hills during his unemployment bliss. That's when he first coaxed a hesitant Miriam to sneak off with him to a deserted and distant plantation line shack. He'd found the shack on a coffee field map in Snake's primitive office.

"Good thing you are so nosy," Miriam teases Sterling. "That map's been there forever, and I never gave it notice."

"Being with you keeps me on my toes, my dear."

Miriam has liked this smooth, older American from the start. Both of their minds already have rushed light-years ahead to many happy days together, but Miriam is determined not to be a pushover. Nevertheless, the first line shack visit leads to others, each one friskier than the last. "You're fun," she's always quick to tell Sterling.

During one shack visit, he proposes, "So here's a fun idea ... I don't suppose you'd care to let me practice my hypnotism drills on you, would you?"

"Wow, that's about the last thing I thought you were going to say. Is that supposed to be romantic?"

"Snake says I have to work at this with someone I trust."

She laughs. "Hey, boy, you don't think I've had that game played on me before? Living around here, hypnotism heaven, with Snake as everyone's guru?"

"All right," Sterling says with a shrug, "so I don't get points for originality. But I'd like to think you and I have something going on that all those players only could dream of, right?"

"Come on, sweet-talking man, you know we have something going on—just don't be getting your hopes up too high too fast. And I won't be doing anything I don't wanna be doin'."

"What, are you saying I want to seduce you by hypnosis?"

"Can you imagine such a thing?"

"Girl," he intones with faux indignation, "I never would dream of such a thing!"

She pushes him down on the antique weathered bed. "I'm sure," she purrs, entwining her body with his. Between a few kisses, she whispers, "Now don't be taking this as some kind of promise of anything to come. Just a little kissin'."

"Only if you come will I."

It takes young Miriam a moment to catch his drift. "Is that right?" she eventually responds. She's all in long before he even attempts any hocus-pocus. They're all over each other, removing clothing as they go. Sterling is amazed and humbled to find that this legendary young beauty has remained a virgin till now.

She shrieks and goes giggly at the sight of her blood trails. "I need to capture this," she laughs.

"You're bad," he laughs back as she snaps a picture.

Sterling's visits become less frequent, with extra work brought on at No Worries by brushes with some tropical storms, bringing a few injuries to his clinic. Eventually, though, hurricane season ends.

Surface life settles down, and Sheryl decides to take a solo journey to the jungle for a day of bamboo rafting, telling Sterling she'll use the little excursion to clear her mind. As a couple, they have been discussing how by next week she'll be at the outer limits of any abortive surgical procedure that could be performed.

"The rafting will do you good," he agrees. "You'll figure it all out."

Even while talking to Sheryl, Sterling focuses on his unexpected opportunity to be away from her watch. Once she is gone, he pries a few hours off duty from Ronny Walker and heads for the hills.

After a line-shack tryst, Miriam waits till passion cools to spill some news to Sterling. "I'm pregnant," she says softly, her eyes seeking his.

"What?" he exclaims in knee-jerk fashion, though he heard her perfectly well.

"You heard me," she replies, staring him down. "I knew this would not be good news to you. I just knew it. Suddenly, this is not so fun or romantic for me anymore."

Beyond stunned, Sterling tries to gather his splattered thoughts. He has nothing to say.

Miriam, though, has plenty enough to say for both of them. "Stupid, stupid me!" she laments before bursting into tears. "And it's all the worse," she sobs, "since you're never around anymore, especially when I need you most."

"I am here now," he finally utters, enveloping her in his arms.

"For now," she interjects. "I was a fool to believe you were not using me, but no more."

"I've never felt anything but love and compassion, despite what you think."

Miriam steps away from him in the tiny shack, seemingly blocking out his voice. Talking more or less to herself, she says, "All the girls say nothing can happen the first time."

"No, my dear," Sterling says, unable to keep from chuckling at her naïveté, "I'm afraid that's an old wives' tale. First time, any time, can be your time."

"I realize that now. It doesn't exactly ring true in practice."

Sterling's mind races through obvious repercussions. He mumbles, "Snake is gonna be pissed! He'll think I've overstepped my bounds—betrayed his fine hospitality."

"No lie!" Miriam interjects in agreement, shaking her pretty head in trepidation.

"And he wouldn't be wrong."

Miriam shudders. "I'm sure he didn't have this in mind for me quite so soon. And he rules, boy. Cross him and you find out."

Sterling's mind flashes from one delicate situation to another, thinking secret thoughts of the Sheryl situation and now this. New thoughts blast from further back in time, his action-packed months at Makeup Is Us. He's been down this path before, that summer. But at least then he was similar in age to the girls he romanced, with only one of them getting pregnant. This time, with the age gap, there's more than a tinge of guilt for Sterling. Miriam is so young.

For the first time ever, Sterling feels like a real cad. Traces of guilt flutter in his thoughts of Sheryl, even as he feels tight up against the ropes standing before Miriam. He's in a double bind with trouble ahead from each of them. "Talk about unfaithful," he mutters, momentarily disgusted with himself.

"What?" Miriam asks.

Stressed, Sterling snaps to attention and caresses her face. "My dear, my mind was wandering around, out of control."

She searches his eyes. He looks back into her eyes, gently. He tries to send a sympathetic thought way deep into her psyche. Verbally, he softly adds, "I'm faithfully here."

Even as Sterling scolds himself, he knows he better get on the ball. Miriam's surprise news was so out of left field. Her eyes now seek guidance. She's in trouble, in need of a holding hand, his holding hand. He embraces her and tries humor. "So you don't think he'll be too happy with me?"

"Ha!" she exclaims, laughing in his face.

"Figures. I'd feel the same." Sterling stalls momentarily and then smoothly says, "We need to discuss our options."

"Options? Like what, an abortion? Me? I, uh … I don't know."

"I know it's not what you'd want to do if given a choice."

"Gee, really?" Pain manifests all over her face.

"Sorry, really. All I meant was—"

"Careful!" she interjects.

He takes heed and proceeds gingerly. "All I mean is this is pretty unexpected, right? And depending on what you—we—decide to do, it could affect the rest of our lives, right?"

"Either way it will affect the rest of my life."

"So," Sterling says, forging ahead, "I'm sure you know of girls getting them done on the sly."

"Right," says a wounded Miriam, "on the sly."

Sterling senses his insensitivity. "Hey, baby, sorry again. I didn't mean it to sound so bad." He reaches for her, but she pulls away repulsed.

"Whatever," she snarls in retort. "But you're wrong to think that this is so unexpected. I mean, come on, mon, are you kidding me? We were totally careless! Under your leadership, I might add."

"Hey, it takes two, and you were game."

"I was game?"

"I forced nothing."

"That better not be your story for Snake."

"What story? I should be telling him I forced myself upon you? That ain't gonna happen. Listen, Miriam dear, if you do both the right and smart thing, we won't need any story."

Miriam sees where this is leading. "Look, even if I okay an abortion, you're forgetting Snake."

"I assure you, that's the last thing I'm doing."

"You are afraid of him, this I know."

"Well, that's for sure. Who wouldn't be?"

"You better be."

"I am."

"Then think of this, smarty Yankee man, Snake knows every midwife and doctor from here to Kingston. People know me too."

"Point being?"

"You still think we can keep this quiet?"

Sterling, befuddled by fear of a vengeful Snake, still insists, "Why not, if we're smart?"

"No, my dear." She chuckles heartily but with overtones of misery. "This cannot be kept quiet. It will be front-page news here."

Sterling knows she is right. "The right idea will take hold," he offers reassuringly.

Miriam wants him to stay the night—needs him to stay the night. But of course he can't stay. Little does Miriam know that Sheryl awaits Sterling at No Worries with more trouble of a similar nature. Sterling sees Miriam home from the line shack and returns to No Worries.

Come morning in the hills, Miriam joins Snake for breakfast. He senses that his little sister is on edge and demands to know what is going down between her and Sterling.

To the point, she says, "I came up pregnant, Snake."

"What?"

By noon, Snake and Miriam are motoring for No Worries in his aging Toyota. An unwanted distraction looms darkly on the horizon, a postseasonal hurricane. Already not so far off, it builds strength in promise of catastrophic trouble. Radio airwaves buzz with warnings.

Inside the Toyota, all weather issues take a backseat to Snake's preoccupation with Miriam's condition and how she came to be in such a fix. As they zip downhill in the creaky car, thoughts of what to do about Sterling ricochet around inside his brain—murderous thoughts.

He snarls to Miriam, "I thought I could trust this American man of medicine and did so with my own sister." Choking beneath the dignity of a revered, holy man, he asks, "Please forgive me, girl. I know I can never forgive myself."

"Snake, this is life. There is nothing to forgive."

Snake composes himself. "To think I would have been glad, proud, to have Sterling as a brother-in-law through proper channels of respect—despite the age spread between you two. Now I only feel outrage."

Miriam smiles at her big brother. "It is good to see you in your dangerous mode. You are so powerful when you get this way. I am so proud to be your little sister."

At No Worries Beach Resort, Sheryl sits at a lobby table near the reception desk, finishing up frantic paperwork for a nervous but grateful man, a JA Tours client. She's just gotten him a flight change that gets him and his family out of Jamaica right away, free and clear of the hurricane. Sheryl wishes luck to the stressed tourist as he runs off to tell his wife and kids the great news.

Wondering what crisis will spring up next, Sheryl scans the open-air lobby and spots an aging Toyota double-parking outside, to the irritation of the head valet. Taxis, shuttles, and freaked-out travelers already clog the driveway. The Toyota blocks the only avenue around all the vehicles loading up people and luggage for treacherous runs to the airport in Montego Bay.

An impressive duo climbs out of the Toyota, a towering man with salt-and-pepper dreadlocks and a stunning young woman. Both are obviously angry and in a hurry. They are in no mood for listening to the valet, who follows them into the lobby.

The Rastafarian man tosses his keys to the valet, firmly instructing, "Move it yourself. And you better not lose those keys on me, mon, or there will be trouble." As the valet turns to go, the tall man calls after him. "Is Dr. Sterling Jackson around today?"

The valet, overwhelmed with masses of badgering guests, has no idea as to Sterling's whereabouts. He looks relieved when Sheryl steps in to help.

"Can I help you?" she asks the man amid the tense atmosphere.

"I'm looking for Dr. Sterling Jackson. Do you know where he could be found?"

Sheryl sneaks a glance at the young woman before answering. "No, but if you'll give me time to check, maybe I can find him for you."

"That would be appreciated," says the man, calming down a bit.

"Who shall I say is asking?" asks Sheryl.

"Tell him Snake and Miriam happened to be in the neighborhood—thought we'd say hi."

"Right," replies Sheryl, not believing a word of it. She smiles at Miriam, thinking she notices a tiny baby bump. She notices Miriam likewise examining Sheryl's growing condition. "Well," continues Sheryl, "let me see what I can do for you. I'll be right back."

Sheryl exits outside, wondering about the reasons behind this unexpected pair's search for Sterling during the chaos of an approaching hurricane. Her early warning system already has her suspicious of any forthcoming explanation from Sterling, provided he can be found.

She heads for Sterling's beachfront bungalow near the pounding surf, making sure Snake and Miriam are not tracking her movements. Confident they're still in the lobby, Sheryl turns down the path to Sterling's digs, mindful of swirling debris in the air. She develops the strange feeling that she's seen Snake and Miriam before somewhere. She's certain of that.

"Up in the mountains," she suddenly mumbles, "that's where."

⧟

In the bungalow, Sterling stuffs clothes into a suitcase. He has to kneel on the top to get it closed. Grabbing his passport and cash from a closet safe, he rushes outside and begins running down a lush pathway away from the beach.

"Look!" screams one scurrying guest among many. "It's getting closer!" The sky has darkened to an ungodly hue that screams, *Get out of my way!*

Guests are scampering all over the resort property in various stages of panic, many towing suitcases. Tropical landscaping sways in the increasing winds, with the menacing clouds casting sinister shadows on the resort's many brightly colored guest buildings. Heard everywhere are panicked voices in varying languages, speaking to the crisis's international flavor.

At a path crossroads, Sheryl and Sterling run into each other. She grabs him on the fly. "Where are you going?" she angrily demands.

Antsy and wanting to keep on the move, he thinks fast and barks into the wind, "To the lobby to find you! Thank God you're here! Get your stuff and let's get out of here!"

"And where are we going?"

"Beg, borrow, or steal us a flight to anywhere, fast! Or at least let's get to the airport and be first in line once the debris is cleared."

"Sorry to say," Sheryl snarls with a glare, "but I think the lobby's the last place you want to be right now."

"What're you talking about?"

"There's a rather unusual couple looking for you there."

"What?" he stammers, fearing the worst. "A couple of what?"

"A couple of Jamaicans—Snake and Miriam. Ring a bell?"

Sterling flushes, knowing the jig is up. "Oh …"

"What's this 'oh' all about?"

"It's a long story—let's leave it at that for now."

"Okay, listen," she says forcefully, "for now we will leave it at that. There's too much going on to squabble. But this will be revisited, soon!"

⧟

Sheryl has no intention of leaving this alone for long. She suspects the worst—that this involves Miriam and that little bump. Whatever it is, as much as she'd like to argue now and part ways with him forever, Sheryl has been through these storms before and knows that at this point it's the luck of the draw. Anything bad could happen. All hands are needed on deck. Survival mode rules. Personal troubles are trumped.

Sternly, she instructs Sterling, "Get over to Little Italy. It's our best hurricane shelter for anyone in the know."

Sterling glances first at the increasingly dangerous horizon and then checks out the Italian-themed restaurant down the path. Staffers and platinum-level guests are ducking inside.

Sheryl testily adds, "I'm putting you in the know."

"Maybe you're right. It's crazy to be out in the open."

"There's no maybe about it. I'll send your friends off to a different shelter."

"And then what?"

"We'll deal with this after the storm blows through."

"Fine," he says, apparently acquiescing.

"Whatever's going on, we both know it isn't very fine."

"You're right," he admits. "And we'll face it head-on right away."

She stares him down and then snarls, "I'm still on the clock. We'll reconnect later."

As she scoots for the lobby, Sheryl's mind is a fog of competing memories and visions. Job responsibilities outweigh everything else, though, and she wants to shake off Snake and Miriam as fast as possible. Then she'll take on that other snake, Sterling. Sheryl angrily indicts him based on his expressions alone. *He looks like he's on the run from everyone, everything.*

As if that's not enough, sudden memories of her bout of morning sickness earlier today prompt self-flagellation. While on the run during this storm, she almost forgot she's pregnant. In an instant it all comes back, leading to the familiar questions: *What am I doing? How did I get here?* She's powerless to answer, until a strong inner voice rings out: *You know.*

She does. That needy night with Sterling haunts her. Against the background of another dazzling sunset, their pulses raced, taking them to the brink. She crumbled in his arms, desperate for love. Sheryl tears up upon recalling her desire to be cuddled.

Panicking and bewildered, she asks, "How could I have let this happen? What a sucker I am, all for the beach under some coconut tree with a joint and the moon." She shouts into the storm, "What a dummy!"

Sheryl enters the lobby through a side entrance carrying the weight of the world. In self-chastising mode, she blinks off tears that are so far camouflaged on her rain-soaked face. Shaking off regrets over her inexplicably wanton behavior that just might damn her to hell, she puts it all behind her to face a swarm of panicked JA Tours guests pressing in on her from all directions. Responsibilities rule. For the moment, she back-burners Snake and Miriam.

⟡

Outside, Sterling reaches Little Italy. With a quick look back toward the resort's open-air lobby, he verifies Sheryl is inside, totally occupied. Abruptly, he changes course, getting off the heavily beaten paths of fleeing foot traffic. In stealth mode, he skirts the lobby exterior, passing deserted swimming pools and turning onto an employees-only maintenance path.

At a fork in the path, one choice leads to a deserted beach with monstrous breakers crashing. The other path leads away from the beach in the general direction of the resort's approach driveway. Sterling sees some empty tourist shuttle buses arriving. Most importantly, he sees that the shuttle loading zone is clear of Snake and Miriam.

Hustling to the driveway curb, he notices Snake's Toyota parked nearby. The chief valet spots Sterling as he runs past with a suitcase. "Hey, Doc— where are you going? We need you around here!"

"I'll be right back. I'm taking this to a friend who is leaving the island. Don't panic!"

"Be careful, Doc!" The valet takes Sterling at his word and gets back to work.

⟡

From inside the lobby, Sheryl happens to catch sight of Sterling on the move among the shuttles, suitcase in tow. She's not surprised to see he has lied to her again. Next, she spots Snake and Miriam at a VIP customer service alcove. There, they wait for Dr. Jackson, who is being paged.

With Snake and Miriam preoccupied, Sheryl runs to the driveway and cuts off Sterling just short of a shuttle loading people making a last-ditch dash to the airport. "Whoa, buster, where do you think you're going?"

"I changed my mind, for us. There's a killer storm bearing down, and I don't want us to meet our maker! Get moving. I'll get us a taxi while you quickly pack."

"I don't think so, Sterling. You look like a man with bigger worries on his mind than a tropical storm."

"Honest, girl, the summer storms spooked me, but I thought they were done. This is the worst of all! Our number could be up if we don't get out of here, now!"

"Don't bullshit me, Sterling. What's with that old Rastafarian in the lobby and his daughter or whoever she is? Tell me now because it will come out anyway."

"Looks like it's coming out already."

"Afraid so, and it's better I hear it from you, right?"

"I guess so," he concedes. "And she's his little sister, not daughter—although he treats her like a daughter. Anyway ... they're gonna say I got her pregnant."

"What?"

"Like I said, that's what they're gonna say. That doesn't mean they're right. But maybe they are right."

"Maybe they are right? What?"

"I met them when I was gathering data for a medical journal article about jungle medicine. He's some kind of Blue Mountains shaman, Snake Gibb."

"That's where I've seen them before," Sheryl exclaims, "at a coffee plantation excursion last year. We traveled through this little village and stopped for a magic show, all part of the excursion. Both of them were in it."

"Whatever," grumbles Sterling. "Just understand—he had her sneak into my room when I was asleep. She had her way with me before I even realized it wasn't a dream."

"Get out!" Sheryl spits at him. "That is some kind of creative bullshit, I'll give you that, but you're really dreaming if you think I'll swallow that crap."

"Honey, honestly!"

"You must think I'm an idiot."

"Sheryl, I don't think you're an idiot—far from it."

"Well," she chokes, "I feel like an idiot, trusting you."

"Don't—"

Disgusted, she promises, "Sterling, unless you face the music here and now, right after this storm, I'll never speak to you again!"

Sheryl is thankful that all the people running in circles around them are too focused on their own troubles to notice the couple's angry interplay. She wonders how many of them, if any, were living out serious life crises of their own when interrupted by the angry weather gods. She slips into a trancelike state as she looks around at the numerous vacationers panicking in the bull's-eye of the powerful storm. Many are beyond tears. All have exposed fears.

Suddenly, she realizes that Sterling is speaking. "All right, all right, my dear. Yes, you're right—always right." He agrees to meet with Snake after the storm passes.

Sterling attempts to touch Sheryl, and she pulls away, repulsed. Here they are again, in the middle of another unwanted pregnancy with him as the root cause. Sheryl, fearful for her own situation, empathizes with beautiful young Miriam.

"Get going," she commands with disgust and a nod toward Little Italy.

Backing away, he suggests, "Maybe you can soften up Snake a little for me?"

Finding his request incredibly nervy, Sheryl dismissively snaps, "Go hide out in the spa—lie low. With any luck, they'll get back to the mountains, fast."

Surrounded by ever-growing pandemonium, Sheryl is glad to have the distraction of work. She ditches Sterling for the lobby. Her main concern now, beyond the crazy weather and shepherding her tourist sheep, is what will happen if Kearns hears about this Miriam and Snake stuff. She remembers having had a touch of doubt the day she vouched for Sterling. But she ignored the angel's warning and now is paying for it.

In the lobby, loudspeakers tell those lucky tourists previously scheduled to leave today that they still will be going. This means a couple buses' worth of mostly North Americans. Everyone else, the loudspeakers boom, either should secure all loose items in their rooms and hunker down or go to one of several storm shelters on the property.

"All right!" shouts a dad to his drained wife and brood, heading for the driveway.

Mother Nature's whirling-dervish clouds are visible through a windowless skylight, keeping the crowd in a panic. Sheryl, a hurricane veteran, remains calm, though in a daze, as she seeks out Snake and Miriam at a VIP alcove.

When she reaches them, Sheryl defuses the moment, saying, "Sterling has owned up to what your visit is about. I'm appalled and so sorry—but he needs to be doctoring emergency cases right now. And I personally vouch he won't leave the island till all parties have met."

To her relief, Snake admits that he and Miriam indeed are anxious to get back home. Finding Sterling isn't worth being out in the open during a hurricane. Snake says, "I hope I can trust you. Where will I find him after the storm?"

"Just contact me here. And don't worry, procedure after a hurricane is no days off till things are put back together. So he will be here. I'll see to that."

"Tell the not-so-good doctor that we will be back. And no more hide-and-seek, not with me. That would be his gravest mistake, ever."

"I'll be sure he understands."

Snake is out of words. He offers no handshake either. "Let's go," he tells his pregnant kid sister.

The valet hands them their keys, and they vroom off in their creaky Toyota to join weather refugee traffic.

Sheryl fears she just lied with her assurances of Sterling's whereabouts. She wonders, *How, it seems, can I guarantee anything with him now?* Sheryl feels terrible guilt by association with the scoundrel she's helping hide from Snake's wrath.

Sheryl leaves the VIP alcove for the frenzied main floor of the lobby, where she unexpectedly encounters Sterling. "What're you doing here?" she barks. "Get to the spa!" He probably never went to the shelter, she figures, and was just waiting to see Snake and Miriam leave before reappearing.

"Come on, baby, it's like I was raped!"

A few nearby ears perk up at that vocal burst.

"You know there's nobody for me but you."

Sheryl rolls her eyes. "Don't be giving me that," she warns. "I've heard it all before anyway. It's meaningless from you."

"Baby, come on."

Abruptly, Ronny Walker interrupts their conversation. He reports they've lost a shuttle driver for the last airport convoy. "Johnny headed for the hills!"

"Who can blame him?" Sheryl replies. She knows what's coming next from Walker.

"You're licensed on shuttles, right?"

"I am."

"So can you help me, us?"

"It's kind of out of my hands, Ronny. Sure, I'd be helping you, but JA Tours might consider me AWOL. I've got lots of guests under my stewardship."

Walker laughs. "It may surprise you to know, Sheryl, but I have a majority stake in JA Tours, so don't worry about them. I can assign a resort staffer to cover you. That's if you want to. It's strictly voluntary. No worries."

"Right—no worries, just a little old hurricane, that's all. And me driving a bus full of pants-pissing tourists at their wits' ends. What's to worry about there?"

Suddenly, though, she sees that this gives her an out, a sudden advantage born from adversity that affords her a chance to ditch Sterling for good, which she knows is the right and prudent thing to do. It could be now or never.

"Tell you what, Ronny, I'll do the shuttle run, with the understanding that an airborne seat out of here awaits me at Sangster."

"I can arrange that," Walker promises.

Sterling looks ready to drop everything and run with her. "Let's go," he says. He turns to Walker. "Get one for me too."

"Like hell, Sterling," Sheryl says. "You're staying here to make a plan with that girl."

Walker tweaks an eyebrow in apparent interest. "I don't want to butt in, but I'll be hard-pressed to come up with even one seat for Sheryl."

Sterling shrugs. "You can't blame me for asking."

Walker pointedly gets in Sterling's face. "I'm caring less about you by the minute, but you're gonna stick around and play doctor—even though I'm having my doubts you know a scalpel from a toe clipper."

Sterling looks indignant. "You know better than that. You've seen the quality of my doctoring."

"Let's not even go there. Just get your ass to that spa, pronto!"

Walker, on an authority binge, additionally instructs Sheryl, "I need you in that first shuttle. Take ten minutes to pack, whatever."

"Gee, thanks, I think."

"Good luck! I'll get the bus loaded in the meantime." With that, Walker double-times it to the driveway.

"Aye-aye, sir," Sheryl shouts in his wake. She turns to Sterling and talks fast. "Seems like there's unholy pregnancies everywhere you go. So I'm out of here and done with you. Don't try to get in my way."

Sheryl bolts to her room to pack, never having felt so bold in dealing with calamities. She even seems to be getting a thrill from it. Seeing Sterling skulk off toward the spa felt gratifying. She's ready to hit the adventurous road to Sangster and get out of here fast.

ও

Sterling, walking along the path to the spa, has never felt so unready for anything. His route takes him near his own bungalow, where he's surprised to see Snake nosing around some windows. Sterling stoops low behind shrubbery and slinks away before Snake spots him. Feeling trapped, he barges in on Sheryl at her garden-view room.

She is clearly annoyed as she finishes up her rapid packing, ready to run. "Don't you get it?" she taunts. "Get away from me! And stay away from me."

"Snake's prowling the grounds looking for me!"

"And I hope he finds you!"

"Nice, thanks. I thought they'd left!" complains Sterling.

"Apparently not," snaps Sheryl. "Fine! Hide under the bed for all I care. See if he finds you there. I'm out of here, mon." She opens her door and stops.

Snake looms outside, waiting. His hateful glare homes in on Sterling. Snake steps to the threshold, body language conjuring up evil spirits. "You think I'd let you get away?" Snake snarls.

Sterling is speechless.

"I'm here to see justice is done," Snake continues.

Sheryl tries to edge her way outside, calmly saying, "Snake, do with Sterling as you will. But I have a job to do. Lives are at stake."

Snake blocks her path. "Well, his life is at stake right now. I can say that for sure."

Sheryl questions, "But we're cool, right—you and me?"

"Nobody moves," he responds, "not just yet." But as widespread panic continues to play out among tourists in the background, Snake gestures with his hand for Sheryl to go on her way. "Good luck," he says.

"Same to you and Miriam," says Sheryl as she leaves.

⊷⊷

Sheryl sprints out of the room not caring what might happen to Sterling. In a state of shock, she cuts through the lobby toward the driveway, mixing with panicky guests and resort employees toting clipboards along the way. The open-air room bulges to capacity. Fear still dominates.

⊷⊷

Back at Sheryl's room, Sterling, angered at the thought of Sheryl and Snake more or less being teammates, is at a rare loss for words.

Snake stares him down, obviously furious over Miriam's condition. "You call yourself a man of medicine?" Snake roars. "You are a thief—a thief of hearts and trust." He pops a swift, solid double stiff-arm to Sterling's chest. Sterling takes it like a man.

"And thanks to your betrayal of trust," continues Snake, "we've had to leave the safety of our mountains today with a hurricane coming!" He hits Sterling in the chest again.

This time, Sterling instinctively shoves back, pushing Snake into the path of a gust-blown coconut that hammers his head. Snake falls to the ground and remains there, limbs splayed out. Sterling cowers at the bloody sight. An involuntary argument breaks out between the modestly good and decidedly bad sides of his brain.

You killed him! I can't believe it.

You're crazy! Who says he's dead?

Look at him! He's not moving!

The coconut did it anyway, not me!

The coconut would've missed him if you hadn't pushed him! That's obvious!

Wonderful. And does that make you my accomplice?

Whatever. Aren't you going to see if he's dead?

It feels like the twilight zone for Sterling. His head spins, and his heart seems to skip a beat. If Snake is dead, "murderer" will be a new line item on Sterling's résumé.

He exhales, uttering, "Well …" Wordlessly, he takes a closer look and feels for a pulse, which he doesn't find. Acting like he imagines a doctor would, he holds a finger beneath Snake's nostrils—nothing. Snake surely seems dead to Sterling.

Panicked, Sterling scans the surroundings. He sees no witnesses. Everyone is in the lobby, in the shelters, or by the buses. Feeling safe for the circumstances, he feels calm come over him. *Deal with it, Sterling*, he orders himself.

Back at the driveway, Ronny Walker is supervising a handful of resort employees when Sheryl arrives, ready to go yet overwhelmed; being busy helps. Together, she and Walker efficiently guide the anxious departing guests, helping with the loading of luggage and the filling of seats. Two buses remain curbside. They'll be the final shuttles to go.

"You're on the lead bus," Walker tells her.

"You think that's a good idea?"

"The guy behind you got his license last week. You're in charge, Sheryl, as usual. You'll pull it off, no sweat."

"We'll see. Thanks, Ronny."

"Good luck, girl, and get away from Sterling for good."

They hug. Sheryl feels like she's onstage with crowds watching from the buses. This unexpected pressure helps hold her emotions in check. She climbs up onto the driver's seat of the lead shuttle.

Sheryl watches through her side-view mirror as Walker loads her luggage into the bus belly, seals the compartment, and visually checks with the second bus's driver. Turning back to Sheryl, Walker gives her a thumbs-up. Security opens the gate.

Sheryl gingerly accelerates the bus away from the curb, dutifully mimicked by number two's rookie pilot. The two No Worries buses join other shuttles fleeing nearby resorts. They gather speed while driving in formation on a tight roadway through scrub jungle, away from the land of beach resorts. Quickly, traffic stacks up approaching Ocho Rios.

Ocho Rios market vendors are battening down their tents or their shutters on tin shacks. Tourists trapped away from their resorts run the street, desperate for transportation. Local citizenry flee by foot, bicycle, motor scooter, and aging compact cars, not paying much attention to normal traffic courtesies. A horn-blasting chorus accentuates total chaos.

Sheryl and the rookie take it slow, ambling carefully around town through tiny road openings in the third-world bottleneck. Traffic clogs to a halt at a shantytown bend in the road. For Sheryl behind the wheel, time momentarily stands still. The No Worries buses and the rest of the jam inch forward around the bend into a straightaway. Traffic flow opens up as everyone barrels out of the bottleneck and out of town. Pedestrians grittily forge ahead on dirt shoulders, barely flinching—there is an air of "been here, done this before." *My God*, Sheryl thinks, observing all sides of the story.

She slows her bus again, approaching a turnoff for the Port of Ocho Rios. Care is called for as fleeing dockworkers run through traffic seeking higher ground. Riding her brakes, with lulls in forward progress, she steals seaward glances and spots a departing cruise ship. *Get a move on*, thinks Sheryl; the mega ship suddenly appears fragile in light of the approaching mammoth storm. The only vessel in sight, it aims for a bright speck of light in the distant western horizon through raging seas. To the east, things look much worse—dark, foreboding, threatening to bring inevitable death and destruction. *Come on*, she mentally tells every person or vehicle in her way.

Finally reaching the lowlands on roads winding close to the sea, Sheryl maintains a steady pace, all the while keeping an eye on the rookie behind her. He seems up to the task. So is she, Sheryl proudly realizes, though frightened stiff. *What a trip!*

As they drive along a suddenly somewhat open road, a somber silence descends over the bus's interior. Sheryl, still getting her bearings in the driver's seat, spots a radio system and powers it up. It takes a few moments to find an on-air station. A loud weather update suddenly announces, "Hurricane Victor confounded experts last night, breaking from its northerly track to now threaten nearly all of Jamaica."

Her passengers already are too stunned to noticeably react to the announcer's beautifully accented report. Heavy raindrops pelt the windshield. Sheryl flips on the wipers and concentrates on the narrow, congested road.

The announcer continues, "Outer bands from this surprise postseason hurricane already have hit the north shore hard, bringing heavy rains to Ocho Rios and eastward to Port Antonio. Forecasters say the category-three storm now raking Hispaniola will regain strength once it crosses back into open waters. Look out!"

Sheryl clenches the steering wheel as nearby palm trees bend in successive wind gusts that are gaining strength and buffeting her bus. Her eyes dart between jungly mountains on the left and wild seas to her right. Feeling weightless while narrowly dodging a pothole, she can't fully suppress her anxieties. "Oh boy!" she exclaims over the little rush in her tummy. She checks her overhead mirror; shuttle two still trails closely behind her. "Good there," she says quietly.

A two-way radio squawks from a perch on the dash. It's Rudi, the rookie driver of bus number two, all hopped up. Sheryl stiffens a one-hand grip on the steering wheel and reaches with her other hand for the handset.

With worry in his voice, Rudi says, "Sheryl, mon, we are running late!"

"No!" objects Sheryl. "Don't be talking that way, mon. I need to make my flight."

Rudi asks, "How did you get a ticket so late?"

She answers, "I pulled a favor from a ticket agent and shot to the top of standby."

"How can you be standing by? You're not even there!"

"I'm there, all right—as long as we arrive on time."

Sheryl notices that her riders have stirred from their silence. They've broken into scared blathering all over again, with increasingly strong expressions of fear.

Rudi asks, "What you gonna do if Byron's a no-show at Sangster?"

"I'll be leaving this bus in your care, my friend. No way I'm missing that plane."

"You gotta be crazy! What am I gonna do with two buses in all this weather?"

"Sorry, Rudi, but I'm out of here if my plane's allowed to go. I'm on it!"

Drowning out their talk is another hurricane update broadcasting to both buses. "Expect coastal flooding and road washouts all along the north shore."

"Wonderful!" moans a fearful passenger on Sheryl's bus. "That's us!"

Sheryl tells Rudi, "Let's knuckle down on the road, Rudi. Block out whatever craziness might go on with the passengers, and be focused."

"Aye-aye, boss," acknowledges Rudi. "Over and out."

"Over."

Within moments, a collective hush sets in as Sheryl slows at a gawkers' traffic snare. The object of interest is the burned-out hulk of a once-pristine tourist shuttle bus just like those from No Worries. The derelict vehicle is shoved off onto a narrow dirt shoulder, its front end crumpled like an accordion from a head-on crash. The entire superstructure, inside and out, is burned to a crisp. Sheryl knows that every shaking tourist must be thinking the same thing: *Who could survive such a crash? There, for the grace of God, go any one of us.*

Half-mesmerized by the mournful roadside sight, Sheryl sets up poorly for a roundabout ahead that spins off to Montego Bay's Sangster International Airport. No matter how many times she's driven British-style on the left, she still gets confused by the clockwise spin to this roundabout's flow. Horns honk as she gets back with the flow. Rudi remains fine all along, even blocking for her. They circle the intersection cleanly.

Traffic stacks up as they approach the airport entrance. Overloaded vehicles of all sizes creep along till the buses reach a jammed arrivals curb that's in total chaos. "We're here!" a passenger screams from behind Sheryl, and everyone jams the aisle at once.

Sheryl and Rudi jump out of their respective vehicles to help adrenaline-rushed passengers who are pushing and shoving at the buses' cargo hatches. People grab their bags, hurrying inside the terminal in a collective frenzy. Sheryl extracts a final suitcase, her own.

Even with Mother Nature's wrath closing in, Rudi takes the time to tease her. "Sheryl, mon, how you gonna take all that cold and snow?" He feigns a shiver. "You'll beat a fast path back here before you know it!"

"Don't hold your breath, Rudi. I've had enough tropical storms and hurricanes for a while. Seems like there's always another one in the chutes, even off-season."

"It happens, sometimes. This is such a time."

The pair of drivers are looking to the ever-worsening sky when a rusty sedan with bad brakes screeches to a stop at the curb. Out from the front passenger seat hops Byron, and the woman behind the wheel—his wife, Sheryl presumes—pulls away immediately. Byron walks straight to Sheryl at her empty bus.

"Hey, girl," Byron says, full of nervous energy, "you best appreciate how I give up my one day off to drive this tank of yours in a freakin' hurricane!"

Sheryl smiles and nods appreciatively. "I do appreciate it, Byron—you know that." She adds, "And the boss appreciates it even more. Thanks. I'd have felt bad abandoning it here."

Rudi interjects, "Not from what I heard!"

"Well," she agrees, "you got that right. Good job, Rudi!" They hug good-bye.

Sheryl gives Byron the bus keys and a quick hug.

Byron tells her, "Don't be forgetting us up there," and then turns to Rudi. "We gotta go now! There are mudslides on the Queen's Highway."

"Get gone!" insists Sheryl. "Both of you, find cover."

"Don't be worrying," assures Rudi. "We're gone!"

Byron and Rudi climb behind their elevated steering wheels and abruptly inject both buses into already-crazed traffic, like true Jamaican drivers, with Byron in the lead.

The rain's intensity picks up, and Sheryl hotfoots it for the terminal with her suitcase. Scanning the scary horizon one last time, she can't keep herself from mumbling. "Shit, mon."

Sheryl's uniformed and armed connections guide her to the front of the standby queue at Conch Airways. The grumbling from others quiets to a minimum once her escorts' glares shut them down. Sheryl skirts through loosey-goosey customs checkpoints, hustling to grab one of the last few planes on the tarmac. Barring a last-minute scratch, they remain scheduled to get off the ground. "It'll take a miracle from here!" someone shouts.

Sheryl settles into a seat by the head. Outside, the raging storm closes in on Sangster. Strong gusts stiffen a taxiway wind sock. Her plane moves up in line.

"Get us out of here!" a voice cries out.

The sudden roar of jet engines accelerating tells everyone they just might survive this yet. Sheryl, stressed beyond belief, involuntarily thinks of Sterling and how she never wants to see him again. But the plane's bumpy sprint down a rain-splattered runway quickly takes her mind off personal woes. Everyone aboard goes silent. Numb, Sheryl prays, *My God, please help me through all this!*

Once they are airborne, the pilot banks sharply toward western skies. As the plane levels off in flight, Sheryl already feels safer. *Thank you, Lord.*

Fading behind them in the sky, the powerful gale still gives chase, but it's losing ground on the airliner. However, Sheryl knows that back at Sangster International, torrential rains are ripping sideways across deserted runways, and all of Jamaica is battening down hatches, plenty nervous; this act of God threatens anything and everyone in its path.

Disasters of a different nature storm back into Sheryl's troubled mind. *Let's see*, she ponders, still terrified, *I'm pregnant by Sterling, though God knows I can't believe it! Plus I've passed on a career-making offer, also thanks to him. Good going!*

At least she is not fearing imminent death anymore. Sheryl's thoughts spin off into a seemingly endless loop, alternating between dread and sadness. She knows that, at best, she has two weeks left to decide if she should end this pregnancy safely in America and, in the sad process, cut all ties to Sterling forever. That latter part of the equation seems so desirable, and the nightmarish thought of actually having an abortion starts to seem justified—she thinks. Then again, who knows?

No worries, mon, she thinks sarcastically before exhaustion puts her asleep.

Chapter 8

ROE YOURSELF GENTLY

Sheryl and Sterling read the dessert menu at their tucked-away corner table of the American Cuisine Grill; it is full winter outside while the Arab Spring blooms back in Cairo. Sheryl's bloodshot eyes are pools of sorrow as she sips tea, mulling dessert choices. Abortion memories have taken hold, tearing her apart—what's left of her, anyway. Even after all these years, there's been no reconciliation between her mixed emotions. She senses she's losing her grip. "No doubt about it," she mumbles to herself.

Sterling breaks her train of thought. "Hello over there. What's it gonna be?"

Sheryl is surprised to see that their waiter has returned and is awaiting their selections. "I ... uh ... guess I'll go with your all-American apple pie à la mode," she tells the waiter.

"Seems appropriate," concludes Sterling. "Let's make it two." As the waiter leaves, Sterling says, "Doesn't get any more American than apple pie à la mode—a perfect crown to your homecoming dinner."

"This is one homecoming I wasn't taking for granted," says Sheryl. "But I suppose someday Cairo will be just another close call—like my mad dash from Jamaica."

Sterling recalls, "Yeah, mon—that was some storm chasing you off the island, all right."

"Storm nothing," she clarifies. "It was you. The hurricane just gave me the fuel to go."

"I see—and you really thought you'd ditched me. I know."

"You know what?" Sheryl asks sarcastically in a singsong voice.

"I know that you really left me hung out to dry with Snake."

"Yes," replies the still-soft but ever-hardening Sheryl. "How well I remember."

"Hey, hey, hey, ditching me—never gonna happen, girl, eh? We're committed for life."

"We should be committed, all right. Anyway," she clarifies, "for sure I should be, because there you were two weeks later at my door—and I let you in!"

"Of course you did, dear. You were feeling so bad."

"I was feeling bad that you'd made a liar out of me with Snake."

"Come on now, admit it—you were missing me."

Sheryl sadly states, "I've spent half my adult life doing just that."

"Doing what?"

"Feeling bad and missing you."

"Oh, baby, that hurts. Not true. I've always been there for you."

"It hurts, yes—and it's all true. And were you there for me because you were already around, having ignited whatever? Like I said, the whole Jamaican thing—who could forget such a mixed bag of memories, all the highs and lows including the wild aftermath?"

"Yes," Sterling says, "who could forget, indeed?"

"And don't think I ever will!"

"I'm sorry I brought it up."

"I'll bet you are."

Her edgy tone produces a moment of stony silence, allowing Sheryl to recall how Sterling had tracked her down in Lincoln Park so soon after her white-knuckle escape from Jamaica. Startled by the sight of him at her door, Sheryl couldn't get her body to react fast enough to keep pace with her brain, which was screaming, "Slam the door! Run!" Today, she silently demands of herself, *What was I thinking?*

It's way too late now, with nothing to be done about any of it; however, she can't avoid remembering that crisp autumn day—walking with Sterling through Lincoln Park with a cool breeze off the lake, hearing how right after Sheryl had hit the road driving the shuttle, flying storm debris seemingly had killed Snake. After the storm, though, Snake was very much still alive. Apparently, so the story went, that coconut had delivered only a glancing blow.

Snake was found by Canadian tourists who were hunkering down. They brought him in out of the storm. Snake came out of an apparent coma in Sterling's own No Worries emergency clinic. Sterling reminisces with a shaking of his head, "If it weren't for those Canadians dragging me inside, I would've gotten away clean."

Sheryl listens, disgusted by his concept of clean.

Sterling rattles on about having been trapped by Ronny Walker. Since there was no way out, there was no way around Snake's squeezing a healthy cash settlement from Sterling. By then, Snake mostly just wanted Sterling off the island, but with a steep price. "I thought I was a goner," chuckles Sterling.

"So did I," quips Sheryl in a tone that says she had, in fact, hoped he was a goner.

Blocking out his presence across the table, she recalls how after returning from Jamaica, she'd just reached a decision about having an abortion before his unexpected arrival. It had become clear what to do over two weeks of pondering. His being there changed nothing.

♋

"I have an appointment with a scalpel tomorrow," she tells Sterling.

"You're kidding!" he quickly replies.

"What's the surprise? We're done. The child would be a painful reminder for me of you. I doubt I could take it. Besides, you don't want a child anyway."

"You're wrong about me, dear, and I'm sorry to hear you say that. But I understand."

Strangely, Sheryl suddenly can't say she isn't glad to see Sterling, although she hates to admit it to herself and wouldn't want him to know. She fantasizes that maybe some responsibility is all it would take to straighten out his act for good. Now that they are back home in familiar surroundings, in the light of day, with no Jamaican sunset to influence anything, who knows what might be possible?

"Maybe this can work after all," she abruptly dreams aloud, startled by her own voice.

He says, "Listen, my dear."

She braces for major bullshit.

He continues, "Don't think I wouldn't be there to help with the kid's needs. So you don't have to do this, Sheryl. Just please be sure of your actions. That's all I ask."

She is immediately repulsed by his company again. "That's it?"

"Pardon me?"

"That's all you'll ever be to our kid, after-the-fact money as a costly lesson for a fun time with Mommy? Or better yet, you hint, just get rid of it now. We'll all be better for it. Right?"

"Come on," he whines, "we never talked about fathering responsibilities. But if the kid comes around looking for Daddy and knowledge of the world, I'll be there. No question."

Unimpressed, Sheryl frowns. "Wow, how big of you. And how naive of me to think you had something more substantial to say, like 'we can do this together, honey.'"

"Wow, there's a surprise, to hear you want to bring a kid into the world with me as Dad."

"How cheap does that make our nights on the beach seem? I thought you were genuine."

"Baby, I was genuine. Come on now. You twisted my meaning."

"What exactly did I twist?"

"All I'm saying is it's a lifelong step, and we never discussed kids. That's all I'm saying."

"You've said plenty."

"Well, anyway, we should've been more careful."

"Oh really, like being careful was on your mind at all."

"Takes two, dear."

"This is meaningless, Sterling. You're damn nervy. What happened did happen. But it's done now. Over. Don't worry, my mind was made up days ago. I'm not wavering. You're off the hook and mean nothing to me."

"I messed up," he confesses.

Sheryl's glazed eyes can't blink. She feels catatonic as her mind wanders. *Who needs him to tell me what to do, anyway?*

Sterling moves into the rationalization stage. "What can I say? The islands got to me, I guess. It'll never happen again. You know that."

"Oh?" questions Sheryl. "I know that, do I? Who'd want to find out now, anyway?"

A stare-down ensues. She's sternly mute, thinking there's a lot going on in his head, but she's not sure she wants to hear any of it. "Humph," she snickers with disgust.

With the ice broken, Sterling says, "Sheryl, please … I'm a fumbler when it comes to you."

"Yeah, right."

"You know I am! And the truth is, I'm elated you haven't done anything yet—that I'm not too late, the more I think about it, really."

Emotionless, she responds, "Well, I'm overwhelmed."

"Aren't we both?"

"What's with the big change of heart?"

Sterling wraps an arm around her and gives her a gentle hug. "Jamaica is something else, a whole world unto itself, but"—his voice turns emotional—"so is this, becoming parents together of God's child."

"Really?" Despite suspicions over his mood swing, Sheryl finds herself wishing this could lead to a lifetime together with Sterling and the child—maybe even multiple children to call their own. What could be better? Full of hope, she exclaims, "We could make it, Sterling, don't you think? You, me, our baby. We could make it, I'm sure."

"Sure I do, dear, of course."

Excited, she reiterates, "Don't you think?"

"We could make it," he assures her. But after a moment, he adds, "Then again, maybe not. Who knows? And then you have to think of the kid."

Sheryl is slammed, blindsided, by his callously contradictory comments. "I've been right all along," she retorts.

"You've been right about nothing," Sterling claims.

"You're the wrong man for bringing my children into the world, and I'm right about that."

"What a thing to say. I'm surprised how easily this abortion seems to be coming to you."

"You think I've dreamed all my life of having an abortion, much less being pregnant out of wedlock?"

"Who's saying that?"

"I really don't care what you say or think. The fact is I'm pregnant; we're pregnant. Our child should have a chance at life. But Sterling, you've turned into such a despicable person, I can't believe I even know you, let alone am pregnant by you."

"Maybe—"

"Maybe nothing. Nothing's meant to be here, Sterling."

"Look, all I really meant to say but didn't know how to say is … you have to think about dealing with a mixed-race child. I've seen strong couples break in the glare of that. We must consider all angles before making a decision."

"Are you kidding? You're back there?"

"Back where?"

"You're the one always talking race relations, even while playing the race card."

"Maybe you've got a point there, but I've had a lifetime of needing to keep all these cards in mind. No offense, but what do you know about anything outside of your white-bread world?"

"How like you to make such generalizations."

"What can I say?"

"You could say, if that's how you feel and if it's so obvious we have little in common, why you've pursued me all over again." Not waiting for an answer, she states, "You're wasting time for both of us."

"It's not about how I feel. I feel hopeful like you. It's about being realistic about stuff I've seen all my life."

Sheryl feels deflated all over again and quickly returns to her previous tack on her upcoming appointment. All consulting is concluded—no more talking it out, no more thinking it over, done. Perhaps. But she fears the heartbreaking act will bring haunting repercussions for years to come. Silently, she freaks out. Aloud, she says, "Sterling, I need to be alone."

"As you wish."

"None of this is as I wish. It's the pits."

Watching him catch a bus relaxes Sheryl a bit—he's gone. Sunshine exploding from behind a passing cloud brightens her beloved Lincoln Park, which all these years since moving to the neighborhood has been her extended front yard. That it runs down to the great lake is a bonus. *This place has saved me*, she thinks gratefully of countless walks here in all seasons.

Sheryl ruminates about how despite Sterling's sudden reappearance in the picture, she already has done her homework, tracking down the highly rated Michigan Avenue Specialists Group. She's thankful that the Magnificent Mile location demands the best of conditions, as opposed to a Jamaican hut in the hills. All things considered, she's ready, she thinks. But who knows? *Lord, help me*, she desperately prays.

Calls to motherhood echo in her subconscious. She wonders how many chances one might be allowed to squander before coming up sterile. It's not like she doesn't know anyone who came up barren after a botched procedure. She speculates as to why her generation has become such a leader in this field, with no answers. *Some legacy*, she thinks with disgust, turning for home.

The Proverbs resonate within her: "A just weight and balance are the Lord's ... a froward heart findeth no good." Haunting her further is a Sunday sermon she recently saw posted: "Everlasting Punishment." Yet Sheryl's hopes for forgiveness come from the book of Psalms: "For thou, Lord, art good, and ready to forgive; and plenteous in mercy unto all them that call upon thee … For great is thy mercy toward me: and thou hast delivered my soul from the lowest hell." If God could forgive David for the Bathsheba episode, surely He would forgive her if she changed her ways. She vows, *I will change back to the good, Lord.*

But while she sleeps overnight, a devil invades dreamland and by morning has convinced Sheryl that she should take one last shot at rehabilitating Sterling. *Forget the abortion*, she thinks. Coming together as a couple and forming a family is preferable to eliminating a fetus. For all his flaws, she believes that Sterling does have enough moldable clay to turn out a fine man, in her hands. She's to be his sculptor. *And we're both still young enough to pull it off*, she fantasizes.

Showering and dressing, Sheryl figures she's confused enough that she should seek another opinion. With her back to the wall on time, she can think only of running everything past her big sister, Gloria. Gloria is free that night, so they plan a sisters' reunion over dinner at a favorite burger haven, Heaven on Harms, a halfway point for the two of them.

Gloria picks up Sheryl in her BMW at the Skokie Swift train station. Although it's been a while since they've been together, the two easily fall into sister-chat rhythms in the car. They talk family gossip, which mostly centers on tensions involved in planning for brother Jon's impending marriage, his first. In-laws-to-be all are in snits with each other.

Gloria, a veteran of two marriages, commiserates with their brother in absentia. "Talk about stress," she says authoritatively. "Been there, done that."

Negativity about marriage is not necessarily what a spaced-out Sheryl needs to be hearing. Thinking she's stressed plenty as it is, without having been there and done that yet, Sheryl responds, "Yeah," without any punch behind it.

Inside Heaven on Harms, over cheeseburgers on rye piled high with grilled onions, Sheryl teases Gloria for having left thirty behind. Gloria dishes back, "Your day will come."

Sheryl, as baby of the family, is still hanging onto twenty-five, she's quick to remind Gloria.

"By a thread," Gloria retorts, knowing it won't be long till Sheryl's next birthday.

Gloria, no teetotaler like Sheryl, orders a glass of wine. She lobbies the idea to her straight-arrow kid sister. To neither's surprise, Sheryl politely, if a bit sanctimoniously, declines to imbibe. She wonders what Gloria's reaction would be if only she knew that her refusal this time was for more than just usual reasons. This time, she's not-drinking for two.

Gloria, sampling her wine, asks, "What's new?"

Sheryl wonders where to begin, pausing for thought as Gloria enjoys her wine. They have never really chitchatted much about sex before, partly because Sheryl always played the virgin when homebound. Then there was the six years between them and the religious overtones.

They've always talked about everything else, though, and Sheryl is finding this harder than she thought it would be. Resultantly, Sheryl decides on no specifics for Gloria right now, maybe none ever. "Oh, I don't know. Not much."

"In town for long?" asks Gloria, not suspecting trouble.

Sheryl, unsure of where she stands at KTC, reports, "My freelance connections have jobs for me down the calendar, and Kearns might have something next month. But there's nothing going on right now—same old. How about you?"

"Same old for me too—working around the clock, as usual."

"Still on the condo board?"

"Of course—what a drag. But come on. Tell me about Jamaica! You were there forever."

Sheryl can't suppress a smile. "Yeah, well, it was just something I'd never done before, going bamboo. But I'd thought about it and just decided to let it happen in Jamaica. Perfect timing, ripe conditions, very relaxed."

"That's what I hear."

"It's true, and I really needed the break."

Gloria, who never has gone without working full-time, says, "Yeah, how nice. I'll have to get down there someday."

"Do go! One thing was that I got into interesting conversations, being a minority white girl everywhere I went—everywhere."

"And blonde, at that," observes Gloria with a suggestive grin.

"Right," Sheryl says, grinning back just as suggestively. "Anyway, that's all the kind of stuff we'd never discuss over dinner here, that's for sure."

Gloria titters. "Is that right? And tell me—did any of these conversations get beyond talk?"

"Let's just say I heard some interesting pros and cons on interracial marriage and mixed-race babies. What are your views on the subjects, Gloria?"

Gloria looks taken aback. "What? Did this come from you, my little baby sister of innocence? Are you holding out on me?"

"Huh? Get out. I'm just talking. What's your opinion?"

"I suppose it might differ depending on whether we're talking about this playing out over time in Jamaica or the US, don't you think?" asks Gloria.

"Maybe … sure … I don't know. Shouldn't it play the same everywhere? So since you've never been down there, to JA, how do you feel about it all as it would be up here?"

"I know how we're supposed to feel with the changing times, and I'd like to think I'm pretty liberal. So of course, I strive to see interracial marriages and biracial kids as normal parts of our contemporary world."

"That doesn't tell me a thing about your feelings. We'd all say that one way or another."

"Well, I guess I'm just looking at things from the perspective of being in my second marriage. Who would've thought? What I guess I'm saying is, in romance, there's still this little thing about the already steep odds against any relationship working. Why increase the odds with misunderstandings due to differing backgrounds, if longevity of love is your goal?"

"I understand. And how well has the similar-background thing worked for you?"

"Yeah, right … very funny," replies Gloria without laughing.

"So back to the example—what about their kid? Is the world getting more accepting of racial diversity? Maybe these kids will excel purely thanks to having a mixed background."

"Maybe, but take it from a firstborn: being a trailblazer at anything is tough hoeing."

"Get out," laughs Sheryl at Gloria's familiar lamentation.

"Why is this topic suddenly so fascinating for you?"

"It's just the type of stuff that comes up when you travel as much as I do."

"I see," Gloria says whimsically. "Do tell."

Sheryl holds back at first but knows this is why she's here. "Well, to tell you the truth, I'm pregnant."

"What?"

"You heard me. And cutting to the chase, it's a black man."

Gloria looks stunned but intrigued. "Is he Jamaican?"

"No, someone I work with."

"Wow."

"Yes, wow."

"What do you know about him?"

"Actually, I've known him since that summer at Makeup Is Us."

"Oh really? And I've never heard of him before?"

"Oh, we were out of touch for a long time. Kind of just recently reconnected."

"So it would seem. Again, though, what do you know about him?"

"He grew up in Cabrini Green but worked his way through medical school and is now a doctor, currently without a hospital. The one he was at, in Indiana, went bankrupt."

"Too bad about that, but as a licensed physician, he should be able to land somewhere."

"He's not worried. His main pursuit is a clothing company he and his cousins have formed. They have some hot designers, and he's in no hurry to get back to doctoring."

"Really? Interesting. What about his dad—have you met him? You can see a lot of what he'll become by looking at his dad."

"He died in a car accident when Sterling was a kid. He was pretty much raised by his uncle, who I haven't met, but it seems like he did a good job. Sterling idolizes the guy."

"You know, you can do background checks online now. You never know what might be in a person's past. I would do one on any man I might date these days."

"Yes, well, we're kind of past that, I think." She cradles her slightly bulging belly.

"Sheryl, I don't want to be forward on this, but if you're considering different options, I would say absolutely do what's best for you. Nothing's ever too late. Sometimes these men come and go in our lives. And the goings can be as important as all the comings in the world."

"I get it, and maybe you're right. But I really just don't know anything anymore."

Before long, they are parked outside the Skokie Swift station.

Gloria asks, "Have you talked with anyone else?"

"Just a doctor who confirmed everything. I'm so scared."

"Oh, Sheryl, what are we to do?"

Sheryl has no response. Her chin begins to quiver like no chin has ever quivered before, fast and unrelenting. A chill rushes through her.

Gloria stretches out both arms across the console to give her a warm hug, sharing tears. "I wonder what Mom would have to say."

"Better not to bother her," Sheryl figures, thinking of the health challenges their mother is already dealing with.

"It's a tough call," Gloria admits. "Obviously, I'm not Mom. But I'm here for you, sis."

"I know. Thanks, Gloria."

Riding the rails home, Sheryl longs to talk with her mother about all of this. But her tendency has always been to avoid approaching Mom about anything personal. She prefers keeping her life as private as circumstance allows. One thing is for sure, though: nobody in the family ever would have suspected Sheryl of having pregnancy concerns outside of marriage. She actually wonders if they even might be less surprised to hear about Sterling's race than to learn that she's pregnant.

The next day is gloomy, with the lake shrouded in a sinister fog. The atmosphere seems appropriate to Sheryl, who feels like a criminal as she rolls up in a cab at the curb of the Michigan Avenue Specialists Group. Sterling is with her and actually pays the driver as he and Sheryl exit the car.

The building is steel and glass—cold. They verify the floor number on the lobby directory. Sheryl says, "Let me go on my own from here, Sterling."

"No way, baby. You'll need me up there."

"All I need is to get this done."

"Oh, come on now."

"Come on, nothing. Take a walk or cool your heels in the lobby. You can play hero later. Right now I want peace and quiet. Please give me what I want."

"Of course," Sterling quickly responds. "I'll take that walk for a while, but I won't stray far. In my mind, I'll be with you."

"Sure ... well, try being with God for a change. It could make a difference for you."

An elevator arrives, and Sheryl hops aboard. Upstairs, she finds her way down long hallways to the entrance of what she feels will soon be a crime scene, given the action she's taking. Before opening the clinic's door, she gathers herself and then leaves the rest of the world behind. Closing the door behind her, she realizes, *No turning back now.*

In the waiting room, Jackie Gleason and his orchestra provide Muzak cover for anyone wishing to converse. Sheryl finds herself sitting beside a woman near her own age. Frightened little girls have come out in each of them, two nameless strangers sharing the weight of the world, equally fearful that anything could go wrong.

The stranger confides in a whisper, "I think my first time here I was so much in shock about even being pregnant I hardly gave fear for myself a thought. But I had some bad spotting hours later, and the worst starts filling your head."

Sheryl's mind spins back to the Jamaican hut. "I think I know what you mean. Are these guys good?"

"Oh yeah, don't freak out. The spotting was kinda normal, I guess. They probably warned me, but I was in a daze."

"Sure. Thanks. That's good to know."

"You here alone?"

"Uh, kinda—yes and no. My partner in this achievement dropped me off and will be picking me up. That's enough for me."

"That's good. Good enough, right? That was me the first time too. This time it's with my true love. He also drove me here and, you know, will pick me up too." Her eyes spill over with tears. "He doesn't know about the other one, of course."

"Of course. There's no need now."

"Sure. Maybe later, but surely not now."

They turn silent as another patient arrives. She checks in and sits across the room alone, seemingly intimidated. A nurse arrives and calls for Sheryl's new nameless friend, by number.

"Good luck, dear," Sheryl says to this sister-in-arms with an upbeat tone of voice.

"Thank you," chokes the stranger. "Good luck to you too."

Naturally, they never will see each other again.

❧

Meanwhile, Sterling, out for his urban walk, revisits Uncle Austin's oft-repeated remarks about how a pregnancy helps a con seize psychological control over a mark, even if only for the short term—although long-term control can and does occur often too. *It's what Austin calls "keeping them confused,"* thinks Sterling, proud of himself.

Along the same lines, abortions allegedly rank high in gaining mind control of a mark. "More often than not," Austin claimed, "there's something connecting about going through trying circumstances together. Keeps a psychological bond growing stronger against all odds."

Sterling figures Sheryl could be toast any number of ways, if only he were to bring down the hammer, like he's often been tempted to do. He determines, though, that there is no need to rush.

Back in the clinic, Sheryl gets the nod from the nurse. Her time has come, ready or not. With trembling thoughts she trails the nurse, convinced that hell awaits her, for sure.

Chapter 9

ALOHA, MOM

American Cuisine desserts are but a recent memory for Sheryl and Sterling. They sit silently, sipping tea, like any couple with little left to discuss publicly after a lifetime together. Extreme mental exhaustion factors into their silence—for Sheryl anyway, what with all the reminiscing at the table, inwardly and shared, and since she is still suffering jet lag and battle fatigue.

Sterling, seemingly to break the ice, asks, "Care for more tea, dear?"

"Sure, thanks," replies Sheryl with indifference.

She loathes seeing him discover that the teapot is empty. His mannerisms in flagging down their waiter are all too familiar. Her mind, thanks to abilities honed through travel, clicks into solitude-in-a-crowd mode, drifting back to the most definitive moment of her life—a moment when he was not tagging along, though his lurking in her mind's background overshadowed all.

Sheryl's mother, Ruth, was still alive. The two were together in Waikiki Beach, Hawaii—Mom and daughter number 2, plus one hundred conventioneers under Sheryl's watch. It was the time of their lives together, a very private time for them despite Sheryl's duties. Her working hours gave Ruth opportunities to roam paradise alone, the being-alone of which was unique and likely thrilling in itself for her. She and Sheryl would meet up off and on throughout each day.

Ruth has her own luxury corner suite, with Diamond Head visible in the distance. All expenses are on Sheryl, who is treating her mom to airfare and accommodations, bought with her most valuable fringe benefit at work: mileage points. They are lounging on the balcony, enjoying the stupendous view.

"Best birthday gift ever," Ruth assures the baby of her brood.

"It's a thrill to provide for you, Mom—you've provided so much for me. I'm just glad you're so happy with it."

"Happy I am. Thank you, Sheryl."

Sheryl's suite adjoins Ruth's in case they ever feel like opening the door and sharing space, but for the most part they're maintaining separate quarters. This lets Sheryl's mom find total relaxation in her hot tub, when she's not coming and going, and also allows Sheryl to use some of her sparse free time for meditation.

As her mom yawns, settling into her chaise, Sheryl decides to return to her own suite. "See you later, Mom. And rest up—tonight should be lots of fun!"

On the edge of sleep, Ruth lazily replies, "See you later, dear."

In the privacy of her own room, Sheryl soon settles into the quarter lotus position on plush carpeting by her own balcony's sliding door. Only now does it hit her how sorely she needs this alone time. *Lots to figure out*, she thinks as she gazes out at the deep blue waters beyond the nearest beach. She stares without focus to relax her eyes along with the rest of her body. Her mantra is "om, the mind never sleeps, just be sure to rest the body, om." Its gentle repetition has proven to be a relaxant for her in the past. She's hoping this session will put her mind at peak efficiency, allowing her to achieve a calm state of consciousness that will unveil solutions already staring her in the face that she's just missing. That's her plan, anyway.

An oft-playing vision starring Sheryl and Sterling as a couple against all odds fades into her subconscious. She's familiar with the plot but can't ever figure out the end. As of the run-up to this Hawaiian trip, Sheryl is on again with Sterling. This time is different; she's gone in on the clothing venture for $20,000. She has stock certificates and an executive future. It's hardly what her dad would call collateral, though, she knows—that is, if her dad even knew of Sterling.

Sterling has never been much for meeting the family. They don't hang a lot with any of Sheryl's circle of friends, either, which probably works fine for Sterling. The less anyone knows about him and his offers of a fast buck, one would think, the better for him. Still, despite not knowing her family, he constantly berates Sheryl with accusations of racism against all of them.

"How presumptuous of you," she has said, defending family to the end. "You've never even met them. What do you know? They're not like that at all."

"Some things you just know through osmosis," he tends to snap in reply.

Sheryl wrestles with bewilderment over the hold he has on her. It's the most confusing aspect of her life, this constant re-upping of their relationship in regular rhythms over the years—so damaging yet irresistible, so inexplicable, so inescapable since Jamaica. *What's the deal?* she wonders. *Because when we're good, we're good*, she self-counsels, hating how melodramatic her life sounds. At the core, however, she knows it all stems from Jamaica and the tragic fallout that followed, when the only shoulder to cry on totally openly was his.

The reality is—the part of her life with Sterling has gotten out of control, although there are times she's so glad to be in his company. It's always a good time when she lets down her hair. *Is it Stockholm syndrome?* she wonders in a clear meditative state, hovering above the beach. *Did he kidnap my self-control?* She concludes that there's a certain intellectual stimulation between them that fans the flames, or there's a familiarity that breeds re-upping for more of the same—that theory is a strong contender too.

In years past, pre-Jamaica with Sterling, whenever Sheryl would get back to Chicago with limited time before her next trip, varied groups of longtime companions were a valued hometown commodity. She enjoyed fun, reunions, and variety and soon was back to international work.

Now, once she returns from wherever, Sterling swoops in, smothering her with total companionship. This has its nice points, in the romancing and partnering around, but as a result, many of Sheryl's friendships have suffered. *That's just a fact*, she sadly reflects. By default, Sterling has become her entire circle, more so than ever now that they've also gone into business together. With anxieties erased in the core of her meditative state, Sheryl homes in on some of the more pleasant memories she has forged with Sterling. There certainly have been good times, times of naturally growing together, even recently, such as with Sterling's first camping trip just this last summer.

Sheryl has been camping since childhood. Her family and several others routinely took over corners of campgrounds at small glacial lakes scattered around the upper Midwest, a week or two at a time. Prior to her trip with Sterling, it admittedly had been a while since her last camping trip, but she was certain it would be like riding a bike. Conversely, Sterling had never set foot in a tent.

"We're going to change all that," she said, challenging the urbane Dr. Jackson. "You've got to get out in nature!"

Sterling smiled and replied, "If it'll make you happy, I'm happy."

They set out with rented gear for Devil's Lake, near Baraboo, boyhood home of the Ringling Brothers. Pitching their tent not far from some ancient effigy mounds, hard up against the forest, Sheryl took glory in finding a favored but isolated spot strictly from memory.

"Not half bad," he admitted while trying out the large air mattress.

Before nightfall, they quickly hiked the bluffs up to the Devil's Doorway, an ominous portal to the sky high above Devil's Lake. Spectacular panoramic views induced hand-holding before the two started their descent back down the trail that had led them there. Come campfire after dinnertime, the stars seemed as bright as any Sheryl remembered from Jamaica, and she said so.

"Baby, that's gotta be a maybe," insisted Sterling. "Those stars were like no others."

"And that ganja was pretty good too, right?" laughed Sheryl. "Maybe that was it."

"Well, I don't know," he said with a chuckle, "but this right here is nice. And so are you. I'm just happy you've allowed me to stick around long enough so you can get to know the real me."

"Is this the real you, really?"

"Really."

"I knew a little Mother Nature would do you some good."

"Is that right?" he asked mischievously, moving in for a fireside nuzzle.

At week's end during the long ride home, Sheryl succumbed to his business pitch and let down her guard over an emergency fund she'd built up over the years. She agreed to invest $20,000 in Sterling's company. Buyer's remorse set in even as they visited her bank the next day to put the money in his hands. But she vowed to take the regret as a temporary state of mind and roll with the well-considered decision she had painstakingly arrived at in the car. *It has to work!* she told herself like a true believer. Besides, a week in the woods had convinced her that he really did love her.

The flame first lit in Jamaica, before Snake and Miriam came into play, before Sheryl's own unplanned circumstances became known, had been reignited. Sheryl believed that everything to do with Snake and Miriam had been an aberration, and she wrote it off to going bamboo, of which they both were guilty. It just had gone to his head a little more. *After all*, she told herself, *he was kind of a local celebrity. Maybe Miriam's whole family did throw her at him.*

Maybe, maybe not, but Sheryl's stance was that he was back to being the interesting, fun guy she had known to begin with at Makeup Is Us. They laughed and got horny when out dancing at the Drake and choked up together at sad movies. Walks through Lincoln Park always felt romantic, but despite that and the lathers they reached on the dance floor, he was not pressing her for intimacy, a wise move on his part. She was far from ready for that.

"But I am pleased," she told him, "to feel redeemed about giving it all away to you that night on the beach. After you turned so unsweet on me there, I never would've dreamed I'd be saying that."

"My hope is that someday you'll forget about that whole episode, and we can bury it."

"That would be nice, I'll admit."

Sheryl was relieved to put her hometown drama on hold awhile to take care of business. A tour to Switzerland followed rapidly by a South African one created an absence during which her heart grew fonder of Sterling. Into the fall, more trips followed elsewhere. When she was home, the two were like newly introduced lovebirds. They were touchy-feely, and she had an "everything is coming up roses" outlook. She concluded that a person can overcome tragedy, forgive, and move on, if not entirely forget.

Sheryl comes out of her quarter lotus position and refocuses on her suite's elegant decor. She wonders if she's not supposed to entertain such heavy thoughts while meditating, although for her, meditation works for such considerations. Clarity helps, she hopes, and she's feeling a burst of clarity now, burying thoughts of him by looking ahead to tonight's luau with her mom.

"Just Mom and me, no Sterling—or anybody else for that matter."

But the part about nobody else being around isn't quite accurate. When Sheryl later joins her mom at the luau, which is playing specifically to Sheryl's group of conventioneers, she is technically still working. But for tonight's luau, hotel staff have everything under control. The event is routine to them, so Sheryl is able to relax and give her mother a hug as the first course is served. Traditional music warms the background.

"Sorry I've been on the run so much, Mom. This group always keeps me busy."

"Sheryl, dear, don't worry about a thing. Enjoy the food and show." Dancers in grass skirts join the musicians, moving their hips to the music.

"I'm just hoping you're not bored all day while I'm working."

Ruth laughs. "You needn't worry. I absolutely love being here without also being on-call for everyone's emergencies as mom, wife, or whatever the crisis calls for."

Excited, Sheryl exclaims, "That's just what I'd hoped for you on this trip."

"Listen," says Ruth, as if letting Sheryl in on a secret, "I've been to enough of these conferences with your dad to know you've got your hands full. But I'm sure you're also having fun while at it, right?"

"Absolutely, Mom. Thanks for always seeing everything so clearly."

"What I'm seeing here is how you're advancing in your career. I'm impressed." Ruth gives her daughter an encouraging smile. "Honey, I'm so proud to watch you in action. And I'm grateful for this precious slice of life's pie, heaven here in Hawaii—and it's all your doing, this treasured birthday gift from my baby daughter. Being on my own like this, believe me, I'm having the time of my life."

"Aw, you're choking me up, Mom, but in a good way." Sheryl beams upon seeing how relaxed her mother looks, as relaxed as she can remember. She asks, "Then everything's good? Need anything?"

Ruth says, "Thanks, but I don't need a thing. This is so relaxing. You just don't know."

Sheryl doesn't know. She suddenly wonders if something is bothering her mom and, if so, for how long. How to bring it up, though—that's the hurdle. Sheryl figures there's always another day for such talk, especially in Hawaii, where they enjoy ideal conditions.

So it goes for more than a week. Ruth routinely shops or sunbathes at Waikiki and maybe does an excursion. Sheryl works her fun gig, and they join together at night. On the second-to-last day of the convention, Sheryl grabs her final chance to sneak a few hours alone with her mom. Once the next day comes, Sheryl will be overseeing the morning scurry as everyone rushes to prepare for airport transports. This evening, though, she has arranged for a hotel intern to cover her over dinnertime and for a few hours beyond into the night.

"Tonight is for you and me, Mom," Sheryl proudly announces.

"That sounds lovely, dear."

They dine at dusk, overlooking Waikiki Beach and Diamond Head. "What a sight, huh, Ma?"

"What a sight is right," Ruth agrees. Lazily, she recounts, "And it's so nice not to be on a schedule. Gorgeous views everywhere and nothing to do but take it all in."

"I hear you, Mom. That's how I felt those six months I went bamboo down in Jamaica."

"Jamaica, yes—you've never really talked much about Jamaica, Sheryl."

"Talk about no schedule."

"How long has it been by now?"

Sheryl questions herself for having headed in this direction. She answers, "We'll have time for that tonight, Mom, if you want. How about first we have dessert down on the beach? It's all arranged. We'll be just in time for sunset."

"Good job, Ms. Tour Director. What could be finer?"

They find their reserved chaise longues, which come at a premium. Further, thanks to favors Sheryl has pulled, they have scored a nice forward position on the beach. The sinking sun glows brightly off Diamond Head, painting a shimmering stripe atop the sea. Surfers and massive canoes filled with tourists still ride the waves—synchronized chaos and gaiety. Overhead, wispy clouds collaborate for a stunning spill of sun into the Pacific Rim.

Mother and child let gravity pull them deeper into their chaises as a steady stream of waves crash upon their heavenly slice of land. From beyond earth's edge, the sunken sun reflects off the wispy clouds' undersides in spectacular fashion.

Awestruck, Sheryl asks Ruth, "Isn't it all so reassuring, Mom?"

"That's exactly what it is, Sheryl—reassuring. And I sure am grateful for life."

"Same."

"I can't remember when I've felt so decompressed."

"That's way overdue, Mom. You've worked so hard."

"Let's just say it's been a long time. But that's being a mom. And I have no trouble with that." She smiles. "It's all good. I'm making up here and now for lost time."

"Glad to hear it, Mom. Our being together here means a lot to me. It's really special."

"Yes, Sheryl, it really has been special. Once-in-a-lifetime special."

"Mom, you know, I've been seeing how relaxed you are here, and I'm starting to feel the same. I've been on edge awhile, more than I thought and for longer than imagined."

Ruth gets that motherly look. "Tell me all about it, dear."

"I don't know, Mom. It's a lot to tell and would be a lot to hear, especially after all you've been through." Sheryl mentally kicks herself over that last remark. She scolds herself, *Why remind her of her health issues? Especially now with her so relaxed and refreshed!*

Ruth sees her daughter's discomfort but doesn't waver. "Take your time, dear."

Sheryl chokes on her words, saying, "Um, let me think this through a minute."

"Of course."

They concentrate on the invisible sun's colorful but fading curtain until it gives way to nightfall and twinkling stars above the Pacific. "Unbelievable!" declares a lone voice in the beach crowd. Ruth and Sheryl people-watch under a starlit full-moon night.

After a while, Ruth coyly asks, "So ... were you going to tell me all about Jamaica?"

"Oh yeah, Mom ... err, make that 'yeah, mon'!"

They share a good laugh. Sheryl has no idea what her next words will be, but she senses that her mother feels more like being a friend or sister tonight, pressing, as she is, for inside gossip on Sheryl's love life. Sadly, for Sheryl, that's what Jamaica boils down to: gossip fodder. She knows this isn't the type of gossip her mom is ready to hear. Sheryl also fears the heavy burden that keeping this story top secret would place on her mom. If Sheryl is ready to share her truths, it will have to be with complete confidentiality.

Ruth interrupts her thoughts. "Are you all right, dear?"

Sheryl didn't realize she was spacing out; under the gun, now, it's fact-facing time. Who else does she have for the sharing of such secrets? It has to be Mom. Sheryl has been wanting to talk with her about Sterling and her abortion for ages. The problem is, she's never really decided whether or not talking about it all would be the right thing to do.

Inwardly, though, Sheryl reasons, *Maybe this is my only chance. I have to take this chance.* Staring down Pacific rollers, she suddenly states aloud, "I could dance around a lot of stuff that happened down there, Mom, but the basic thing of it all is ... I got involved with a man. Pretty seriously too, and he's a black man."

Ruth looks unfazed. "Dear, your father and I both know you must run into romantic adventures on the road—I mean, that would be expected. And if you're in Jamaica, I suppose the odds are it would be with a black man."

"So you understand?" asks Sheryl.

"Of course, dear," Ruth says with love yet concern.

"Would Dad?"

"You should talk with him yourself."

"I don't know where it's going, Mom, so why bring it up with Dad? I just thought I'd run it past you. So please, keep it between us—okay?" Sheryl is on the verge of tears.

Ruth pauses for thought before answering. "I'm not used to keeping secrets from your father, so the thought of it stresses me greatly. But of course, Sheryl—just between us girls, I promise."

Overcome with emotion, Sheryl takes Ruth's extended hand and clarifies, "By the way, Mom, he's not Jamaican. He's American."

"Oh."

"Does that make a difference?"

"I don't suppose it does. But with him being an American, at least you have that in common."

"Right," concurs Sheryl, figuring her mom means they must have little else in common.

"For starters," Ruth says in an upbeat way, "that's good to have that bond, considering how internationally you travel." She laughs and continues, "It will remind you you're still American. What else can you tell me about him? What's his name?"

"He's a licensed doctor and an entrepreneur, a very interesting guy. Worked his way up from nothing. His name is Sterling."

"I see. He does sound interesting. Tell me how you met."

Sheryl starts from the beginning at Makeup Is Us and then recalls the long period in which they went their separate ways, starting off their careers, until the KTC reunion that led to his being hired for the Jamaican run of tours. She spares no details as she talks of her detour off the straight and narrow, starting with the moonlit night she first tried ganja.

"Oh my," declares Ruth, appearing dizzy over the whole scenario.

"I know, Mom. I know. It gets worse." Sheryl describes her frisky behavior under beach palms, and Ruth appears to be nearly in shock. Luckily for Sheryl, who knows the most shocking revelation is yet to come, the steadily cresting waves become an auditory and visual distraction. They periodically break the conversation under the light of a brilliant moon glowing down upon Diamond Head not so very far away. Surfers and canoeists have disappeared. Peace. Hawaii.

Underneath it all, however, Sheryl aggressively questions herself about the wisdom of having laid out so much, so fast, for her mom. She can imagine how confusing it must be to hear of one's sometimes-Bible-thumping daughter holing up with some guy in Jamaica, virtually on a sex romp from a mom's point of view. Sheryl's tortured imagination spins.

She struggles to say, "Mom, you're being wonderful about this."

"Nothing about this is easy, Sheryl. I'm really struggling to understand you now."

Sheryl stammers, "Oh, I just … I only wish there wasn't more I have to confess, but—"

Ruth cuts her off. "Wait a minute now, Sheryl—you don't have to confess anything to me. That's never been the case. Your option is to not say another word. You know that."

"I know."

Ruth sighs, adding, "But I'm here to hear it if that's your intention."

"Which I appreciate," chokes Sheryl. "That's why I'm talking so much, Mommy." She breaks into tears. So does Ruth. Metronomic wave action masks their teary discussion from the beach crowd. Everyone seems to be in their own little world.

Sheryl cries, "I've been carrying shameful secrets. It's just too much for me to bear alone. I have to tell somebody." Her tears fall faster, and she begins hyperventilating.

Ruth reaches for her hand. "Oh, my little girl, please, just tell Mommy."

"I don't know how."

"Just let it out."

"I've had an abortion."

"Oh my God," Ruth reflexively responds before going speechless.

Sheryl fears that her mother, who was so relaxed, now has been staggered and stunned. She can only hope her mom will handle these new stresses that Sheryl has brought upon her as well and routinely as she's always managed to handle everything else. Sheryl is pretty stunned in her own right.

Finally, Ruth speaks. "It's hard to find the words, Sheryl, but I'm sure you've paid quite a price. You can't punish yourself forever. God forgives as long as we've sincerely changed our ways. You know that, so now remember that."

Wondering whether her mom simply forgot to say that she forgives her daughter too, Sheryl only manages to say, "Thanks, Mom," while struggling with her emotions in public.

There are, in fact, still no people watching them. Most gazes remain cast upon the moon or on a lover's spellbound eyes. With their chaises huddled close together and set off a bit from others, Sheryl regains a sense of privacy and begins to calm down. She also thinks better of sharing her investment news with her mom on top of everything else.

Recollecting the worst days of her life, Sheryl never has felt so ashamed. She is grateful when the trade winds pick up and gently massage her temples. Once more, the perpetually rolling Pacific takes command of her senses. Its steady wave of relaxing rollers further hypnotizes the entire beach crowd, already lost in admiring the astral nightscape.

Somewhere on the beach, a lone ukulele plays "Tiny Bubbles." A stray voice with training picks up on vocals to everyone's amazement. So goes another magical night in Hawaii.

The mother-and-child reunion lulls into its final countdown, their relationship now seeking new comfort and discomfort levels. With packing, shuttles, and a long flight ahead, this vacation officially ends now. In more than a few ways, it has been one for the books.

Later, in her bed, Sheryl sobs into her pillow. "Aloha, Mom. I'm sorry."

Chapter 10

MEXICAN STANDOFF

American Cuisine Grill's revolving door spews out Sheryl onto the shoveled and salted sidewalk. Lingering thoughts of Mom and Hawaii have her thinking of how that initial $20,000 investment in Sterling's company by now has more than doubled in size. But she still has nothing to show for any of it except more stock certificates and paperwork promising luxury vehicles soon to come. Verbal promises also abound—of marriage, kids, and a great house near the lake.

The revolving door next deposits Sterling outside behind her. The blustery winter weather has calmed, as though the eye of a wintry hurricane has settled over downtown. Silently, they trudge along Diversey past other hardy pedestrians blazing trails, everyone all bundled up against the cold. Some people must be in better moods than others, puffing out clouds of air while going wherever it is they are going.

Sheryl is not so energetic. Her mood remains reflective. It seems this day is nothing but memories. It is as if her life is passing before her eyes, her thoughts darting back over the years, taking advantage of the continued silence between Sterling and her.

She thinks of Acapulco, always a favorite stop this time of year. Acapulco is also memorable for having been her first destination trip after the tragic encounter with a scalpel.

Her fondness for Acapulco makes it an ideal location for regaining her travel legs while recovering—on the surface anyway, at least physically. She hopes that a solo getaway trip there will help her emotional wounds as well.

La Vista Hermosa del Mar Hotel sits on lushly landscaped grounds elevated high above an impeccable beach. Everything sparkles. It needs to—because Sheryl is far from sparkling mentally. She distracts herself with a brief private tour of the facilities, given that she also is scouting this new beachfront resort for KTC in trade-off for some of her expenses.

After the tour, a tropically dressed Sheryl puts on her dark sunglasses and leaves behind her junior suite with a great view, heading for the grand veranda she saw on the tour. It overlooks a large infinity pool packed with baking tourists and the beach even further below. Along the way, she pauses at a makeshift bar dealing out free margaritas. Sheryl thinks, *What the heck? When in Rome, eh?*

Drink now in hand, she wanders through a partying pool crowd, eventually reaching an ornately tiled staircase down to the sandy playa. Barefoot traffic moves both up and down the stairs, some revelers stepping in beat to the party music pulsating in the background from the pool. Everyone is seemingly having a good time; the crowd is energetic yet very laid-back.

Sheryl sheds her sandals, spots an available *palapa*, and beats a beer-bellied competitor to the sheltered lounger. He bows out like a gentleman, though with a forced smile. She stretches back in her private beachfront perch and takes a long sip on the margarita.

"Ah, so refreshing," she can't help saying aloud. *Jeez, I'm drinking*, she thinks in sudden wonderment, mildly aghast at the thought. *Well, just this one*, she thinks, and she means it.

Sheryl spaces out on the great visuals of the beach and the bay itself, thinking that best of all about this Acapulco jaunt is that she's not working. She told Sterling she was but more truthfully told Kearns she needed time away, solo. He asked no questions and got her a great deal. "Here's to Thomas Kearns!" toasts Sheryl to the breeze, thinking what a wonderful boss she has had in him. *I have to get back to thinking more of my career again!* she resolves. *This whole pregnancy crisis with Sterling really took me off-track. Sterling took me off-track, period.* Luckily for her, it seems Kearns remains open to her full-time return.

Lounging in comfort, thinking of how many beaches she's enjoyed through the years, she admires the bay and its jaunty, nautical traffic. A few whitecaps are pleasing to her eye, just as a cacophony of sounds from the bay pleases her ear. Gradually, Sheryl notices a well-tanned couple in their fifties relaxing in the shade of a neighboring *palapa*. They've already noticed her.

"Welcome," says the man in a Canadian accent. "I'm Jack. This is my wife, Irene."

"Nice to meet you, Jack and Irene. I'm Sheryl."

Irene asks, "How do you like it so far?"

"I was thinking it couldn't be any better."

"That's the spirit," agrees Jack.

"The whole truth," warbles Irene.

Approaching from down the beach is a large balding man, in his fifties like Jack and Irene. Obviously anxious and disturbed over something, he's also crisply sunburned. He speaks urgently with an Italian accent. "Hey, Jack, you seen Carlita?"

"Not today, Marco." Turning to Irene, Jack asks, "How about you, Irene? Seen Carlita around?"

"I've been here drinking with you all day, Jack. If you haven't seen her, neither have I, you know." Irene seems ambivalent about Marco and most certainly about Carlita.

Jack, though, shows genuine concern. "Sorry, Marco. We'll keep an eye out for her."

"Thanks. If you see her, tell her I'm looking for her."

"Of course," promises Jack, "but don't worry, man—you'll find her."

"Yes, sure," mutters Marco as he walks off, burned skin glistening in the sun.

Jack dishes, "That Marco there, what a guy, down from Toronto. He has a little girlfriend here he visits once a year. Quite the ladies' man."

Sheryl can't see it. "This Marco guy?"

"Believe it. Always some kind of trouble going on here for him," Jack quips, "but he keeps coming back for more. And he's about as Italian anymore as you or me. He's been in Toronto twenty-five years but never lost the accent. Thinks it's good for business." Jack becomes distracted by a group of women in thongs passing in front of him on their way to the shoreline.

Irene doesn't skip a beat in response to Jack's mental departure. She dutifully takes over, telling Sheryl, "Marco's got a landscaping business and a wife and kids."

"Yeah," Jack chimes in, "and every February, he's down here for a landscapers' convention. He got hooked up with this little Carlita five or six years ago."

Sheryl asks, "What's his excuse now? This isn't February. It's prime season back home."

"Well, he's pretty busy down here right now," snipes Irene, turning back to her glass.

Jack speculates, "Who knows what he told the little woman back home? But there's trouble here in paradise, it seems, no denying it—with this Carlita and her family."

Irene snaps, "She's pregnant. Bet on it."

"Oh, come on now," counters Jack.

"Come on where? That's the trouble here," insists Irene. "And what a show she put on prancing around the bar the other night in those cheap sheers, like some sexpot."

Jack chuckles. "By golly, she sure did make hotel security nervous. They don't much like the local ladies partying with guests on the premises."

"That's understandable," Sheryl says. She finishes her drink. "Well, I think I'll check out the rest of the beach." Getting up, she gives a slight wave. "See you around."

"You betcha," Jack and Irene respond together.

Sheryl walks the shoreline along with an eclectic mix of vacationing foreigners, plus all types of locals, from panhandlers to the moneyed. Volleyball games and Frisbee-tossing beach bums are scattered along the beach. Parasailers fill the overhead sky. Boston Whaler rentals cruise with the big girls of the bay, a large double-decker booze-cruise boat and a three-masted sailing ship, the latter being a Mexican Navy midshipmen trainer. WaveRunners dart everywhere.

Sheryl nears a pier at the far end of the beach that also attracts foot traffic from a nearby retail strip. She thoroughly enjoys her surroundings, taking it all in, including the sighting of a young girl walking a barking dog. The happy mutt longs to run, but his pubescent master maintains control of his leash.

A shuttle bus arrives at the retail strip and begins to unload. Sheryl spots someone she recognizes among the emerging passengers: Marco, the Italian Canadian from the hotel. He's not alone. Keeping pace with him in choppy little steps, thanks to stacked-sole sandals, is a little Mexican woman in hot pink short-shorts. Sheryl figures this must be Carlita. At around twenty-five, Sheryl guesses, she sports a second-trimester tummy peeking out from beneath a short blouse.

The interesting couple heads for a little taco shop. Sheryl watches the two order through one window and then step to another to wait for their food.

Seeing Carlita's little baby bump brings memories of Sheryl's unexpected pregnancy and the recent ending of it, draining all the fun out of what till now has been a great day. Her sad experience is a very new add-on to her life, always below the surface, resurfacing in waves of grief. *So this is how it's going to be*, she reflects sadly. *Reminders will be everywhere.*

She finds a bench and sits down beside a local woman. They trade smiles before Sheryl retreats to the drama playing out inside her head, a drama that now costars Carlita. Like a new word that suddenly keeps popping up, making a person wonder why she has never heard it before—Sheryl now worries that's how it will be for her with pregnancies, never before much on her radar but now ever popping up, encroaching upon her life with unwanted memories. *What a fate that would be*, she thinks, torturing herself.

Desperate to reset her day, Sheryl hops onto an architectural tour boat readying to launch from the pier. After all, she's on vacation, right? Why not be spontaneous? As the double-decker tour boat departs to the scenic bay, she silently tries to cheer herself. *Let's brighten up!* Nevertheless, she frets, *Maybe I have this suffering coming—my sentence.*

Glorious sunlight drenches Sheryl on the large catamaran's upper deck, helping melt her melancholy. The tour guide of the good ship *Aca Tiki* gives, in English, a complete history of all the hotels they are passing along the hotel zones. He also shares a wealth of knowledge about various harbors, navy docks, and once they are past all the congested areas of the bay, the many infamous private villas looking down from the cliffs high above.

Sheryl can't recall taking this excursion before and finds the rugged coastline breathtaking. She plans to add the two-hour cruise to her next working itinerary here. As *Aca Tiki* docks, a trolley arrives at a stop at the turnaround by the beach. Sheryl retrieves her sandals from an oversized handbag and runs for the trolley. "Let's see where it goes," she excitedly tells herself.

Sheryl is pleased to see it goes to the Avenida Costera Miguel Aleman, a main drag she knows well. Hand-painted VW Bugs and aging Toyotas doing duty as cabs dominate traffic. The trolley clinks along past open-air-lobby hotels, money exchanges, and a diversity of Mexican and international restaurants. At one stop a flashback to another Acapulco night hits her. "Oh my," she exclaims to herself, "this is where we caught the surrey!"

She sighs softly over a full-moon memory stirred by being here, a night she has never quite forgotten, one night at which she's often wished to have had a second crack. *Good luck there, foolish heart.* Yet tonight's ride brings it all back.

Matt Ayers, a handsome wealthy American expat whom she had met through friends, sat close to her in back. The rig's driver was headed for the world-famous La Quebrada Cliff Divers. Matt, half-local but with the explorative spirit of a tourist, was acting as her personal guide. This would be Sheryl's first chance to see the daredevils she already knew by reputation.

"I can't believe you've never seen them for all your visits here before," said Matt.

"It's a mystery to me too, I'm afraid. I'm just a bit freer on this trip, I guess, not tied to a scripted schedule."

Sheryl read Matt as a gentleman despite his rebel's reputation. The surrey deposited them into a large crowd at a lighted parking lot. Sheryl felt his hand take hers so naturally as they navigated the crowd, which flowed toward a torch-lit gorge overlooking the wild Pacific Ocean below. Matt had a way of slipping through the crowd so that before Sheryl knew it, they stood front and center at a railing-rimmed overlook above the gorge.

Tidal swells rose up close to them before slipping away back to sea, creating a great need for precision with any cliff diving. The leaps were soon to be made directly across from them on the rocky face of a great cliff. Looking around from the incredibly close-up view she had in comparison to others who were still vying for position, Sheryl gave silent thanks to Matt with a warm smile, betraying how much she was impressed by him—especially with the way he formed a protective shell for her from the crowd, standing strongly behind her, arms providing a backrest. *Could he be the one?* she wondered, albeit not too seriously.

Across the gorge, a group of young divers who had gathered at a shrine in prayer became everyone's focus. They came out from their prayers, and without much haste, the first diver stepped to a mountain-goat perch. Studying the tidal waves' comings and goings below, he launched into a swan dive of massive proportions, hitting the drink at a perfect moment. The crowd exploded.

As cheers faded, the crowd noticed that other divers across the way had moved onto numerous rocky perches. In a dazzling display with perfectly timed intervals, they launched into a flawless series of dives, mixing both individual and team dives.

After the finale, Sheryl exclaimed, "What a thrill!"

"Heightened by seeing it with you," responded Matt.

She turned to face him; his arms assisted in the move, holding her steady. Her knees collapsed a bit, but she had no worries in his gentle grasp. He stole a lingering kiss she was in no hurry to let go of, but they were, after all, in public. Still, they continued kissing.

The kiss ends only when the real-time trolley bell signals its next stop. Sheryl exits her daydream and wonders what it would take to track down Matt these days—*if he's even still here*, she speculates. She fondly figures, *I could say he really was the one who got away.* She fully remembers how fun he was—and a gentleman at that and such a great kisser. Regrets tinge her mood.

Sheryl's several adventures with Matt may haunt her, but she forces a smile. At least she's been out there living life to its fullest, she concludes. She figures she easily has twice the memories of anyone triple her age, with all that she has seen and done, the many places she has been, the many people she has known, and much of it all priceless, a true wealth of experience.

Still, she inwardly complains, *here I find myself alone again in yet another crowd, this time on the dodge from Sterling. Lord only knows why he had to come into my life in the first place. Just look what that's brought.*

The trolley stops at a dusty old flea market, where a sign reads, "El Mercado de Pulgas de Juan & Eduardo." She's been here before with Matt. It looks much the same, but she finds no connection to her previous self. She held her head high then as a young woman of principle and standards, even with a dashing young millionaire showing her the town. *I still lived as I preached*, she thinks. *Not like now.*

Impulsively, Sheryl gets off the trolley to navigate a series of open tents covering half a block, all filled with cheap merchandise. She distracts her harried self by hovering over the goodies with tourists and locals alike. Displays beckon on either side with things she'd normally barter for to bring back home as gifts. But she is in no mood to buy anything. Just passing time.

Since the reminders brought by Carlita earlier today, Sheryl's self-worth has descended to new lows, and she is haunted again over her loss of motherhood. Walking Tent Avenue, she scolds herself, *Geez, can we find a bright side somewhere today? I have to work my way out of this!* Sheryl determines to anticipate everyday reminders of her indiscretions and be ready to stand strong in the face of them before they put her into a tailspin. *Relax*, she instructs herself. *I made some mistakes, but I'm not making them again! Repent! As I learn, so I grow."*

She turns up a path between two tents and soon is examining onyx board games under the largest tent around. Onyx board games always catch her eye. The buying bug bites. But before she can decide on a purchase, she finds herself in eavesdropping mode. She faintly overhears some men arguing in the near distance. Speaking many languages gives Sheryl an advantage in such situations. She understands convoluted conversations in situations where she often is not expected to understand. So she is often under the radar.

The muffled banter nearby between a couple of angry men doesn't seem to interest other bargain hunters. They move on to other tents. Sheryl, however, looks around till she spots a tin shack beyond the large tent, from which the voices seem to be emanating. The overheard but unseen argument continues. A threatening voice growls in Spanglish, "To treat my niece this way? You are dead!"

A second man with a macho Italian accent says, "I told you you'd have your answer by Friday. Don't push me any faster."

Sheryl pretends to check out a variety of onyx chess sets scattered on tables all over the large tent while she edges nearer the shack.

The first voice responds in a steady voice. "To be clear—if you don't do as I say, you will be dead, señor, very dead. Take me seriously or not, at your peril."

The flimsy shack's door creaks open, and Sheryl ducks behind a fat tent pole doubling as a poster board. Watching from behind a poster, she sees a man step outside, slamming the door behind him. It's Marco. He's in a huff. The door reopens, and Carlita runs out after him in tears.

Marco hears her coming and waits impatiently for her. "If Eduardo keeps it up," postures Marco, "he's the one who'll be waking up dead."

Carlita, in surprisingly decent English, implores, "Don't mess with him, Marco!"

"He should not mess with me!"

"I don't think you remember too well—he has many bad men to do all his dirty work. No matter how tough you are, they are tougher. Believe me, I have seen how tough."

She reaches for him, he melts, and they hug without concern about any onlookers, of which there appears to be just the one, Sheryl behind the pole.

Carlita catches her breath and tells Marco, "I don't want our baby to know so much badness. This is no life for anyone."

Marco breaks their embrace and storms off up the path. He grumbles over his shoulder, "Let's go. I need a drink."

"Me too, but you know I can't," she laments, massaging her baby bump. Carlita shuffles after Marco. Once she catches up, she stays a step behind, single file. They reach the curb just as a city services bus arrives.

Back in the large tent, Sheryl steps out from behind the pole, jaw agape. "Wouldn't Irene like to know," she mumbles to herself.

Peering into the bus as Marco and Carlita take seats, Sheryl can't help but think that perhaps Marco is not long for this world. In him, she might almost be seeing a ghost. *Because come on*, Sheryl thinks, *how long will this local thug allow Marco to back-talk like that? And I thought I had problems.*

Sheryl foots it to the curb as the bus pulls away. She stands by, ready for whatever type of commercial vehicle arrives next. Mentally, she knits together the raw factors involved in this little drama unwittingly playing out before her. It seems Carlita is the flea market owner's niece. She's pregnant. Uncle sounds nasty. He's extorting something, details unknown. *Money, no doubt*, she guesses, filling in the blanks with Jack and Irene's background information on Marco and Carlita. Whatever is going on, they seem ready to kill each other.

Back at La Vista Hermosa del Mar Hotel, Sheryl keeps an eye out for Jack and Irene. She feels a need to tell them her story from the flea market. It's beyond gossip. Threats to life in both directions have been witnessed. Jack and Irene, though, are nowhere to be found.

The next day, Sheryl rises early to comb the beach for seashells. She also does plenty of strolling ankle-deep through the water as gentle waves come and go. This is the most exhilarated she's felt in a long, long time. She enjoys the view of all the hotels and condominiums lining the broad sandy playa. Other early risers jog and walk the shoreline in both directions.

Despite still having Marco on her mind, Sheryl is feeling sexy in her suit under the sun, ready for nothing more today than hanging around the beach. *For sure I'll run into Jack and Irene*, she figures, shuffling concerns for Marco behind her beach-combing pleasures.

Sheryl completes the outward leg of her down-and-back beach stroll and turns around. Some of the normal risers are out by now, and a few commercial vendors have already set up shop. Through the growing crowd she spots a battered Marco, one arm in a sling, stumbling past a volleyball game. From the looks of it, he's lucky he didn't stumble right into the game.

Marco manages to wait out a landing parasailer at the waterline, only to be nearly run down by an out-of-control WaveRunner headed for a wild landing. In saving himself, Marco loses his balance and falls; he slowly picks himself up, covered in sand but lucky to be alive. With a glance at the WaveRunner, which has now come to a stop without killing anybody, Marco resumes his beach stroll at an unsteady pace. He looks both wired and weary, with a wary eye out for everything all around him.

Sheryl is shocked by Marco's down-and-out condition. She calls, "Marco!" before he even sees her coming.

Marco squints into the sun behind her.

"What happened to you?" she asks.

He steps closer for a better look at her. It's clear she needs to remind him who she is.

"I'm Sheryl, a friend of Jack and Irene. We met yesterday at the palapa row on the beach."

"Oh yes, sorry. I'm a little preoccupied. Good to see you again, but I have to go."

Before he can get away, Sheryl is quick to say, "What happened? How can I help?"

"Nobody can help, thank you. Damned if I wasn't mugged last night— drunk and out too late at the wrong place, so it's my own fault. That's the long and the short of it."

"I'm sorry, Marco. Have you gone to the police?"

He laughs, which seems to cause him pain, and replies, "Who are the police in Acapulco? Do you think you know the true answer? No, I didn't tell no police. I wouldn't know who, or what, to tell. I was so drunk. Somebody had a gun, and maybe they clubbed me with it."

"Oh no, that's horrible! What about your arm?"

"It's my shoulder, mostly. But my elbow kinda needs to be immobilized too. The sling helps. It could have been worse. I am alive, for now."

"Marco, you poor guy!"

"Yeah, tell me. I woke up in the gutter, bleeding. The hotel doc says somebody stabbed me. Just missed a major artery and didn't go too deep. He gave me some stitches and a shot. I've been self-medicating a little too."

"Marco, please don't take this wrong, but … I mean … like, I know I'm young enough to be your daughter. But honestly, don't you think you've had enough to drink?"

"Of course, I think so." He shakes his head in disgust. "That's how this all happened in the first place. Too much booze, always, down here. Like I said, nobody to blame but me." Marco suddenly looks dizzy.

Sheryl takes his good arm and stretches it across one of her shoulders in support. "Let's find a place to sit down," she suggests comfortingly.

The hungover and aging landscaper's knees wobble. Sheryl steers him around to head in the direction of their hotel. The hulking, hurting Marco leans on her heavily. Some passing beachcombers stare; others pretend not to see. Sheryl spots an outdoor café right on the beach. A resident dog steps out from behind a shadow, watching silently as the two new customers approach.

They find a shaded table, and a waiter soon arrives. Sheryl orders two large coffees and a combination plate of appetizers. She figures a little food with his booze will help Marco, who now uses the table for support.

He says gratefully, "Thank you, Sheryl. I know I do need some kind of rest."

The waiter scoots off with their order up a slight sand hill to the café's cooking shelter. In amazement, Sheryl checks out the awake but zoned-out Marco.

He gradually becomes aware of her scrutiny of him. "Hell," he mutters, "I wouldn't go into an area like that back home, on a bet. But here? How stupid! This town is losing its charm for me."

"How did your Acapulco routine start up, Marco?"

He leans back in his chair to regain his equilibrium. A tear streaks out from behind his sunglasses. "Nobody knows this story. Now it'll be just you and me, I guess."

The waiter interrupts with coffees. "The appetizers are soon, my friends," he announces quickly.

"Gracias," Sheryl says as he walks away.

As they sip their coffee, Marco chokes up and freezes.

Sheryl says, "If you don't want to talk, Marco, that's cool—and understandable. I was just being nosy, anyway."

Marco smiles slightly at her. Sheryl suspects that he's glad to have a friendly neutral ear, so she pours on more charm with a glowing smile. He relaxes a bit more.

"I do want to talk," he assures her. "Maybe it will help, somehow. The burden has been so great, and I need to share it. A stranger like you is probably the best way."

"Sounds logical, don't you think?"

"Maybe so. I wish I'd never fallen into some unhappy knowledge seven years ago that changed my life. I would've been far better off to never have known all the truths behind my life, what I'd thought was a happy life."

"How's that?"

"Because that's why I came down here for my first convention. I'd always skipped them in the past. First time in my life I ever wanted just to get drunk. Back home, even today, I don't drink a drop—just here, once a year."

"I believe you, Marco. If you drank like this all the time, you'd be dead."

Marco stares into his coffee, still looking dazed. "I was stinking, rotten drunk on the town one night and met Carlita at some jazz joint. And to be honest, it's also where I got mugged last night."

"Don't go back there!"

"Right, easy to say. I tell myself the same thing. But that night—bam. She was wild in bed. It was some night."

"I see. And the rest is history, so to speak."

"Exactly—my own little rough-and-ready annual fling with a Mexican peasant girl. It makes me sick thinking of how that all started. But I do love her now. That's what's happened over the years."

The waiter returns with their appetizers. "You will like these, my friends."

"Gracias, and here," she replies, forking over some money. "You keep the change."

"Thank you, my friend!" The waiter leaves, and Sheryl and Marco sample the finger food.

"And now," Marco continues between bites, "she is pregnant."

"Marco, I don't want to insult your lady, but who says you did it? You come here once a year. She may tell you she loves you, but what is she up to the rest of the year?"

"I asked the same question, of course. But after slapping me for having such thoughts, she counted back the days for me, very animated like an actress, to this year's visit." He shakes his head in self-pity. "The odds are strong, very strong, that it's me."

"Still, that's a lot to take on faith. Once the baby's born, get blood tests done."

Marco fixates on a parasailer's beach landing, seemingly looking right past Sheryl. "Anyway," he says like a zombie, "this isn't the worst of it. Her uncle is demanding twenty thousand dollars to smuggle her to the States for an abortion. Or I'm a dead man."

"Again, I think you should go to the police," she insists. "Make a complaint."

"This is Mexico, my naive young friend."

"You know he'll pocket the money, and she'll have some back-alley abortion that costs him peanuts." Sheryl chokes up, flashing back to Michigan Avenue.

Marco nods in agreement. He mindlessly nibbles on their appetizers, stopping to remove his sunglasses and rub his sad eyes.

Sheryl is upset just from hearing the story. "What are you going to do?" she asks.

"I keep asking myself this question—just like I asked once before in my life."

"You've been blackmailed before?"

Marco snickers and cracks a wry smile. "In a sense. I just didn't know it at the time." He looks out to sea and blinks back tears. "You remember I spoke of knowledge I wished I'd never gained?"

Sheryl grimaces empathetically and nods affirmatively. He looks numb.

Marco continues, "Twenty years ago, my wife, Sophia, who was not yet then my wife …" He hesitates. "No, let's forget about this history lesson. I am here now."

"Ain't that the truth—the here and now? What else can it boil down to, Marco? So keep it that way. Put all that history stuff behind you." Sheryl feels like such a hypocrite offering those words of wisdom. But they do sound good. She will have to give the advice a try.

Marco seems to give it all some thought. "Right," he says without conviction. "Sure, just put it behind me."

"Yes," coaxes Sheryl, full of hope for them both.

Marco sighs. "So okay, this no longer is the one big blight on my life, agreed. Now there is this newer blight. Poetic justice. My life in a nutshell." His head drops into his hands. He cries.

Sheryl worries she's making him feel worse, and she remains concerned for his safety. There is still no sign of Jack and Irene. She feels duty-bound to pump him up. "Marco, you have to be alert and concentrate on this Mexican standoff with Carlita's uncle. Then do right by her. And start your life over. Day one. Be strong."

He takes a deep breath and scans the horizon over the ocean. Some of the sadness and fear disappears from his face. Still plenty serious, he says, "That sounds good on paper. We'll see. Thanks, though, Sheryl. I'll figure this out now."

"You're welcome, Marco." She checks her watch. "Let me walk you to the hotel."

"I appreciate your concern, but I'm much better. Thank you."

"Of course, but are you sure you'll be okay?"

"I need to think, and this is a good place to think."

"I understand. Find me if you need me."

"Thank you, for everything."

"My pleasure. Good luck."

Sheryl leaves Marco on his barstool alone with his troubles. She takes her own mind games on a walk to the shoreline. It seems true that there's always someone with it worse than you.

⌖

The present day interrupts Sheryl's memories. It is again the dead of winter in Chicago. Sheryl and Sterling reach her building. He starts to open the door for her, but even before she knows she's doing it, Sheryl pushes him away. "Back off, Sterling," she demands in a sour mood.

"What's with this?" he complains.

"At the least, understand I'm still jet-lagged from the most traumatic trip of my life. I'm bushed and want to be alone, so good-bye. Thanks for brunch." Reveling in his state of confusion, Sheryl leaves Sterling flat-footed behind her. Once inside the foyer, she's glad to see the doorman is absent from his lobby post. Not up for face-to-face contact with anyone, Sheryl grabs an elevator fast.

As she rides up to her floor, thankfully alone, her thoughts jump back to poor Carlita and Acapulco. More to the point, she remembers how really it was Carlita who brought Sheryl back together once again with Matt Ayers. Sheryl's fear for Marco's life inspired her to track down Matt for his local knowledge and contacts. She stirs aglow in memories of finding him with help from the hotel concierge.

⌖

The concierge chuckles at her gratitude, saying, "Finding such a wealthy US expat who is pretty well known around town, even if nobody does know his business—it was pretty easy, I'll admit."

She tips him nicely nevertheless, thrilled to know Matt indeed does still live in Acapulco. When she finds Matt, she learns that he's married now, but his Canadian wife is visiting family up north. So he volunteers to ride shotgun for Sheryl as she follows a hunch in tailing Marco that next night after his mugging. She's worried he'll return to the site of the mugging, El Club de Jazz. "I'm sure he'll be stumbling in there again," she explains to Matt. "He's thrown caution to the wind—only now he's a bigger target than ever, all banged up like he is."

Matt warns, "I've been to this joint before, and it's not the wisest place for a couple of gringos to be—especially a beautiful blonde like you."

Sheryl, typically more adventurous on the road than at home, responds, "Well, it's not totally unheard of, right?"

"Of course not. You've got me there. Plenty of tourists hear of it, and some check it out."

"Then that's us," she declares, gleaming. She hopes that her happiness about hanging around with Matt under such serious circumstances does not make her a potential home-wrecker type.

Arriving at El Club de Jazz, Sheryl opens the club's squeaky screen door. Several locals look up as she enters, followed quickly by Matt. The club is crowded and smoky, and a Santana CD is subbing for a band that's on break. They happen to enter during a brief sound gap between tracks. The couple takes two of the last three stools at a cramped bar as the next song begins.

"Dos cervezas, por favor," Matt orders.

A gnarly bartender cracks their beers. The bar's other patrons soon bore of gawking at the latest gringos and drift back to minding their own business, or planning mischief, as it were. Sheryl, figuring she has to go ahead and drink the beer if she's going to fit in while undercover at a seedy bar, toasts Matt. They chat while scoping out the place, trying not to stick out too much in the crowd.

Sheryl says quietly, "Interesting group, like you predicted."

"And that includes us, don't forget."

"Hold on." Sheryl has spotted Carlita exiting the ladies' room.

Despite Carlita's very obvious condition, several drunks hit on her as she makes her way to the bar, ignoring them all. She takes the one remaining stool, apparently hers to begin with, near Matt and Sheryl. Carlita sips at a half-full glass of beer. Sheryl privately tsk-tsks over a sad sight symbolic of anything but Madonna and child.

An occupied stool between Sheryl and Carlita opens up, and Sheryl sidles on over next to Carlita. "Mind if I sit here?"

"Suit yourself, pretty white girl."

"Thank you, Carlita. How are you tonight?"

Carlita looks at her, perplexed. "Do I know you?"

"No," Sheryl admits as Matt protectively reseats himself next to her. "It's more like I know of you, sort of—I'm a friend of Marco's. I've seen you with him."

Carlita stares at Sheryl blankly, sheds a tear, and turns back to her beer. She takes a chug and says softly, "I guess you have not heard yet."

"Heard what?" Sheryl asks with trepidation.

Carlita, eyes straight ahead, whispers, "If my Uncle Eduardo learns you are here talking to me, it is big trouble for you. He owns this place."

Sheryl discreetly scans the crowd. Nobody seems to be watching at the moment. She assures Carlita, "That's a chance I'll have to take. I'm concerned about Marco. I thought he might show up here tonight. That's all."

"Well," Carlita says, choking back tears, "you can stop worrying—Marco is dead."

Stunned, Sheryl blurts out, "What?" A few eyes turn their way.

Carlita answers, "He collapsed at the beach today from untreated internal injuries and was dead before paramedics arrived. He's gone, for good. And I can't believe it."

"Oh no. But I saw him on the beach today—talked with him and helped him ride out the morning. He'd been drinking."

"He always was drinking a lot, for as long I knew him."

More local eyes zero in on their yapping lips.

Sheryl asks, "Was it from that beating here last night? He was banged up badly."

"Yes," answers Carlita. "So if you saw him, then you know all about that."

"That's why I'm here—in case he came back looking for trouble. The more I thought about his mood and situation, the more worried for him I got."

Carlita says, "I am touched by your concern for my dear Marco. Thank you."

"I know he loved you. He told me so just this morning."

Carlita, obviously on edge, appears overwhelmed. "That is so nice of you to tell me. Thank you again. But I am worried that Uncle Eduardo could show up any moment. If that were to happen, I really would catch it from him if you are here."

"I don't want any trouble for you, Carlita."

Carlita asks, "Are there any other reasons why you are here?"

"To be honest … yes." Sheryl pauses for a glance at Carlita's baby bulge before continuing. "I see you two were close enough that you should know better than to be drinking beer tonight."

Looking ashamed, Carlita puts down the glass. "Believe me, this is the only drink I've had since I learned of the baby inside me. It was just too much for me with Marco's death."

"I know, but I think he would want you not to get drunk over him."

"Believe me, there is nothing more I want than this baby. I think God will give me no more chances if I lose this baby."

"What do you mean?"

Nervous, Carlita sneaks a peak around the room and says under her breath, "I don't tell you this, comprende? But since I was very young, Eduardo has forced me to work the tourists. I learned English this way. If these men don't make me pregnant, Eduardo knocks me up himself."

"What? And Eduardo truly is your uncle?"

"Sí, some uncle—verdad?"

Sheryl feels devastated for her. "I don't know what to say, Carlita. This is a horrible story."

"It is a true life story."

"So," guesses Sheryl, "he scares the foreign men with blackmail to make them come back here to face the music?"

"Sí. And his deal always stays the same—come up with the monies or die."

"And everybody pays?"

"One guy has refused."

"Marco?"

Carlita shivers at the thought and nods. Sheryl follows suit with the shivers. Matt, from behind, places gentle hands of support on Sheryl's shoulders.

The bartender is beginning to look nosy, and Carlita mumbles, "I cannot talk anymore in this place—too many ears all around here for me."

"If you leave with us, wouldn't that look suspicious?"

"Of course, but less dangerous for us than if we keep talking here. I will think of something later if it comes up with Eduardo."

The band, looking buzzed, comes back from its long break. The musicians start tuning up, which distracts everyone else. Carlita and her new benefactors make their exit.

Outside, a cab pulls up at the badly cracked curb. Matt has the driver take them to Avenida Costera Miguel Aleman. The traffic at this late hour is dominated by the usual VW Bugs and Toyota cabs. Their cab rolls past familiar open-air-lobby hotels, money exchanges, and varied Mexican and international restaurants.

"Drop us up there, por favor," Matt requests of the driver, pointing out a late-night restaurant at the next corner.

"Sí, my friend," the driver responds.

Inside at a comfy booth with few other customers around, Carlita details how the baby deals get set up over time. "It always happens at some nice resort with a man who wants to think I am his own."

"How many other women are involved?"

"I stopped counting. But anyway, unfortunately, I am Uncle Eduardo's favorite," she says sadly but with a tinge of swagger. "I bring his best results." Suddenly overcome, Carlita bursts into tears.

Sheryl hugs her. "It's okay, dear."

Sobbing, Carlita says, "Señorita, you do not understand. I must get my abortion this weekend, with a real butcher this time. A very bad reputation. Plus, this will make one dozen times—twelve abortions. I will burn forever in hell. I need a priest."

Sheryl strokes her hair. "If we put our heads together, maybe we can save the baby and get you both out of here. Can you put your hands on any money?"

Carlita stifles her tears and laughs lightly. "Kind lady, you don't know the life of a cheap Mexican whore. Uncle Eduardo, he controls all my money."

Sheryl never has felt so helpless or so sickened by someone's sad circumstances. *This really takes the cake*, she wants to say but holds back out of respect for Carlita.

"Listen," Matt interjects, "there's only one thing to do. Carlita, let us get you out of here tonight. No going home. I have friends in Mexico City who will help you get a new start. I have enough money to fund you awhile."

"Oh, Señor Matt, why should you do this for me?"

"Why should I not? That's the question."

Sheryl is as excited as Carlita. "Girl, when a man like this steps forward for you, don't step back."

Carlita quickly concludes, "You are right, of course!"

Matt and his contacts deliver as promised, which is how Sheryl sort of comes to terms with herself over Jamaica and Michigan Avenue. She is proud to have been the conduit between Carlita and Matt, and boy, she still swoons for him. She wonders how in the world she let him slip away for some other woman to marry.

I must have been nuts, thinks Sheryl as the elevator ride ends.

Stepping out onto her floor, still with Carlita and her by-now middle-school daughter in mind, Sheryl takes pride in having done someone some good in this world. The nature of her good deed has returned some balance to her life. Unfortunately, the realities of today lead her to hang her head in misery. Too many wrong turns have led to a mountain of financial misery, which complicates every other facet of her existence. It's a hard sell to herself that her time on earth has been fruitful.

Sheryl's shoulders sag as she approaches her apartment door, key in hand. *Been here, done this*, she thinks. Crossing the threshold always reminds her of everything gone wrong in her world, starting with thoughts of Sterling's fine Lake Shore Drive condo.

"Oh boy," she huffs sadly, thinking, *Here we go again, home sweet home.* Profoundly depressed, she turns the key. Chin quivers kick into overdrive.

Chapter 11

REALITY, THE PRESENT TENSE

Sheryl enters her apartment and flicks on a light in her tiny entryway. She's mentally and emotionally exhausted from Sterling's visit, on top of a sleep-deprivation hangover following her exodus from Cairo. She is fully spent. Not even a day has passed since she touched down at O'Hare. Already, though, Cairo sort of feels like a lifetime away.

Regardless, she knows nothing has changed here. Magazine and newspaper stacks line the walls of her little front hallway. Clutter gathered from around the world competes against childhood mementoes of family and friends. High-end art pieces on corner stands mix with cheesy golf-outing giveaways stashed on a shelf. More mismatched stuff fills out the claustrophobic entrance hall to her formerly efficient, neat, and orderly one-bedroom apartment.

Maybe this time home I'll really get around to thinning out some stuff, she thinks. All this stuff presses in upon every fiber of her body, sapping her strength. In what once was a shipshape, comfy home, she judiciously looks before stepping along her cleared pathway through all kinds of bits and pieces. She ventures forward haltingly into the overstuffed congestion of her tiny dining area, made smaller by somewhat organized squalor. "Oh, how," she groans, "can I go on living like this?"

Her messy surroundings would prevail over those of any legendary cat lady's Victorian. Standing at the junction of her hallway, with the living room to the right and another hallway to her left that leads to her compact master bedroom, Sheryl is flooded with memories of Sterling promising to get them "that big house in Hyde Park, soon!"—whatever "soon" means to him. But the promise was that he would see to it that Sheryl had a place to display her world-collected treasures, the good stuff.

"Damn him!" she shouts to the loneliness of her congested world. So why did she allow things to continue—not only continue but even grow worse, monetarily? Just once, she only needed to have found the strength to walk away. So simple, it seems now. Just change the locks; stop taking his calls. Avoid his hangouts, which would've been easy. "Even if it's easier said than done," she tells herself.

How this could have been and could still be today is beyond her. As with today, there she sat, looking into his eyes from across the table. Admittedly, though, today is not a good example. This plays like the end of the road. Back in the day, she thought the road went on forever, always allowing one last chance to exit. But no, she has found, sooner or later there's a dead end.

Memories flow fast. Sheryl remembers how Sterling struck while the iron was hot after Devil's Lake, working on her for additional cash investment in his clothing company.

Sterling tells her he's being ripped off by a Chinese company stealing his company's designs. The State Department is involved, and all assets are tied up in taking the Chinese corporation to court. But not to worry, the judge is sympathetic to all American companies, as per her lengthy record in such cases.

"We just need a little shot in the arm from some outside investment, till those Reds are sent packing back to China," Sterling confidently states.

"No way!" Sheryl retorts.

"But—"

"No buts."

"All right, understood," he whines, "but how about letting me explain it so you'll understand what I'm all about?"

Foolishly, she relents. "Fine, go ahead." Hook set.

"It has to be hush-hush," he insists conspiratorially, "because my mainstream competition doesn't know about these Chinese knockoffs, or even that my company exists!"

"How cloak-and-dagger," she says, unimpressed.

"Listen," he predicts, "we'll take them all by surprise once this court stuff is over."

"Sounds fascinating but not too plausible. How long will this be in court?"

"That's hard to say, of course."

Sterling talks fast enough to get in promises of big titles, inflated salaries, and plenty of travel for them as a couple. Her days of having to work her way around the world, doing the bidding of others, would be done. Others would be doing her bidding from the highest level.

∾౷∾

Back in the present day, Sheryl sadly recalls how over time she began to believe some of Sterling's blustery financial forecasts. Then there was one magical night of change, in Grant Park. It seemed the whole city was there as extras in the electrically charged atmosphere ushering in the new administration. Sterling's promises of matrimony set her heart aflutter.

Her scattered mind jumps to the memory of giving up Thomas Kearns's big-time offer of a cushy position in Florida. It was what she'd dreamed of plenty of times, before Jamaica with Sterling. "Why, oh why? That would've changed everything."

She bums out over having allowed Sterling to kill her ambition and encourage that bad move, only later to have her time with him in Jamaica end in complete acrimony. Postabortion, she somehow allowed him back in her life with lovey-dovey talk about a ring and a child or two, to reflect their love for each other. Over time, he painted his marriage and family assurances as pledges to erase the tragedy of their aborted darling.

"Whatever in the world did he mean by that? How can one erase such things? But I fell for it, every word. What bullshit!" She thinks about all the fine things he was going to buy her, someday, with all the millions finally brought in by their clothing company. She thinks about that maybe nonexistent company, she now realizes, into which he ultimately conned her to invest. "Stupid me!" She slaps her forehead, and her chin begins quivering again.

Sheryl's eyes bug out at her encroaching stuff. She laments, "It's so hard to do anything around here when your heart is broken, totally broken for too many years." The contrast with her lap-of-luxury lifestyle on the road, on the boss's dime, hits hard. This is the dismal reality. *That's bad enough, sad enough*, she thinks. But throw in day-to-day destitution for having lived beyond her meager means while helping cover Sterling's monthly nut, and her life is a mess, driving her to solicit loans from long-unseen friends, even casual acquaintances. The whole situation is untenable. *But of course*, she tells herself, *it's nobody's fault but my own for believing that asshole and his infinite fast talk. Lawyers and lawsuits!*

More than ever, she doubts this company exists. *Those times he took me to court and had me wait in the lobby while he went into a courtroom, he could've been dealing with other issues—or just sitting there as a spectator!* Sheryl's stomach turns, again and again, not so unusual lately. *How naive of me.*

She can hear Sterling now: "But honey, they have my corporate money all tied up. This stuff takes years. But the payoff will be immense! All we need now is another few months of carrying some of my bills." Invariably, she has always succumbed to his needs.

"Asshole," she mumbles, knowing she'd likely advance cash from her dwindling line of credit if he came begging for money tomorrow. "It's like a sickness! I'm sick!"

Sheryl squeezes her way down a narrow living room path forged through countless objects, including a shrine to her now long-dead mother, Ruth. Photos from their Hawaiian trip dot the bookcase display, among other shots of Ruth spanning her lifetime. "Oh, Mom," Sheryl groans sadly. "I need you, Mom."

She reaches the front side of a sofa that defines the living room section of her tiny abode. The sofa backs up to what would be a fine dining table and chairs given the proper setting. Wearily, Sheryl pushes aside overdue bills and dunning notices that cover the near end of the sofa. She flops onto the cleared corner cushion. The winter sun sets early, robbing all remaining natural light from the room. Sheryl reaches for a lamp on a crowded side table and turns it on low.

Eerie shadows highlight mountainous accumulations of inconsequential material things. In the dimly lit room she glances at career-tracking photos with her on top of the world, in all corners of the world. Not in the mood for such reminders, she kills the light, wiping out the better-day images collectively staring her down. "Successful days they were," she emotionally recalls. "Somehow, they should have led to a better now for me than this!"

Soon, outside nightlife backlights her apartment. Shadows different from before dance across the room. Out of nowhere, Sheryl reflexively text-messages Sterling. "Hello," she types, not knowing why. Angry at herself for foolish knee-jerk texting, she stares blankly at the cell's screen till it goes black. "Damn." She continues staring at the dark cell phone.

Shortly, with no response forthcoming, her shoulders sag. She buries her tired face against the sofa's armrest, sinking deeper into despair. "This is the worst … oh God, just the worst." Squinting through tears, she scans her smothering sea of materialism-gone-hoarder-mad. She is overwhelmed. The collective weight of everything sits more heavily than ever upon her weary shoulders, bringing pure misery and hopelessness while accentuating her loneliness; it feels like hell. "Sterling," she cries aloud, writhing about in the sofa's corner, "what have you done to me? And why—why me?" After hyperventilating for a minute, Sheryl slowly calms down, though the sense of hopelessness remains. "What's the use?"

With an affected onstage groan, she suddenly twitches into a figure of someone approaching the edge. Hyperventilating again, she moans herself slowly into a fitful sleep. Soon, rolling dreams take her one moment to New Zealand, the next somewhere else. A black-and-white kaleidoscopic mindscape opens a peephole into her life.

"Get me out of here, Muhammad!" she mumbles in her sleep to her Cairo airfare connection. "I can't take it anymore!"

The night-vision jumble of images jumps back five months.

∽✑∕

Sheryl had recently convinced Gloria to front her a few thousand dollars, after being as effective in selling her sister on Sterling's company as he earlier was in selling Sheryl. Gloria even met Sterling once in the process, at his charming best. However, lack of follow-up details on the investment has led to friction between the sisters.

Yet just before leaving on a London tour, Sheryl, in need of emotional support from someone other than Sterling, tells Gloria about her destitute situation. Over burgers again at Heaven on Harms, she says, "In a nutshell, I've gone from having my condo paid off to having two maxed-out lines of credit on it. I'm broke and living under a pile of dunning notices."

"What happened? You were so proud at your mortgage-burning party!"

"It's a question without an easy answer." The long story short, she explains, is that during the mortgage frenzy that led up to the big fall, under pressure from Sterling, she secured dual lines of credit. He was always running short and in need of help.

"How could you even get all that credit on your condo?" asks Gloria, incredulous.

"Sterling had some mortgage broker who made it all so easy," Sheryl whimpers.

"Unbelievable," says Gloria. "Then again," she quickly adds, "maybe not so much. The more I learn about him … well, let's just say I'm not totally shocked."

Sheryl, on the verge of tears in public, nods in agreement. "I don't know what to do."

"Let me talk to Dad and Jon. We'll figure out something. Meanwhile, just stay away from Sterling and don't give him another dime."

After Sheryl returns from London, Gloria, Jon, and their father, Oliver, take Sheryl to meet with a bankruptcy attorney, who gives her homework for their next meeting. "Pull together as many records about your dealings with Dr. Jackson as you can," he instructs. "And I wouldn't worry too much about losing your home just yet. Foreclosures are jamming the system, dragging everything out. And politics play against the banks right now for having given out so many shaky loans."

The family lunches after the meeting. Sheryl feels a little better already, although she's plenty embarrassed to have all her dirty laundry out for display among her family. "Thank you, Dad, for finding this lawyer. He makes sense and gives me some hope."

"Of course, Sheryl—but the burden is on you to pull those records together for him. Otherwise, you're handicapping him from doing his job."

"I understand. I'll get to it."

Gloria says, "Think about letting me put you in touch with a great counselor I know. You should be talking about this with a professional too, not just us. These are mental games he's been playing with you, and you really need help from an expert in that field."

Sheryl says, "I understand all that too. Let me think about it."

The turnaround time to her next tour, dearly loved Switzerland, is only a week. So no records get gathered right away. A month passes with Sheryl still accomplishing nothing in that arena. Plus, she breaks a firm appointment with the lawyer that was made specifically to push her into action. Shortly thereafter, she lets it slip over the phone to Sterling that her family now knows of her desperate finances and unsecured investments with him.

Sterling is livid. "Why'd you tell them about our deals? With everything good going on in court and finally coming together, their uninformed interference is the last thing we need."

"Last thing we need or you need, Sterling? My patience's wearing thin."

"I can understand your stress over a few bills, but keep the faith. Hang in there with me."

"What do you think I've been doing—for years?"

"Have you ever thought there might be things you've done, maybe slightly misrepresenting some facts here and there, that mean you should stay out of the spotlight? Bankers weren't the only ones spinning yarns."

"Yeah, another fine mess you got me into with that broker buddy of yours."

"If I were you," warns Sterling, "I'd be shredding records instead of turning them over to some lawyer you don't know."

"Don't be trying to turn the tables on me over this. I want my money. I need it—now."

"All right, I tell you what, how about you give me six months to make good on every penny you've ever loaned me, with interest? I'm that confident over things in court now."

"You've got to be kidding. I have to go."

"Last thought—are you sure you'd like them to know about our child in heaven? It was so tough on your mother. I think that was the slow beginning to the end of her time on earth."

Sheryl hangs up on him and breaks down crying, curled up in the corner of her sofa.

Another week passes. She avoids Sterling's calls and doesn't return his messages, all the while procrastinating on the daunting task of pulling financial records and all the corporate paperwork on Sterling's deals for the lawyer. Her filing system leaves much to be desired.

At the first of the following week, Gloria calls on behalf of the family. "We're doing our best, Sheryl, to give you support in all this stuff. But you need to let us dig in and really help."

"Dig into what?"

"Let's do lunch again and talk it all through. We're thinking today, down by you."

Sheryl panics. No family or friends other than Sterling have been in her place for years. She's adept at steering get-togethers elsewhere, quipping that her place is a mess on a short home layover between trips abroad. Well, that, plus it's on the small side. Small, they all understand. Mess, they have no clue.

Gloria continues, "Think of where you'd like to eat; we'll be there at noon."

"Okay," Sheryl responds involuntarily. "Text me when you get here. I'll come down."

The call ends, and Sheryl immediately chastises herself. "Great! Now what am I going to do? What if they want to come up here? Damn it!" She looks at the clock: ten o'clock, two hours to go. "Oh boy."

Her cell rings again. It's Sterling. For some reason she answers. He's anxious to see her. She agrees that he can come by at noon; they'll do lunch. "Wait for me downstairs," she says, neglecting to mention there will be others for lunch.

Sheryl is unexpectedly giddy over the prospect of her dad and Jon finally meeting Sterling. After all, how often has Sterling said that someday he wants to meet her whole family? He recently even said as much to Gloria when the three of them had tea at the Chicago History Museum. Now, it seems, fate will bring them all together come noon.

This is Sterling's last chance to prove he's the man he wants me to think he is, Sheryl thinks, fantasizing about a long shot. Maybe, just maybe, this spontaneous encounter will be the thing to push him along, to make good in front of the family. Allegedly, he one day wants to join them. *Seeing all this happen would be so superior*, thinks Sheryl, *to forever being labeled a sucker*. There's the illogic, she realizes, as to what keeps the abused coming back for more.

Noon approaches. Sheryl receives a "hurry up" text from Sterling, who has reached the lobby. After texting him to relax with a magazine, Sheryl receives a text from Gloria: they are parking at her corner and will be right up. Sheryl replies, "I'll meet you in the lobby!" She picks up her pace and gets out the door to an elevator.

When the elevator reaches the lobby, the doors open, and Sheryl steps out, suddenly afraid of the challenge ahead in bringing Sterling together with her family unannounced. She spots Sterling sitting in a stuffed chair, topcoat off, with his banker's pinstriped suit in full display as he reads a magazine. He looks impatient and hasn't noticed her yet. Sheryl then sees Donald the doorman buzzing in her family. The buzzer catches Sterling's attention, and he looks up at the door just as Jon enters the lobby. Sheryl watches as her dad enters next, and she can tell that Sterling doesn't realize who they are. But once Gloria enters, Sterling's expression turns to stupefaction.

Gloria looks equally stunned. "Sterling," she says, "I wasn't expecting to see you."

"You sure of that?"

Jon steps up directly to Sterling and stretches out his right hand, which Sterling takes reflexively. "Hello, Sterling," snarls Jon with a firm grip. "I hear you've been looking forward to meeting the family. Well, here we are. I'm Jon. Can't say I'm all that thrilled to meet you."

Sterling suddenly rails against Jon, full of street venom. "How dare you call me that, you racist son of a bitch!" he shouts, likely looking to plant thoughts in the doorman's mind.

"Nice try," Jon replies as he begins videotaping the interaction with his cell. "Please be sure to speak clearly so we all know exactly what it is you have in mind. Now," he intones, "what was it you claimed I said?"

Sheryl, momentarily dumbstruck at the elevator bank, sees Sterling ignore Jon and switch his attention to Oliver, who is slowly approaching, his gait unsteady. Sterling taunts him, "So, old man, how does it feel to have been such a racist bastard all your life?"

"What?" asks the hearing-impaired Oliver.

Sheryl jumps into the middle of the fray and loudly demands, "What's going on here?"

"I'll tell you what's going on here," says Sterling. "Your family is crucifying me!"

"Yeah, right," says Jon.

Sterling is cornered, outnumbered, and obviously unhappy about the newfound scrutiny from Sheryl's family. He brushes past her seemingly intent on going on the offensive. He threatens Oliver's space by getting in close to his face, snarling, "You'll rot in hell for it too."

Oliver stumbles backward, away from the threatening affront. He makes a fortunate fall into the stuffed side chair Sterling once occupied.

Jon, seeing that his father is shaken but safe, spits, "What a con man!" to Sterling's face.

"What did you say?" Sterling screams, splattering spittle.

Gloria tries playing peacemaker. "Come on, Sterling. Let's not take this somewhere that we'll all live to regret."

Jon steps back to allow his sister space in approaching Sterling.

"You've got nerve," claims Sterling with an eye to Gloria.

Gloria angrily tells her sister, "Your friend Sterling is out of control."

"If that isn't the pot calling the kettle black, I don't know what is!" Sterling shouts. "I'll have you all arrested before today is over!" Sterling starts pacing back and forth, mumbling, "Here we are again—plain intimidation of a black man in full view of witnesses, with no justice in sight!"

Jon keeps filming. Gloria and Sheryl check on their dad, who seems all right, aside from being shocked and speechless. His face is ashen, his eyes bewildered and sad. Gloria looks to be restraining herself from unleashing a tirade against her sister.

"Dad," whispers Sheryl, crouching low. "Are you okay?"

Oliver looks into her eyes, detached. Gloria fights tears. Everyone else in the most public space of Sheryl's longtime communal home fights tears too, except for Sterling. He paces. Donald the doorman maintains his cool.

"So it was," recollects Sheryl, now half-awake, sinking deeper into the sofa's corner.

Outside nightlife still backlights her living room with dancing shadows that mix inside and outside material goods. She groans from exhaustion. Still almost dozing, the conscious half of her current state realizes that things never again will be the same between her and her family.

"Things already aren't the same," Sheryl says groggily, remembering the aftermath of the infamous lobby scene. "And will I ever see any of my money?" she wonders. "No!" she realizes without a doubt. "I can't believe what a fool I've been! Such a fool … and worse, now everybody knows. What a joke! On me."

Clearly, Sterling's presence in her life took her off-track from career and child-rearing ambitions. Even more sadly, she knows that the dominant role of her life has been her place in Sterling's life, and it also has been her life's most unheralded role. Virtually nobody outside a small circle has seen her play this part. Yet now everyone arriving late still is in time to witness the third act—wherever that is headed.

"I'm fully exposed," she tells herself, "and that's kind of like being free." She is fully free to imagine, as she often has before, what that child of hers would be up to these days if her one shot at mothering had gone another way; there will be no way of ever knowing.

Releasing a therapeutic sigh, Sheryl awkwardly tosses and turns on the couch in frustration, jumping from half-thinking to half-dreaming and back again and again. Then it dawns on her that it's nighttime and not a crime to call it a night. "Made it through another day," she says, only half-jokingly congratulating herself.

She shakes off the sofa's REM world and struggles to her feet. "Time to hit the sack," she decides, despite knowing her bed will need clearing. Padding along her cleared paths back to her little master suite, she's doing all right till a mirror peeks out from behind a heavily cluttered vanity table, catching Sheryl's eye. The glimpse she gets of herself is so scary that she breaks into tears, wondering, *How will it end, God?*

She sobs, hyperventilates, and climbs into bed. She's lost. With the lights out, insomnia familiarly rules. It hardly fazes her anymore. Moonlight drifts through sheer window curtains, highlighting an eight-by-ten glossy portrait on her vanity of her New Englander man, Jim.

Now there's the one that really got away, she thinks, as she does every time she sees that picture half-hidden by other memorabilia. Loving memories of Jim overwhelm her, as usual. She thinks back to how they met on a riverboat tour up the Seine. How ironic it was to meet the American man of her dreams in Europe! The tingles she felt during those moonlit nights spent together on the Seine have never been topped before or since—unless she counts that moonlit night they spent in a Jacuzzi high up in the Canadian Rockies. *Now that was a night*, she thinks. "None better," she says aloud.

However, that was life on the road—exciting, always new, in complete contrast to the life she lives at home. Jim also traveled for a living, and for every reunion they could arrange at far-flung corners of the world, a painful separation followed. It was not to be. *Best to forget.*

Fluffing a pillow, she settles down onto her backside, throwing into motion a little restless leg syndrome to relax. Next, she tries meditation, prayers, counting sheep, and anything else that never has worked before but maybe will tonight. Flopping around and trying different positions can't hide the fact that on top of everything else, her mattress is shot. *Like so much of my stuff*, she inwardly whines. *Why do I keep all this stuff?*

Finally, as with so many nights before, she gets out of bed and trudges against her will to the bathroom medicine cabinet. There, she finds a bottle of sample sedatives foisted upon her by Sterling. Opening the bottle, she recalls how in a recent moment of weakness, she allowed Sterling to play doctor with her. Now she seems unable to sleep at all without a pill.

Staring herself down in the bathroom mirror, she grumbles, "Here we go again." She puts the pill down the hatch, thinking, *Yes, this'll help. Well, it does most of the time anyway. Let's hope. We'll see. I'm not getting anywhere without it.*

Returning to bed, she rolls onto her back. All her various relaxation and meditation attempts can't get past factor number one: tinnitus. It roots around in her head, playing uncontrollable sounds that range from hearing-test tones to the electronic hum of high-tension wires overhead to whatever. In the quiet overnight hours, without daytime's natural sounds and plentiful background noises to counter the tinnitus, the sounds in her head threaten her sanity.

"I've got bats in me belfry!" she says, even trying humor to lessen her anxieties.

Turning serious, she desperately wonders, *And from what? The noisy jets I'm always on? Too many deafening nightclubs around the world, concerts? And don't forget bombs bursting in air.* She can't help but chuckle as the sedative shows its first signs of arrival. Staring at ceiling shadows, she is mesmerized by the annoying ringing tones in her ears, but not enough to drift off to sleep. Finally, the tones shift to white noise.

Praying for sleep, she sarcastically considers, *Maybe, just maybe, these crazy little sedatives are behind all this noise! I don't remember it much from before!* Sheryl worries, *What other side effects might these pills have?* The pill bottle's warnings flash before her mind's eye: anxiety, confusion, drowsiness, dizziness, depression, dry mouth, elevated heartbeat, thoughts of suicide, rashes. *Nothing all that out of the ordinary*, she thinks sardonically. *Got 'em all!* Paranoia rushes in amid her deteriorating mental state. *Lord, help me!* she prays.

Finally, she falls asleep, or so she assumes. It's hard to be sure, with stray brain waves nagging as they do in the backlot of her dreams. So it is every night for Sheryl. Occasionally, a pleasant dream or two provides some respite from what have become her bleak bedtime realities.

== *Chapter 12*

ISTANBUL ...

The Arab Spring has become a secondary headline. Chicago's own spring nears, soon to clear the air and the remaining piles of slush. One sunny day, Sterling lunches with his sister, Dottie, at his Lake Shore Drive condo with its Belmont Harbor view. It's a quarterly family business meeting.

Dottie remarks, "You'll just have to work a little harder. Hell, you've been riding that handful of accounts so long, you forgot all about new business."

Sterling is annoyed. "No worries—I have some live wires in my sights. Solid stuff."

"Shit, you damn well better have because for sure one of your bread-and-butter gals won't be on the books much longer. She's heading for a fall, and you know who I mean."

"Do tell, like I don't know."

"Face facts then—she's toast, and hasn't got a pot left to piss in either. Time for her to go."

"That's a given." His mood lightens. "But you gotta admit, I drained her good."

Dottie chuckles. "That you have, brother, I have to admit. Just get a replacement."

"Hey, like I wouldn't think of that? I'm working on it. But each case is different, with unique headaches. Any day now, any day."

"Sterling, come on. Don't you think I know one of your stall jobs when I hear one?"

"This is no stall job! Believe me, sis, it's no cakewalk dealing with all these women."

Dottie nearly gags on a mouthful. "Who are you kidding? You enjoy every one of these ladies in all the usual ways."

"Well, true enough." A broad smile takes over his face.

"Now, I know you like variety in your prospecting process, but narrow the focus. Time to cut wheat from chaff and put your hypnotic powers fully into play. They are amazing."

An eye to the lake, he pensively replies, "Good old Jamaica days, turning point of my life."

"For sure, they made your career. But those days are done."

"Yeah, yeah. Listen, fact is I'm going in for the close tonight on my hottest prospect."

"Do tell."

Mischievously, he clarifies, "I mean to say, in the overnight hours I'll be going for the close."

"That's what we wanna hear," she laughs. "Get with it and keep me posted."

"Right. So next … how about the Laundromats? What's the report on them?"

"Brother, you know there's nothing to worry about there, the way I keep them purring. Gotta have some steady count-on money in the game," she brags.

"Keep it up, girl. It is appreciated, especially considering all your nursing hours too."

❧

By midafternoon, down Sheridan off Diversey, Sheryl is taking a service elevator to her building's rear entrance, thus avoiding any process servers she imagines might be coming for her through the front door. She walks to Lincoln Park Zoo pulling a filled-to-the-brim granny basket. Since settling in from Cairo, she never leaves home without the rolling metal bin. It has become a companion of sorts, cradling things of alleged importance. These include Sterling's probably worthless promissory notes and pension-plan paperwork, plus some precious mementoes, in case her home is robbed while she's away. *In other words*, she laughs to herself, *I'm paranoid! My life is an open book.*

Like an escaped prisoner on the lam taking in forgotten sights, sounds, and aromas, she senses a heady rush of optimism, thrilled at being away from the steady stream of overdue bills and dunning notices. But her rush is brief, like all rushes. A sudden and unwelcome recollection of scary foreclosure missives brings her back to actuality. *Maybe I'm not so paranoid*, she tepidly debates, *because the noose is tightening.*

The truth is, she's a near mental case, adrift like a tourist in her own town, simply subbing the granny basket for a suitcase. For a moment, there's a sense of imbalance to her step and a shadow of doubt in her mind as to which zoo this is she's found. *What am I doing out here?* she wonders, confused.

The answer is that earlier, against her increasingly fickle better judgment, she launched herself outdoors to flee fears that Sterling has little cameras all over her apartment, keeping eyes on her. Now it's coming back to her, and she's sure microphones are planted too—not to mention that little peephole in the bedroom closet that inexplicably peeks into her new neighbors' closet, those neighbors being the very people she also suspects are spies for Sterling, with no particular justification. Just like lately she's been thinking that Donald the doorman works for Sterling. *Fear rules*, she realizes, but she can't push it aside.

Losing herself in stare-downs with some monkeys, she sees the desperate circumstances of her life. And clearly those circumstances all are self-inflicted, no self-denial there. Beyond financial ruination, these bitter circumstances have robbed her of a sense of meaningful career accomplishments. She knows she's done pretty well, but nowhere near what her initial potential promised. *These monkeys*, she figures, *make as big a difference in the world as me. Make that bigger*, she reasons, thinking in terms of dwindling primate populations and the importance of each surviving monkey. Futilely, she wishes to be as clutter-free as monkeys in the zoo.

A thought surfaces about having had a beneficial influence over Carlita. *At least I've done that*, she thinks, choking on her emotions. But the burst of pride is short-lived. She notices she's being watched. It's not paranoia. One disturbed monkey stares at Sheryl while urinating in her direction, with twisted facial expressions, seeming to rub it in with relish. Sheryl is grossed out and disturbed at being disrespected by an animal, albeit a pretty parallel species. "Yuck!" she exclaims in the nasty monkey's direction.

Turning for the big-cat house, Sheryl fights guilt over having canceled another meeting with the bankruptcy attorney her family has provided. Although their heartfelt advice makes sense whenever they have her on the phone, it takes little to throw her off the paperwork assignments required for the lawyer's ammunition. *So what?* she thinks, excusing herself. *Another day won't hurt.*

She can't rationalize such procrastination any longer; it's directly opposite the professionalism she's known for on the job. The disconnect between her two worlds has only worsened over the years. She wonders how she's been able to hold it together, taking people on tours around the world while always knowing another siege awaits at the home front.

Staring at a king of beasts and thinking of a few occasions when she just barely did hold it together, she barely audibly utters, "It's been a miracle! Oh my God, the close calls." Tears well up, and her chin gets to quivering. She needs to get out of this building fast and does so, nearly gasping as she stumbles outside of the big-cat house with her granny basket. "Oh my God," she cries aloud to herself.

Sitting at a bench for a break to compose herself and enjoy the view a bit doesn't last long. A disturbed mood persists, making her squirm for comfort, the more disturbed her thinking gets. She returns to guiltily dwelling on her failures for the lawyer. Not only did she just cancel yet another meeting, but as always, she did so at the last minute. She kind of thought she might at least get started this time. However, since the initial fact-finder, she's canceled every appointment. "I'm incorrigible," she upbraids herself.

The cancellation game, though, will have to end soon. The family doesn't seem to believe she's almost done, and they're right; she has barely dented the required documentation. They have been offering help if she needs it, so she just better get it done. She wants to get it done. It's just, well, the cancellations most often have come after heated pleas from Sterling to buy him more time. His lawyers, he insists, finally almost have everything resolved. *And I buy it!* she thinks.

Really, though, beyond buying his bull about the lawyers, it is Sterling's bullying that keeps Sheryl procrastinating. He's made his position clear: "There's no way my name pops up in your bankruptcy proceedings. No way. It ain't gonna happen." Sterling has threatened violence against various Taylor family members if she pursues bankruptcy, the thought of which chills her to the bone. She knows he wouldn't hesitate to harm anyone after his actions in Jamaica. Tiring of the zoo, Sheryl crosses over Lake Shore Drive via the Lincoln Park Passerelle, a pedestrian bridge to the beach, and tries to shake Sterling's threats from her head.

Exiting the bridge, with her overloaded granny basket still in tow, Sheryl hikes with other pedestrian traffic to the Lakefront Trail intersection, where they duel cyclers and joggers in the crossing. A few rude remarks are lobbed regarding her granny basket, which speeders see as an unwelcome obstacle. Eventually, she reaches the still-frozen yet sandy beach. Even rock-hard, it promises that summer is on its way, a thought that triggers more fear.

Wow, that's right, she recalls as new worries attack. *I have to make up my mind soon!* She has to make a decision about returning to work, with two gigs coming up fast. Worse, they're back-to-back. Sheryl senses that Kearns fears she's gun-shy about travel after her Arab Spring break in Cairo. Sheryl won't admit it, but she fears the same.

On top of this, Kearns has no idea about her nearly debilitating financial worries and Sterling blues. Still, only yesterday she assured Kearns that she will be more than ready to get back to work by the first assignment, one of her annual favorites: Magic Pigment Paint's annual convention in Hawaii. What great memories. No problem. *Right!* she thinks now, chastising herself for false bravado. She's frightened beyond belief.

Am I up to it? she asks herself, seeking internal guidance. *That's a good question,* an inner voice answers. She tearfully cries, "Give me the answer, Lord, please!"

Wind-driven Lake Michigan masks Sheryl's mumbling with steadily crashing waves as she stages her drama near two strolling lovers whose bare feet push the season. Great for them, but Sheryl's sighting of the happy couple only makes her lonely, lonelier than usual. Even still, she's concurrently grateful to live in the neighborhood she loves the most of all among the city's distinct neighborhoods. Its welcoming aura over the years, no matter the season, has saved her from the brink of despair more times than she'd care to recall. *And thank God for that.*

Elsewhere in her brain, a work mentality struggles to revive itself. The beach, despite its remaining heaps of melting snow, has her thinking that in three days she's supposed to leave for Hawaii. For the first time since being home from Cairo, the impending pressure to work overseas hits her as real and foreboding. *Truthfully, how will I handle that?* She goes into cheerleading mode. *At least it's just the paint convention. That's a cakewalk compared to Cairo!*

Besides, she has done Magic Pigment's Hawaiian convention twenty-five times. She should be able to do the twenty-sixth standing on her head. *Right?* she wonders, looking for false bravado to gain a legitimate toehold. Just last year, Magic Pigment and the resort honored her longtime service. *Thank God I found their twenty-fifth anniversary broach gift,* she suddenly recollects. *So even that's covered.* She says with growing confidence, "They'll wanna see it. I have it."

At the water's edge where cold foamy breakers die, Sheryl moves beyond thoughts of Hawaii. Another immediate concern is the quick one-week turnaround between her return to Chicago and her next departure, Turkey. That would be tough even for some of the younger tour directors who are still full of energy and not yet down on their luck. However, they'd be absolutely gutting it out and moving ahead without delay, no doubt. *What the hell do they know?* scoffs Sheryl. *Give 'em time.*

Tears fall as she cries softly, "I'm not going anywhere. I can't. I can't go anywhere. My things would be out on the street when I get back!" She weeps, "This may not be Hawaii, but it is home." All the while, visions of dunning notices dance in her head.

Passersby on the frozen concrete-like beach aren't so totally preoccupied with their own spring fevers that they don't peripherally notice the disheveled Sheryl carrying on a self-contained conversation. She feels their stares and shoots back daggers, eyeballs bulging. "What're you looking at?" she challenges one guy. "Move along! There's nothing to be seen here." Even while barking at him, she can't believe she's saying a thing.

"Adios," he says.

Continuing up the beachfront in her own little world, Sheryl finds her thoughts returning to Turkey—and Ilkin, dearest Ilkin. What would he think if he knew she was coming to Istanbul? Maybe he could save her from everything, pay off every penny, clear her name. And then she'd be free to go—go with Ilkin, stay in Istanbul, forever. Leave everything else behind. Start over.

"Maybe it's not too late," she daydreams. "They say it's never too late for true love, and we were that. That we were." Even in her daze, though, she knows the odds are astronomical.

Done with sightseeing, monkeys, and too many worrisome thoughts raised along the way, Sheryl splurges with her only nonfrozen credit card to buy a carryout pizza. Night falls as she hurries home with the pizza strapped atop her granny basket's pile of important stuff.

Entering at the rear service door with her key, she finds the service elevator is being monopolized by a family moving out of the building. Cautiously, not wanting to deal with any people, she ventures to the main elevators, avoiding the lobby. She's in luck—nobody is around; however, the nearest elevator is eight floors up and for the moment isn't moving. "Hurry down!" she blurts out under her breath.

Finally, the elevator slowly descends, just as Sheryl's neighbor from two floors below, Clara, a kind elderly widow with stockpiles of money in reserve, begins approaching from the lobby. Clara and the elevator arrive simultaneously.

Sheryl flashes her famous smile. "Going up?" she pleasantly asks, as though in control of her faculties.

"After you," insists Clara to her younger pal.

As the doors close in front of them, paranoia hits Sheryl. Her smile fades.

Clara hits the buttons for floors seven and nine while observing the fear in her neighbor's eyes. As the elevator stops at seven, Clara gently puts a supportive arm across Sheryl's sagging shoulders. "Now, you just come with me, Sheryl. And I won't take no for an answer." Clara steers Sheryl off the elevator.

Sheryl meekly agrees. "Okay."

"I'll help you with that pizza," laughs Clara.

"Okay," Sheryl repeats as though on automatic.

Sheryl expects an overcrowded apartment, if not a mess like her own. The two have never visited one another's units before, but Sheryl has based her opinion prejudicially on Clara's advanced age, figuring the extra years would have multiplied accumulations for Clara. *That's how it seems to have been with me*, thinks Sheryl.

As it turns out, Clara keeps a neat and cozy habitat, with everything in its place. The layout is the same as Sheryl's apartment two floors above, reminding her of how elegant and pristine her home once was many years ago—another reminder of how far she's fallen.

"Follow me," says Clara, maintaining a slow but steady gait. She leads Sheryl to a dinette set that's actually usable. "Make yourself comfortable, dear. I'll get some green tea going."

"Okay," responds Sheryl listlessly, putting down the pizza on the table. She takes off her coat and pulls up a chair.

Perky Clara sets the table and opens the pizza box. She serves her guest water while the tea steeps. They dig into the pizza.

Sheryl's spirits rise as they eat. "I haven't had a pizza party in years! This is nice, Clara. Thanks."

"You just relax, dear, and enjoy the pizza. It's been a while for me too, and this is a good one. Later on, we'll talk all night if you want to."

After dinner, relaxation, and some time mulling multitudes of things over tea, Sheryl does begin to feel like talking. This surprises her, until she realizes that Clara may know as much or more about her and Sterling as does anyone. She's seen them coming and going for years, sometimes arguing but mostly businesslike in public, never openly lovey-dovey. That was their agreement as a couple: to keep it businesslike around others.

Sheryl senses that Clara must know something and wonders what Clara's observations through the years have detected about her life with Sterling. *Maybe Clara's been worried about me for a long time and by now could be thinking anything—most likely something bad.* Sheryl abruptly catches herself thinking, *Heck, she could be a spy for Sterling!* She quickly beats back the thought. *Can't be, not sweet Clara,* Sheryl concludes with certainty.

More and more in the mood to deliver a soliloquy of sadness about her life with Sterling, Sheryl figures that as long as Clara already can tell trouble's afoot, why not let go of the burden, right? *Everyone needs counseling at some time,* Sheryl thinks, *and this is my time, with Clara so ready to listen.*

Once the words start pouring out, Sheryl gets into more detail than she can believe she's sharing, while only distantly hearing disjointed bursts of her emotional voice sharing details of her pregnancy and abortion. That still haunts her. She also gets into the financial woes coming her way as a result of having invested in Sterling's clothing company, despite his totally shaky collateral—nothing but possibly forged documents and stage-directed scenes, with her as the dupe. "Or so I fear," Sheryl says, holding on to her last grain of hope.

Clara, it turns out, is more a woman of the world than Sheryl would've guessed. The wise, most-tenured dweller in the building tells her just the right thoughts to consider. "This will not be the worst thing you will have to go through in your lifetime, Sheryl."

"That sounds so much like the thinking I grew up with."

"Then you grew up surrounded by common sense, young lady."

Sheryl feels like she's discovered a comrade-in-arms. "I never really thought of it that way before, Clara, because I always felt it was our family's religion that set the tone for us kids. But I guess pure common sense is kind of like the root of all religion."

"The religion of life," chimes in Clara. "Whatever it was, your parents took you down the right path. And as they would tell you today, there's always a path away from trouble."

"Wow. Your words are so helpful, Clara!" exclaims Sheryl. "Perfect timing for me."

Clara smiles tenderly and says, "Don't give up on finding the way."

Clara's words of concern sound motherly, as though they could be coming from Sheryl's own dear late mother. It's almost as if she is hearing her mom's voice. Her mind reels, ethereally infused.

At some point, she hears Clara asking, "Is your family aware of all this?"

"Um, yes, just recently. They're trying to help, but it's hard because they have no idea how big this is. And truthfully, I'm ashamed they even found out about it. I ... I don't know."

"So how much is it in total, dear?"

"Pardon me?"

"In reference to your financial ruin."

Suddenly stunned with embarrassment at having possibly spoken too freely, Sheryl clams up; maintaining equilibrium becomes a struggle. She's close to spinning out of control without having to move a muscle. How could she have spilled her guts like that? Now will the whole building know? *As if,* Sheryl has been worrying anyway, *they don't already know.*

Filled with paranoia and struggling to work up the nerve to make eye contact with patient Clara, who delivers nothing but warmth and compassion with her gentle smile, Sheryl finally answers. "I, uh, really don't know what to say, Clara. I'm touched by your concern for me, but it's all too much for me to bear, and I shouldn't be getting you involved."

"You can, dear, you can. And I already am involved. We're practically family. We've been neighbors for what seems like forever! Now if you can't talk to me, who can you talk to?"

Now Sheryl is really choked up, knowing that the kind woman makes sense and is reaching out, so she must reach back. "Sad to say, Clara, but it would take about half a million just to get square with the world and not lose my home."

"Oh, Sheryl, dear, in today's politics a foreclosure can take years!"

"I don't know, Clara. There are two banks involved on two maxed-out lines of credit. I haven't been working as much, and I've been living off credit cards that one by one have been getting shut down on me."

"Dear, I'm telling you, we'll think of ways to forestall trouble. Don't worry about that."

"Maybe, I suppose, I hope. And if you're really willing to help, there truly is hope!"

"Sheryl, so few people are prepared for emergencies. You'll be fine."

With a sigh of relief unknown to her in recent months, Sheryl hopes Clara is right.

Clara adds, "We're talking, Sheryl. That's the first step. Is there anything else on the list?"

"Um, I also may owe the government something, I think. Got some bad tax advice."

Clara chuckles. "That's what lawyers are for, dear, and I know plenty. I can help you with any paperwork. My husband had me keep the books to his business for decades."

"Oh, Clara," Sheryl cries. "You're so kind, reaching out like this. I'm so lucky."

"You stop worrying yourself silly."

"Okay."

"I really don't know what I'll be able to do, but let me talk to my accountant. Let's see what it adds up to. Maybe I can help some—not all, but something."

Sheryl can't believe this good-luck turn of events. If Clara can help out as now hoped, Sheryl can resolve her major issues without the family looking over her shoulder. That's maybe the biggest boost of all, a way to stop her life from being such an open book with them.

Realizing how late it's become, Sheryl finally takes her leave to return to the ninth floor. Pizza-party vibes dissipate back home when she plays back a voice mail message from Sterling. When he left it, he was angry that she hadn't picked up, unaware that she was not even home and in fact was busy spilling her beans to a neighbor. Sheryl turns ill at the unwelcome sound of his voice. The very thought of how she has allowed him to ruin her life makes her weep once again. Clearly, there are no good vibrations left to this day. She curls up in a ball on the corner of her sofa, her pity perch. "Been here, done this before," she softly mumbles through tears.

Her thoughts return to that awful day in the lobby, her family in a loud standoff with Sterling, Donald the doorman discreetly watching, ready to dial 911.

As Sheryl rushes from her dad's side over to Sterling, she notices that Jon is still recording everything on his cell phone. She steers Sterling through the foyer, defusing him as best she can. "Please, Sterling, don't take this any further," she pleads. "You're a doctor. You can see what this is doing to my dad. Just back away, please."

Not looking pleased, he nevertheless replies, "The doctor in me will go along with what you ask of me, Sheryl. But the man in me will not forget this anytime soon."

"Thank you, Sterling," she says, sending him away outside.

Sheryl returns to the lobby. It's a stilted Taylor family reunion, with everyone stunned from the unexpected and distasteful encounter. Donald still watches discreetly.

"Let's go upstairs," Sheryl suggests to her family with much trepidation. For the first time in seven or eight years, she has no choice but to ask her family up to her place. There's no hiding any longer behind being on the road or saying she's putting her place back together after unpacking. They need safe refuge upstairs, fast.

Gloria tries to help with damage control, quipping, "Well, won't this be the occasion?" She also steadies Oliver as he gets to his feet.

Sheryl panics, realizing, *Now they'll know everything.* For too many years she has worried about her hoarder's lifestyle someday becoming common family knowledge. *If only they knew*, she often thought. Now that time has come.

The Taylors solemnly wait for an elevator. One finally arrives. After the doors open, Clara steps out of the elevator car, looking somewhat taken aback by the large group. She and Sheryl exchange forced but friendly glances with nary a word beyond "hello."

The Taylor sisters help their irritated and exhausted father into the elevator. Jon brings up the rear. Riding upward, Sheryl dryly remarks, "Remember, I wasn't expecting company. So my place could use a little tidying up."

"Don't worry about it," assures Jon. "We understand."

Oliver grumbles, "So far, I don't understand any of this."

Gloria pats Sheryl's back, trying to calm her. "Don't worry, sis."

The elevator opens on nine. "Okay," Sheryl says, trying for upbeat. Ever the guide, she brightly instructs, "Follow me."

Oliver is not amused. "It's been a while, but I still remember the path to your door."

Sheryl stops at her door and faces the others. Her chin goes into overdrive, something no one in the family has ever seen before now, as she tries to stop the oncoming tears.

Gloria takes Sheryl in her arms. "What's wrong, Sheryl?"

Sheryl feels out of control. Her inner core shivers along with her chin. "Oh," she groans, summoning courage to open her door. "Well, here goes nothing. You won't be too happy."

Oliver, hard of hearing, asks, "What's she saying?"

Suddenly unfazed, Sheryl stiffens her spine, unlocks the door, and struts inside to her domain. "Right this way!" she tells her unexpected guests.

Sheryl's feigned confidence fades quickly at the sight of shock and disbelief in everyone's eyes. As her family scans the long and short of their newest nightmare, Oliver, overcome with heartbreak, groans, "Sheryl, what have you done? What's going on here and for how long?"

Jon clears Sheryl's pity perch on the sofa and helps his dad take a seat. Oliver clearly is done in, out of words, but off his feet. He watches his brood snap at each other.

Jon drills Sheryl, "How can you live like this?"

No answer.

Gloria asks, "Why didn't you talk to me? We talk about everything else, or at least I always thought we did. We're sisters, Sheryl. How could you hide this from me?"

"Always about you," Sheryl mumbles. She's numb. Everyone is numb.

Gloria still manages to retort, "Oh yes, let's turn this around on me."

Nobody knows what else to say. Stunned and silent, the guests scope a menagerie of unrelated items stuffed into nooks and crannies in all directions.

Sheryl simply stares off into space. She lives it every day she's not on the road, and she knows each square inch vividly. She understands that there's really nothing legitimate to say. Shortly, the nervous hostess asks, "Anyone want anything to drink?"

Jon breaks his stupor, admitting, "Sure, I could use something—anything cold." Sheryl wonders if he's actually thinking "anything strong."

"Make mine root beer, diet if you have it," requests Oliver.

Sheryl only hopes she now can deliver. Her refrigerator isn't exactly well-stocked. Gloria joins her in the space-challenged kitchenette.

"I'll get some ice going," offers Gloria.

Sheryl remembers that she stocked some pop in her tiny pantry. "Great, thanks. I'll get the pop!"

Momentarily, the air lightens with the flurry of activity. Jon roots around and comes up with a couple folding chairs. He sets them up for his sisters in the living room opposite Dad. He clears a little extra floor space at the pathway and digs out a dinette set chair for himself.

Sheryl, meanwhile, tries remembering exactly where she squirreled away the pop. "Hey, Dad," she calls out from the pantry, "I have that diet root beer!"

Her dad doesn't hear her, and those who do don't bother passing it along. It's more than obvious her visitors are trying to wrap their minds around Sheryl's surreal existence. *How has it come to this?* each seems to be silently asking.

Gloria rations out what little ice she has found and pours the pop. Sheryl rummages through a cabinet until she finds a mixing bowl full of airline peanut samplers from around the world. There's no telling how old some of this stuff is, but it's handy. She puts it on a serving tray Gloria has found and already loaded with drinks. Sheryl adds some souvenir napkins to complete the snack package.

Sheryl clears her throat, readying to make a toast, and says with a practiced smile, "Here's to family." She adds, "Sorry you had to see me like this. But now that you're here, I have to say I'm relieved I won't have to hide this secret anymore."

Her dad asks, "Which secret is that, Sheryl—the one about your con artist boyfriend or the one about how you live like a vagrant?"

Oliver's bluntness stifles conversation. Jon and Gloria turn to snacks to avoid saying anything. Sheryl, forlorn in numerous ways, sits stiffly on her folding chair, eyes locked on the condo building across the street. She wonders if there are any dramas behind its windows comparable to that which is unfolding in her own little place. *Doubtful*, she silently concludes.

Suddenly, Sheryl realizes that everyone's gaze is zeroed in on a collection of shrine-like artifacts displayed within a nearly buried bookcase. Basically, they've discovered Sheryl's shrine to her mom. Photos from all stages of Ruth's tragically too-short life stare out at everyone, peering past unlit candles that overcrowd the shelves.

Oliver is visibly upset and blurts out, "It's a good thing your mother isn't here to see all this. It would kill her." His burst of candor breaks the uncomfortable silence for only those few seconds it takes him to deliver the message. After some moments of group silence, he groans and says, "I'm sorry, but this is too much for me right now. And I've lost my appetite for lunch."

"Are you ready to leave?" Jon asks.

"Soon, yes. I just have nothing more to say." With that, the party's over.

Tenderly, Gloria implores her kid sister, "Calm down, Sheryl. We'll get through this together, whatever it takes. The lawyer is just the start. There's counseling we can talk about, all kinds of things. Get this place cleared out, cleaned up, and back to normal for you."

Jon interjects, "Just get a good night's sleep tonight."

"Okay," agrees a shell of Sheryl. "Can I get anybody anything else before you leave?"

"No, thanks," they all say. Their little visit ends, and Sheryl's siblings and father leave her apartment together.

❦

Back in the here and now, Sheryl remains curled up, in pain and all alone again, on her sofa after the pizza party with Clara. Restless, she starts coming out of a nap. Her vacuous eyes zoom in on her mom's. Photos chronicling Ruth's life come into focus. In a tortured whisper, Sheryl confesses, "I'm a mess, Mommy, really—I'm a mess!" Sheryl hears her own voice, out-of-body, while in and out of consciousness, fighting an awakening to her real-world dramedy.

Slipping into a dream, she stumbles back to a day in her parents' sunroom, only months after Hawaii. It's so much nicer, dreamlike, in the sunroom so many years ago. It's just the two of them again, mother and daughter only. Endless picture windows surround them, overlooking wraparound decking and Ruth's beautiful backyard gardens. Sheryl and her mother have wandered into their first follow-up talk about Sterling.

"There's more to the story, Mom."

"More? I'm not sure I'm ready for more."

Upbeat, Sheryl explains, "It's not necessarily anything bad. In fact, it could be great! It's just a little risky in that it's financial in nature. This is my first grown-up investment, and I just need to confide in someone, and you're the only one I can turn to, Mom."

"You always can turn to me, dear," assures Ruth, who has not been well again lately.

Sheryl is unaware of her mother's downturn at the moment, though, and feels compelled to spill the details about her unsecured investments with Sterling in his clothing company. She's hoping her mom will be impressed by all the potential.

"According to Sterling," Sheryl explains, "I'm guaranteed pension-plan security, plus a lump-sum bonanza once his lawyers get all the annoying lawsuits resolved."

Ruth asks, "What makes you so convinced there are lawyers, money, or even a business?"

"Oh, Mother, don't you think I've double- and triple-checked all that stuff?"

"I was just asking."

In truth, Sheryl has left way too much to Sterling's smooth explanations and legal-looking documents, and she knows it. She's nervous, of course, about the remote chance he's scamming her—but no, not Sterling, he wouldn't. So she still hopes at this time in the sunroom.

"He's even taken me to the courthouse a few times," Sheryl adds, "so I know he's telling the truth about all the legal drama."

"What's gone on at these hearings?" asks Ruth.

Caught off guard, Sheryl admits, "I've had to wait in the courthouse lobbies while he's gone into the actual courtrooms. They've been closed sessions."

Ruth says, "That's not what I'd hoped to hear. Have you ever considered he might have been there for something unrelated to his alleged clothing company? Or just going into a random room as a spectator, doors closed to your view?"

"Letting me think it was his big continuing case?"

"Yes, not such a far-fetched idea when you add up all the known facts."

Sheryl wonders why she's never questioned this before but retorts, "No, Mom, Sterling wouldn't do that to me." She looks down at her hands. "He c-couldn't," she stammers, trying to convince herself as well.

"No?" Ruth gently challenges.

"No, not after all we've been to each other and gone through together." Sheryl rambles on optimistically about what she'll do with all her money once her ship comes in, and Ruth appears to be listening in shock. The mess Sheryl has made of her life begs explanation. Instead, she is giving her mother pie in the sky.

"So anyway, Mom," Sheryl proudly promises, "we'll spare no expenses when I take the whole family on a cruise."

"Of course, dear, but meanwhile, keep me posted on the legal proceedings."

"For sure."

"Get more inquisitive. Ask for proof and details."

"I will, Mom. Thank you for your wise counsel."

"Wisdom seems to come with age," Ruth says, smiling. "But I'm not so sure I like all the other perks that come with it. Anyway, we'll keep this between us, my dear baby girl."

Ruth's voice fades out as though through a flickering echo chamber, all these years later. Sheryl wakes up with a kink in her neck from slouching in the pity perch's tight quarters. Still curled up on the sofa, she stares at the shrine to her mom, guilt-ridden over the extra burden she placed on her at the worst possible time.

Sheryl, so sad now, groans and stirs on the sofa. She shudders, recalling her fears that her mom never would rebound from all the knowledge gained about her daughter. Sheryl's head pounds with self-flagellations about her blind belief in Sterling. How feeble the bit about striking it rich with him must have sounded to Mom. "Unbelievable," Sheryl cries softly to the room. "But she never stopped loving me."

"Never," though, didn't last too long because soon afterward, Ruth's health went into a final downward spiral. Being bedridden in the final months of her life had not been in the plans, so new plans got made. Her memorial service was overflowing.

Changing her train of thought on a dime, Sheryl abruptly announces, "But enough of that—it's time to figure out what to do about those tours!" She had to decide about Hawaii and Istanbul, departure for Hawaii being just three days away. The more she thinks about it, the more she fears going, twenty-five years under the belt with Magic Pigment be damned. It may very well not turn out to be the cakewalk that she's been figuring her experiences there guarantee. But how can she now turn around and cancel after confirming just yesterday? "That's the big question!" Panicked, she placates herself with the reminder that at least there would be no riots, as opposed to her last trip.

That night and the next, Sheryl can't sleep—well, maybe three or four hours each, tops. She staggers through daytime hours pretending to pack for Hawaii, still intending to do that paperwork for the lawyer before she goes. Sure. Such is the plan, but a ticking clock in her head constantly reminds her that she's running out of time to cancel—because she surely doesn't want to go through with it.

Worse, she's freaking out over the one-week turnaround between coming home and leaving for Turkey. Of the two, it's Turkey she sees as more important to her personally. Maybe she should concentrate all her efforts on handling just that one trip, Turkey—do a good job there. No so coincidentally, she again fantasizes about Ilkin. *He could be my savior.*

Sheryl calls Thomas Kearns, who just got off the phone with the paint company's travel agency. He says, "Everyone is looking forward to another year with you at the helm, Sheryl. How goes the packing?"

"Ah, Tom, I just can't do it. It's like I'm still in some kind of shock from Cairo. I really can't even explain it."

Kearns at first is speechless but then reassuringly says, "Take the time you need, Sheryl."

"Oh, I intend to be fully ready for Turkey, Tom."

"That's fine. We'll talk in a week to firm up Istanbul."

"You can count on me, Tom, for sure."

"I know, Sheryl. Please just rest up and don't worry."

As they hang up, Sheryl recollects how years ago she passed up running Tom's Florida office. She would've been pulling down big bucks since long ago and with no travel jitters either. Bad decision. Paranoid now that she blabbed redundantly at the end of her conversation with Kearns, she takes a deep breath and tells herself, "Just do like he says. Don't worry, rest up. I'll be ready."

Her coming week seems to pass in slow motion. Sheryl is as nervous about the Turkey tour as she was about Hawaii. Maybe more so, really. She has additional nontravel worries about whether she'll be able to look Ilkin in the eye, after all the pain she's dealt him through the years. Getting past that still would leave her the unpleasant task of leveling with him about what he surely would view as a shameful life. However, the need to hold off her family as long as possible on bankruptcy proceedings overrides everything.

Pressure from Sterling remains relentless, dark, and foreboding. Every appointment she breaks with the lawyer means breaking appointments with Dad, Gloria, and Jon too. As for the few family strategy meetings she hasn't backed out of, Sheryl is touched to feel they've come together as a team, one for all. The message they're all delivering is that she needs to act fast. Certain bankruptcy options soon will disappear. Yet she continually stonewalls on her homework. "Oh my gosh," says Sheryl with a shiver, completely desperate.

Procrastinating on pulling together what the lawyer needs, Sheryl replays cell-recorded conversations from the lawyer's conference room centering on power of attorney, which on medical issues she has given to Jon. Unpleasant at any level, such concerns suddenly loom in previously uncharted territory.

This type of talk troubles her spirit more than mere financial woes. Though drained of tears, she weeps, "I'm a burden to everyone."

Now that she is outed on several levels, family roundtables get into whether or not counseling should be an option. Even Sheryl knows, though she won't admit it for the record, that she's fragile—mentally ready to slip and fall at a moment's notice. "I'm at the end of my rope," she realizes now and again.

Luckily, since the lobby face-off, she's kept her family convinced that she has finally started cleaning up her place. "I'm making slow but steady progress," she has told them. "It feels so good!" Since Sheryl is convincing about having seen the light, and everyone else has their own life dramas chewing up days, more time is lost, and troubles gain ground. Perhaps using persuasive powers honed from hanging around with Sterling, she tells the story that while allegedly gathering paperwork for the lawyer, she's had to start cleaning house to find records and files. "It's a win-win!" she exclaims in a Taylor family conference call. They've never known her to be a liar, so they take her at her word, and soon it's ten days out from Istanbul, or bust.

Sheryl sits on her sofa, stunned by the contents of a legal-sized envelope from Sterling, hand-delivered by Donald the doorman. It contains a disgusting letter from Sterling touching on many topics, including a denunciation of her allegedly injudicious family. In a fancy font, he also proclaims his long-standing true love for Sheryl, his dearest darling dove. But back to her folks, he rants, "And what was their purpose? Racism!"

"No! You're so wrong," she argues back from her couch at the top of her lungs, arms flailing. "It's you! You're the racist. You've ripped me off all these years, thinking I was some dumb, naive, suburban white chick—and I was!" Oblivious to possibly being overheard but toning it down a bit, she continues, "And now that our secrets are out, your best defense is an offense." She cries, "You're such an asshole, Sterling!"

If he were here, she imagines through her pain, he'd sarcastically quip, "Hey, I don't discriminate. I'm an equal-opportunity swindler." Thinking back to how he betrayed Snake and Miriam and conned Ronny Walker into handing him the doctor slot, she knows that's true.

As Sterling's letter continues, the rants get even heavier-handed. Imperiously, he prattles on about Sheryl supposedly having single-handedly ruined both of their lives. The stylistic text makes slanderous charges against her, alleging much un-Christianly behavior. Tellingly, though, he fails to reference his having bilked her dry. "A minor detail," she snarls in her emptiness.

Sterling's tirade ends, "Our child and mothers above all are in tears, thanks to you."

Sheryl, increasingly frail, collapses on her couch crying, as Sterling no doubt knew she would do, just as he likely knows she soon will cry herself to sleep, which she does—maybe even as programmed by the stealthy hypnotist in her life. Who knows?

❧

While Sheryl sleeps, a bit north in Sterling's living room, he sits reclined in thought in front of the harbor view. Thoughts take him to other harbor views and Jamaica, where he first practiced hypnotism on Sheryl, both with and without her knowledge. She still thinks of him as a clumsy novice good enough for parlor tricks. That she has no idea of how adept he's become at hypnotism over time suits Sterling just fine. Years of field-testing Snake's lessons on his handful of bread-and-butter gal accounts have paid generous dividends.

Really, though, he wonders, *how have I been able to keep all this afloat?* Mind-control games or not, the pressures to produce and pay bills make nothing a cakewalk. His gals' fortunes have ebbed and flowed smoothest without family interference, which always is the beginning of the end. What Sterling knows best about him and Sheryl as a couple is that their history has included incredibly romantic highs that always trump any setbacks between them. Their annual fall bed-and-breakfast road trips circling the big lake through color-splashed forests, from home to Mackinac and back, have created traditionally tender travel times together that let him work his mysterious ways. She seems to have her guard down while traveling for pleasure.

Some good memories, thinks the buried soft side of him. That repressed side of him wonders what might have happened if he had gone straight. *Would she have been the one?* The soft side, never allowed out for long, burrows back deep into his subconscious.

Shed of such sentiment, he thanks the crime lord below that Sheryl's professional life on the run oftentimes has allowed plenty of time for her to cool down and let the heart grow fonder while he attends to his other accounts back home. Meanwhile, the abortion episode slips further behind them in time. They don't discuss it; somehow, though, it binds them together as Uncle

Austin taught him it would. *But that was then, and this is now*, knows Sterling. *Her shelf life's expired.* He only hopes the trigger phrase he implanted in her subconscious back in the day remains active today. Assuming so, all it should take, he figures, is a phone call to get everything rolling.

"Time to find out tomorrow. And maybe do one last little score on her," he chuckles. She does have, he knows, one remaining credit card with money available. "Why not exploit it?"

❦

When Sheryl's cell rings at 7:00 a.m., she remains crashed on the sofa's pity perch, where she slept off and on overnight. Groggily, she checks caller ID; it's Sterling. "What do you want, Sterling? I've had it with you. I don't even know why I answered."

"I was afraid of that, baby, and that's why I called. After I sent that little package, I had second thoughts—hoping it wouldn't upset you."

"Upset me? Are you kidding? You saying it's inflammatory? Disgusting maybe? Well, I couldn't care less anymore about anything to do with you. I'm moving ahead with the lawyer."

"Well, that may be—but just in case there was a tinge of pain, I'm apologizing. Let me take you out to breakfast. You have to follow your conscious on the lawyer thing."

She's not dumb, she tells herself. "Forget it. I'm sleeping in." Being hungry and broke, though, eventually she weakens when he won't take no for an answer. They settle on dinner that evening at the American Cuisine Grill.

"I'll meet you at seven," says Sheryl.

"All right, see you there," he agrees.

That night, sitting at their familiar tucked-away table, Sheryl notices Sterling scrutinizing her overstuffed granny basket stashed in a corner. He asks, "Why are you dragging that thing everywhere you go?"

"Oh, poor baby, are you embarrassed by me?"

"Sometimes, yeah. Your behavior's getting outrageous. You know that? Do you see yourself as others do?"

"Unfortunately, I do, and lately it's not a pretty picture. What of it?"

Food arrives, and they simmer down. As they eat, Sheryl tells him of her latest foreclosure fears.

Sterling interjects, "You seem to be forgetting, my dear, I'm up against it too. In fact, I'm one foreclosure notice ahead of you in the process."

Sheryl knows what's coming next and goes on the offensive. "Don't be coming to me for more money. The well's run dry."

"Like hell it has," he retorts strongly, catching her off guard. "I'm going to remind you of a few things that bind us together, forever, till death and beyond."

Sheryl slumps at the table, exasperated under a suddenly intensified atmosphere in the room. Despair rules her mind.

"Need I remind you, dearest, of that alibi you helped provide for me— in mailing all my fingerprinted postcards from around Europe? You do remember that makes you an accessory to something you'd like to forget about, don't you?"

What little spine Sheryl retains disintegrates.

Sterling spitefully adds, "And those little white lies you told on your line-of-credit loan applications, both of which now are equally maxed-out? Well, something like that also might be of interest to the feds—you know, cheater and liar that you are."

"I was an idiot, but you pushed me into those little white lies right after that whole postcard thing. What I understand now, though, is the truth doesn't matter with you, and the postcard thing never will be forgotten." Disheartened, she remembers how he forced her into those loan lies by threatening to tell Gloria about the abortion, and she knows he's fully aware of what he did. Sheryl sadly rues the day she met him.

Seeking strength and not wanting to totally give up the ghost, she stiffens her backbone and asks, "So what's the latest on all these lawsuits?"

"Look," he says, irritated, "if I could wave a wand and just get them settled, once and for all—yeah, of course, I'd do it! But all I know is my lawyers say the end's in sight."

"That's what I'm afraid of, the end."

"Sounds pretty pessimistic to me."

She doesn't believe anything he says anymore, except where threats are involved. Generally, she sees that his word always has been worthless—no doubt much like her corporate title of secretary and even the company itself. What stands out now is how he seems more menacing than ever. She's become numb to his demands. She can't forget the postcards.

"I'll do a thousand," Sheryl says, caving. "That's it, no more. I'm better at bookkeeping than people think, and I'm telling you that taps me dry. Seriously. Totally."

"Of course," he responds, extending his hand to shake on it. After a beat, he asks, "Well?"

Sheryl, more distraught than ever, frowns at his callousness and reaches for her purse. She retrieves a promotional check from her last credit card and makes it out to Sterling for a grand. Wanting to be shed of him, she feels lethargy set in as Sterling insists on walking her home. She does not even question his sudden desire for exercise that takes them around a block to approach her building's rear entrance. There, they scrutinize the building's back side, including her own windows nine floors up. Under a bright full moon in the shadows of a tree along a fence running beside them, Sterling gets romantic.

"Baby, you know I'm still in love with you."

"How should I know this?"

"Just believe me, there's never a moment I'm not thinking of you. I love you."

"And why should I care?"

"You love me too, I can tell. I know."

She's too listless to laugh. "That letter of yours is your idea of love?"

"Let me take that back and shred it to pieces, so your eyes never fall upon it again."

"Yeah," she responds, "I'll bet you would." Sheryl knows it would be best for her mental well-being to get it out of her sight. However, she might want to keep it around for any number of reasons.

"Honey, please listen."

She interjects, "I'll think about it."

Responding with soft but laser-like eye contact, he gently adds, "Despite some inglorious moments in our linked journey, it's certainly been a one-of-a-kind trip. We've lived a lot of good times together if you just overlook a little bad."

"The bad outweighs the good, Sterling, by far. Face it. I have. And there's nobody to blame but me, stupid love-struck head-in-the-clouds me."

"Oh, come on," he intently intones, "we're seen as the perfect couple in any number of places around town."

"Yeah, like here, for instance," she says with disdain, referencing her building, "especially around the lobby. Throw in a few restaurants and a couple dance floors—big deal."

"Well, you can say what you like, but there have been many wonderful moments. We're a great couple. Not everyone has our kind of connection," he insists.

"Right," she says with a shrug, "lucky for them."

"The point is," he perseveres, "we're one of the great tragic couples." His delivery and timing nudge a little smile from her. He presses on. "You have to admit many of the great couples in history have been tragic figures. That's why they still remain so memorable."

"So we're a Romeo and Juliet story that only the two of us could understand?"

"You got it."

"Well, we are all-tragic, 24-7, that's for sure—and memorable."

"No question," he says as he pulls her into an embrace.

Her half-smile slips into a full-moon grin. For a moment it feels like she's being comforted. Quickly, though, she adds, "But I don't understand. So slow down"—only words aside, she doesn't squirm free from his arms. Sheryl wants to believe, still needs to believe, that years of love and placing faith in Sterling ultimately will be rewarded. As she stands in his embrace under the moon beneath a tree, anything seems possible, once again. *Is it blind faith or blind love that blinds me to reality?* she worries.

"My dear," he whispers close to her ear, interrupting her thoughts, "when the day comes, we should go out together. That would be our crowning poem."

She is creeped out yet touched at the same time. For a moment, the thought seems romantically solemn, maybe even worth considering. Surely, there must be less of a load on one's shoulders in whatever world comes next compared to the here and now. Sheryl catches herself thinking about some of the world's great couples going out together. Certainly, Romeo and Juliet fit the bill, not to mention Antony and Cleopatra. *If it's good enough for the Queen of the Nile*, she nervously quips to herself, *well, why not me?* She answers, *Because what's to ensure that Sterling keeps his end of the deal?*

Her building's back door pops open, as announced by a beam of light from inside. Someone throws some boxes into a compactor by the Dumpster and leaves the door open upon returning inside. The couple notices the open door.

Sheryl suggests, "Probably he'll be back with more garbage. But that's not right."

"Not cool at all, but let's go for it," suggests Sterling animatedly. "Why go around front? Who needs to know our comings and goings anyway, right?"

"Right," Sheryl quickly agrees. "But what's the rush? I have a key."

"This is more fun."

Euphoric still from the moonlit moments and giggling like kids, they dash for the door. Sterling leads, but Sheryl slows for a second to glance at her windows way above and at what lies below, the Dumpster and compactor. She never really noticed before how very directly in line with them her apartment is.

Inside, Sterling reaches a recyclables sorting area, from where he advances toward the elevator bank's back side. Sheryl isn't so lucky. Just as Sheryl comes up the handicap ramp to the door, William, the overnight doorman, appears to close it. Each startles the other. Sheryl suddenly remembers that there is a silent alarm on the back door that alerts security if the door is left open.

William asks, "Out for a walk, Sheryl?"

"Oh, yes," she replies rather nervously. "Nothing special, William—just a little fresh air. It's so nice outside with the change in the weather."

"That's for sure. Good night now, Sheryl," he says warmly.

"Good night, William."

Sheryl finds Sterling holding an elevator for their laugh-filled escape upward. Once they are inside Sheryl's apartment, Sterling's carefree attitude immediately changes. He scowls, letting loose diatribes over her bad luck with running into William.

She doesn't get the annoyance and bites back, "What's the big deal? I've lived here twenty years! It's routine to talk with William."

"Forget about it," he snarls.

"I don't have to worry about what doors I use or who I bring in with me. You're acting strange yourself, Sterling, even for you."

He offers no snappy comeback.

"Cat got your tongue?" she asks with an edge.

Sterling gathers her in close and surprises her with his response. "Hey, baby, maybe you're right. I'm making too much out of this. I'm sorry."

The one-eighty change sets Sheryl back on her heels, literally, as Sterling kisses her comfort-starved lips. Passions that have been on hold too long release in a rush. Never breaking their embrace, the two dance down her crowded halls to her bedroom, where they expand a clearing on her bed.

Afterward, Sheryl sighs, "That was nice," admittedly relaxed.

"Yes, real nice it was," agrees Sterling.

"Are you going to stay the night?"

"Uh, actually, no. I have a big day tomorrow in court. I need to get home and get a solid night's sleep."

"Oh." Sheryl already regrets her actions and suddenly feels lonely as Sterling dresses. She slips on a robe and slippers, following him back through the hallway paths to the door.

At the door, Sterling says with concern in his voice, "Dear, I was noticing in your kitchen last time I was here that you have an awful lot of household chemicals under the sink that could be very dangerous—even hazardous to your health. You should get rid of them, seriously."

"Let's face it," Sheryl says, "there's a lot I should be getting rid of—including you."

"Then I'll make that part easy. I was going to say something anyway. Truth is, your job is done. And you're out of my life."

"What?"

He repeats in a very deliberate fashion, "Your job is done. And you're out of my life."

She drifts into a trancelike state of confusion. "Huh?"

"Plus I'm out of yours—as you seem to want anyway—and as your family and lawyer also would wish. Everybody's happy, right?"

"I don't get it."

"I'll make it simple," he says. "One more time—your job is done. And you're out of my life. Understand me: your job is done. And you're out of my life. Do you understand?"

Dejected and powerless, reeling on her feet, Sheryl manages to say yes.

"Good. And your new orders are—shred, shred, shred till nothing's left to be read. Understood?"

"Of course."

"Oh yeah, one last thing," he snarls to a nearly paralyzed Sheryl. "Your family has been right all along. I'm no good for you, never was. Truth is, all the documents I ever gave you were phony, not worth a red cent. I cultivated you from the start." He claps his hands near her ear and turns to the door.

Feeling like she has just come out of a trance, Sheryl sees Sterling open the door and realizes she's not really sure what he's been saying. She does faintly hear him remind her to lock up behind him. She fantasizes about how she'd like to lock him up, all right, and chuck away the key forever. "Dream on," Sheryl mutters miserably, mocking herself.

Sterling dramatically pauses at the threshold to give her one last condescending glance as he delivers his parting remarks. "This comes not a moment too soon as far as I'm concerned. It's been a real bore these past few years as you've gone deeper and deeper over the edge."

An elevator comes quickly, and he's gone. As instructed, she locks the door behind him. His final comments have devastated Sheryl, contorting her face into a forlorn expression of doom. She already was scared to death that serious change was afoot. Now she knows it for sure.

The next day, nearing the end of business hours, Sheryl has regained some composure after Sterling's visit the night before—until her cell's ringtone makes her jump. It's the boss, Thomas Kearns. She's been trying to get up the nerve to call him all day because only a week remains till she must be in Turkey. She fears answering but knows she can't let things slide to the last day this time.

Struggling with anxiety, she goes for it. "Oh, hi, Tom!"

"Hi, Sheryl. How are you doing?"

"Oh, better, that's for sure. Still a little unsure of what to do."

Very warmly, he says, "Sheryl, I've said all along since Cairo, it's totally understandable if you take extended time off from international trips. I can arrange local tour work for you to get your sea legs back, right here, with no travel pressure. What do you say?"

That's all Sheryl needs to hear. She throws in the towel on travel, officially; it can't get more official. She says she'll let him know when she's ready for some local tours.

Hanging up, she hyperventilates and can't prevent sobbing. Sheryl's sobs turn into a soft whimper as she melodically comforts herself, thinking again of how she has to stick around town anyway to safeguard all her possessions and keep them from being thrown out on the street. *This will all be for the best!* she decides. That is the only way she can look at it.

Shortly, she realizes that her last-ditch fantasies about Ilkin possibly rescuing her are now fruitless—gone with her job down the drain. That hits her and hurts.

Her whimpers fade as she hangs her head. Shoulders slouched, she sighs. "Anyway, sweet Ilkin, no way I can travel."

Chapter 13

... OR BUST

Time passes, and soon a week has gone by. Surprisingly, Sheryl has slept soundly of late, actually awakening refreshed on a couple of consecutive days. Inspired, she sets about gathering files on every one of her dealings with Sterling, old and new alike. She knows for sure that she hasn't thrown away anything; finding the paperwork is just a matter of time. The monumental task takes all day and night over several days running. It gives her something to work at, a job long overdue, though not an easy one; sleep now comes in nap bursts of four to five hours, seemingly enough.

Countless check registers dating back so many years unearth long-forgotten bad memories that don't seem possible even as she stares at the undeniable proof. There are even some private loan agreements with Dad based on bloated income information she gave him under Sterling's tutelage. The sheer volume of checks written to Sterling and their collective amounts astound her. It's tough to see, tougher to swallow. She can't believe all the lies that were told to get money, money ultimately wasted on Sterling. She figures she must have been asleep at some switch for an awfully long time.

Incredulously, she asks herself, "And I wonder how things got so bad?" Seeing it all in black and white, she answers, "What's to wonder? I walked right into it!"

Unpleasant recollections continue unabated as she reviews piles of worthless promissory notes and pension-plan projections plus documents granting impressive job titles and promising windfall profits to come. Everything looks so legal and impressive. Taken together today, it all simply bears witness to years of disastrous decisions, many such decisions long forgotten till now. *My bad, Lord*, she thinks.

Come the wee hours of the fourth morning, her bookkeeping assignments finally are completed. Sheryl takes pride in having pulled everything together. She never could've imagined getting this far along so fast. As a bonus, she even has taken a bunch of stuff to the Dumpster. "I guess I'm not totally out of it yet," she laughs.

She crashes and sleeps till noon. When she awakes, still worn out but pleasantly so, Sheryl spends much of her day recovering from the exhaustive bookkeeping and housekeeping projects, while admiring the orderly folders, files, and notes. She also enjoys seeing tangible results from her forced thinning of things that really had to go—and should have been gone years ago. She can see tabletops.

At dusk, Sheryl retrieves a shredder from storage. She sets it up next to the dining table, which only days earlier she cleared of rubbish to make room for consolidating Sterling's files. By the light of a table lamp, she puts the shredder to work eating up the orderly folders, files, and notes, all the while suppressing conflicting feelings. "Why am I doing this?" she asks herself.

Over the next couple days, she shreds half a dozen large refuse bags' worth of documents. What once looked clear-cut in black and white, on pages upon pages, now is nothing more than impossible paper-puzzles stuffed into oversized plastic sacks. It is mindless work that lets her keep obsessing over how foolish she is to be destroying the only evidence she has of the way Sterling swindled her so badly. Bewildered, she's powerless to stop.

Mentally adrift, she works. Jamaica flashes in her mind's eye for a nanosecond. Next, she's older but no wiser, mailing postcards all over Europe. Then she's back in Jamaica again, turning down Kearns's Florida offer. "Talk about being a fool," she laments. "That was the mother of all the mistakes I ever made, all thanks to Sterling. Everything wrong and bad flowed after that."

Worst of all, she thinks, jumping back to the postcards, she has never even known what the alibi was supposed to cover. Any of several possibilities would be dark, dangerous, even deadly—assuming he did anything at all beyond play her, his specialty. "Deep trouble any way you look at it. Careless me."

On the third morning of the shredding marathon, Sheryl remembers that garbage pickup is the next day. She determines that today she'll set shredding records, clearing out the last chronicles of her long-term lie of a life with Sterling, for good, however bad a thing that might be to do. The number of bags is astounding. More astounding is the story told by her bank records, which show her as pretty much having supported him for ages on lines of credit.

I can't believe what I've done, she thinks while berating herself all day. *I should burn him in court! That's what he fears.* But now that would be all the tougher a task for lack of a paper trail.

Finally, the bagging up of destroyed evidence is complete. After a Dinty Moore dinner, Sheryl turns to the Bible. Of late, she's been avoiding it, not feeling worthy—as a complete hypocrite should feel, in her mind, upon morphing into an unrepentant offender with sins too numerous to list. These acts presumably, or at least possibly, have included some illegal actions, along with many immoral missteps to be sure. She is convinced that hell awaits her.

Try as she may to block such pain from her thoughts, there's no forgetting her multiple woes. It's impossible after Sterling's cleverly timed reminders about everything else wrong in her life, beyond an obvious lack of money. She arrives at the brink of despair. "Those stupid postcards. I'm doomed."

Later, after dark, she schleps the bloated garbage bags via elevator to the compactor outside the back door, next to the Dumpster. Six round-trips of two huge bags each complete her task. A number of neighbors are doing similar garbage-night activities, everyone small-talking about all the latest signs of spring. Her neighbors aren't making multiple trips, so Sheryl uses the same shtick with each group or individual. "Good night," she says to someone new after each of her six trips.

The next night, when the garbage all has been hauled away, Sterling shows up unannounced at her door.

Sheryl, at the peephole, shouts, "How'd you get up here? Go away, Sterling!"

"Just give me one minute, dear, and if you still want me to leave, I'll leave. Promise."

Sheryl wants it to end right now, like countless times before. But as usual, he persists. From the other side of the door, he claims, "Sheryl, I was so out of line and need to apologize."

Sheryl, kicking herself, automatically says, "All right."

Sterling enters full of apologies and romance like she hasn't seen from him in years. She buys his explanation that he's been feeling his own foreclosure pressures and went over the edge. He desperately wants her back, he says. Sweet-talking her, he promises that together they will solve all life's problems.

"Everything closing in on us now will be history in a month," he predicts. "The lawyers are totally confident, good as gold."

"Finally?" she asks with a hint of hope. "Are you sure?"

"I've never been this close to being sure, even when I was sure."

Just as always before, for the moment this sounds so good to Sheryl. Especially in the current crisis mode engulfing her, she craves a little tenderness. The fantasy about long-sought success always seems to convince her to give him one last chance. Just thinking that perhaps Sterling is being sincere can justify much for her in a hurry. She's acutely aware, though, of feeling vulnerable.

Sterling seems to sense her wariness. In a thoughtful manner, he professes, "Life without you, my dear, is worthless. But unfortunately, I can't afford to support you in the style you deserve. This is my shame and our dilemma."

While hearing his claim repeat like a scratched record, she racks her brain, wondering, *What was I thinking a minute ago? Something about what? Darn! Success?*

Sterling looks pleased with himself. "Are you all right, Sheryl? You look a bit confused."

Her defenses hit high alert at the tone of his voice. She barely bats an eyelash before saying matter-of-factly, "My heart is an open sore, Sterling. It may never heal thanks to you."

"Sheryl, I could make similar complaints. I've never given myself so freely and openly before as I have with you, but all I have to show for it is rejection, by you and your family."

She's too numb to laugh in his face. Instead, she remarks, "Well, I certainly reject you now—and the only one you've ever given yourself freely to is you."

"Sorry to hear that. Here I thought, all these years—"

"Thought what?" she interjects. "Give it a rest, Sterling. You outed yourself the other night, remember?"

"Oh yeah, well, you do recall I'm here to apologize, don't you? Because I do apologize. I wrote that thing and said what I said out of not ever knowing where I stand with you."

"Oh, that's rich."

"You're so hostile."

"Listen, Sterling, let's cut to the chase here. For the sake of discussion, it isn't so much that I want to cut off ties. But I'm thinking I have to for self-preservation."

"What if I could come up with a way to prove that I mean to make amends, forever—as in always? Would you hear me out?" He seems so sincere.

"Sterling, you're poison to me. But I'll hear you out."

"Well, as we were saying not so long ago, there's something to be said about being a tragic couple—especially when the couple cements it, the two of them against the world, by going out together."

"What's to be said about killing yourself?" Sheryl often has thoughts of suicide, but the idea of a suicide pact with anyone never has crossed her mind. Yet it almost sounds intriguing, especially once he continues with his pitch and starts talking of their being in the next plane with their child and mothers.

Seemingly sincere, he asks her, "What stronger proof can there be of one's love for another than to fully give up one's own life?"

"And vice versa, you say?"

"Yes, and you have everything here we'd need."

Sheryl is shocked that it suddenly seems they're having a real conversation about taking a suicide oath with each other. How insane! Crazy! But it also feels kind of romantic on a level Sheryl feels dangerously near. Certainly, she's never been here before. But she has been close to committing such madness alone a couple of times, and she almost recognizes and can taste death in their midst, as though the grim reaper beckons with a friendly smile from across the room.

"What's the plan?" she asks. "Just for the sake of conversation, what are you proposing?"

"Homemade poison."

"Simple as that?"

"You got it."

Sterling references her miniwarehouse of drain cleaners, bleaches, polishes, cleansers, rodent traps, paint thinner, and more—all stashed beneath the kitchen sink or in the pantry. Sheryl had no idea how lethal her kitchen had become over the years.

He quips, "It'll be like high school chemistry. I probably can find some pretty good recipes on my cell." Sterling whips out his cell phone, does a voice-command search, and then sticks the phone in Sheryl's face. "Here, check it out," he brags, which strangely she finds intriguing.

She scrolls through several elixirs possibly worth trying, it would seem, with ingredients to spare from her apparent armory. Feeling out of her body and out of her mind, Sheryl hears herself saying, "I say this one," pointing out the recipe link of her choice. "I have this chocolate flavoring in my pantry."

"Well," says Sterling with a grin, "all I can say is pity the poor fool who comes upon our expired, material bodies. Our shorts could be a little soiled, you know."

"At that point who cares?" she laughs, getting caught up in the planning.

"You're hilarious!" he laughs in reply.

They chuckle over the premise a bit. Sheryl, though, feels a need to apply brakes, if she still has any left. "This is crazy talk, Sterling, and it has to stop now."

"Crazy, says who? We're both responsible adults, right? No subject of conversation should be off-limits between us."

Sheryl chortles, "Is that what we're being, responsible adults? You couldn't prove it by what we're talking about—truly, this is insane talk, Sterling."

"I'm just looking at it from the romantic point of view," he rationalizes. "We're star-crossed lovers who've been denied our rightful place in society. Plus here I find out today that my lawyers have no solution after all these years. It's like the rug's been pulled out from under me, and a rude awakening's upon me."

"Upon you? What about us? What about me and all my money? Come on, you've always said your lawyers were sure you'd prevail in the end, no worries. What are you saying now?"

"Ah," he chuckles, "this isn't even about my clothing company. There are some other longtime problems I have to deal with, you know." He grins and adds, "You were there—those court appearances weren't just about any one thing, that's all. You just assumed, sitting out there in the lobbies, that it was always all about the clothing company, right?"

Irritated anew, Sheryl snarls, "And this is how you sweet-talk me into killing myself, supposedly along with you—by bringing up all of your lies?"

"That's the whole point," he says quickly.

"What?"

"Society forces us to most hurt those we love the most. Us, we came together on one plane of my existence, but I had a whole different plane of trouble going on before we ever met."

"Sterling, I'm way past worrying about how we got here, or if you have other saps like me keeping you afloat. But anyway we look at it, my life has become a living hell."

"Mine too! Tell me what is good about this seemingly better level of existence of ours. It's nothing but debt and struggle, with only just a few ever climbing to the top."

"What seemingly better level of existence of ours?" counters Sheryl. "Specifically, I think you're doing just fine." Facetiously, she adds, "If nothing else, you've done a pretty good imitation of being at the top for years—on my money."

"Come on now, Sheryl, that's a low blow, don't you think?"

"Says you. But what does it matter now?" Sheryl fights a big yawn.

"Tired, dear?"

"You kidding? I hardly ever fall asleep before three—and rarely at all anymore without those pills you gave me."

"Oh really?"

"Yes, but sometimes they make me paranoid and give me dark thoughts. So I try staying off them, only it's tough."

"Strange. Those aren't usual side effects. Hmm, when was the last time you took any?"

"Last night, as mostly usual."

"You take one every night?"

"Yes, doctor, except when I'm trying not to."

"You know what—that was a pretty weak dosage I gave you because you're not used to taking medicines. You should double the dosage to get that straightened out. Try it now."

Nervous and wanting to make light of so much sadness, she asks, "What—take pills so that now I can take a nap instead of doing death's song-and-dance with you?"

"Come on, Sheryl, sometimes you say the craziest things. All I want is your happiness."

"Ha, that's rich!"

"Whatever, girl. Just take my advice as a doctor: doubling the dosage still leaves it relatively weak, but it will make a noticeable difference for you. Even if sleep comes slowly, you'll level out your emotions and relax. You need it."

She considers his point. "I am uptight, really uptight," she confesses.

"Dear, I hate to say it, but you're a total fright. Chill now, catch up on relaxation. Sleep."

"You're right," Sheryl decides. "I do need it—some sleep."

"So get some," he says pleasantly. "We'll talk about this new idea of ours after we both get a good night's sleep."

"Sure, Sterling, our new idea. Whatever you say. Good night."

"No rush. Why don't you find your pills? I'll stick around till you get a little drowsy, keep you company."

"Sure, why not?"

Leaving him in the kitchen, she steals away to find her robe. A pocket contains sedatives Sterling has provided. Although she is getting used to them by now, taking her first pill was a real challenge for her, as a lifelong avoider of pills. However, slippage in so many other ways paved the way for more slippage here. Sometimes she thinks she's addicted to these little white pills. "And of course I am."

Downing two pills, a double dose, at her sink, Sheryl can't avoid the mirror and catches sight of dark circles beneath her eyes; it looks like she has raccoon eyes. Her skin is pasty. She touches her normally luxuriant blonde hair, now dry with split ends. Her reflection is hard to recognize. *This is the end*, fears Sheryl more than ever before. *How did it all come to this?* she asks the Lord above, or whoever in another dimension might be listening.

A partial answer comes quickly. *However it came about,* her inner voice says, *it wasn't overnight. It was like a growth apparently misdiagnosed as benign, morphing undetected into the raging cancer that's become this life with Sterling.*

Turning to leave the bathroom, she feels dizzy and lowers herself onto the seat of her vintage toilet. "Only months ago, I was a hero," she tearfully recollects. "Seems like years, though, now," she mumbles, "except when it feels like moments ago."

❧

The Arab Spring's arrival in Tahrir Square starts peacefully enough while privileged partygoers enjoy drinks on the balcony of a grand hotel barely a block away. History, for better or worse, is in the making. Cairo, hub of organized protests across Egypt, buzzes with strident calls for President Hosni Mubarak's resignation. Public-plaza optimists see change ahead for the good. Skeptics fear trouble from many quarters. Realists pulling strings play both for fools.

Leaning against the hotel balcony, a paunchy American in his sixties chuckles, "If this doesn't take you back."

"It takes you back to class, man!" a wise guy hoots. "Nobody ever saw you out on the streets."

Others in the alumni reunion group of gently aging campus hippies share laughs with the wise guy. Bummed, the onetime chuckler has no comeback. The Golden Bear gathering now digs deeply into reminiscences of their Berkeley protest days. Observing everything from the sliding door that leads inside is Sheryl, tour director for this Berkeley booking.

Downwind, downtrodden masses form ever-growing throngs. Dutifully and enthusiastically, they shout rhythmic slogans, waving hope-filled signs while carrying colorful banners. The passionate protestors walk the peaceful-protest walk—till police riot squads suddenly show up, fully armed.

Police release tear gas and open fire with water cannons. Obscenities explode, punctuated by solid strikes from thrown rocks. Both sides give it their all. The police, of course, have the edge, including masks allowing them to breathe. Quickly, they splinter the mob into isolated quadrants of desperate street-fighting resisters.

"Holy shit!" bellows someone up on the Berkeley balcony. It dawns on the California set that the wild scene below quickly could escalate their way. Terrified yet transfixed, they watch live, in person. Some duck below railings for perceived safety reasons, but in truth, such efforts are meaningless. Nowhere in Cairo is safe.

Sheryl shouts, "Don't panic, but everyone, please go back to your rooms." She ducks inside where a ballroom party rages, full of more Berkeley grads of flower-power days. Those dancing the Dirty Dog have no idea that trouble brews outside, homing in, as they are, on their partners with advanced yet subtle groping techniques. At the bar, big drinkers are too busy drinking to notice an overhead TV news update. Other oblivious revelers roam about gabbing and gazing at photos from back in the day.

Sheryl approaches the DJ and asks him to bring down the music and let her borrow the mic. "Sorry to interrupt," she announces to an annoyed crowd, "but you need to be aware that today's protests are turning ugly outside."

That gets their attention.

"Though there is nothing to panic about, I've asked everyone on the balcony to return to their rooms for now. I advise that you all do the same. We will be discontinuing the music, but the food already is laid out, so if you really want to stay here, at least be on the alert. But speaking for Kearns Travel Company, this party, unfortunately, has officially ended."

Someone shouts, "Hey, what about the bar?" A few in the background snicker.

She answers, "That's the hotel manager's decision. I'll check fast and let you know."

"Thank you, Sheryl," one woman shouts to a round of applause.

Sheryl already has returned the DJ's mic, so she waves acknowledgment through the crowd and gets upstairs to her junior suite. Standing at her balcony door, with an eye on the riotous ruckus below, she texts the hotel manager about the bar. He replies that the hotel is safe and authorizes the bartender to stay on duty servicing guests.

With that off her list and knowing time is of the essence, Sheryl calls a trusted ticket agent about changing exit flight plans for her clients. Nothing is available. Disappointed, she calms herself by remembering that this is not her first panic attack in Cairo, having once narrowly missed injury in a minor bomb incident near the pyramids. Additionally, she has been accosted twice on busy streets by roving pickpocket gangs. She knows trouble in Cairo when she sees it. It's here.

As events continue unfolding, daily confrontations at Tahrir Square create unruly crowds at Cairo International Airport. Flights are getting canceled in both directions. Planes on the ground have become scarce. Before long, it's February with no end in sight. For the Berkeley crowd lying low at the hotel, some days run tenser than others, but it's never calm. Power is sketchy; nerves are frayed.

Finally, the US State Department advises all Americans to exit, as if by now the whole world already doesn't know that tourists should leave. Sheryl has known all along. When not working to keep her flock calm, she continues working her cell, seeking flights. One day, she meets with success. "Don't worry, Muhammad! We'll be ready! And thanks!"

She has gained outbound seats for most of her group. The only ones without reservations are those who insisted on making their own arrangements. Some melt into tears as more fortunate ones board an airport shuttle bus. Sheryl counsels the weepers being left behind. "I'm so sorry. Keep trying! And I'll see what I can do at the airport. Something will turn up, don't worry." Privately, disdainfully, she thinks, *Serves you right!* She completes the head-counting of those boarding the bus and climbs aboard after them. Ironically, she herself is one of the unlucky ones without a flight, not that she could leave before the last of her charges anyway. That goes without saying.

En route to the airport, she is praying for a demonstration of God's deliverance from evil when abruptly an incoming call from Muhammad reveals that they have scored two additional plane tickets. Privately praising

God, she's nevertheless highly upset over finding no tickets in it for her and the few remaining others from the alumni excursion. She fights discouragement.

Predictably, it's a long day at Cairo International for Sheryl, who is constantly directing some action or other when not busy interpreting. Shepherding her clients, who are nearly shitting in their pants, drains her to exhaustion. At long last, her final nervous Nellie and arthritic faux-hippie for the day clears airport security. The ashen guy waves appreciatively and disappears from her life.

Amid the vast, stressed crowd, Sheryl stands totally alone. *A tour to remember*, she reflects, overpoweringly saddened, *or forget*. Momentarily unencumbered by responsibility, she wants to collapse in a heap. Yet much remains to be done. She has two tickets to deliver and others to secure.

Back at the hotel, she prays all night. Come morning, there is deliverance again. She secures tickets for the last of the Berkeley crowd, all of whom wisely returned full responsibilities to her able hands the day before. There is still nothing for Sheryl, but ever optimistic—outwardly at least—she boards the bus as chaperone toting her walk-on bag, in hopes that something will pop up before day's end. In transit, she requests, *Meet my needs, Lord. Please meet my needs.* She maintains full faith.

The hot and sticky terminal hums with panicked tourists. Five thousand strong, they clog open spaces and all eateries. Pandemonium reigns. The last Golden Bears somehow don't take too long to send on their way. Once they're gone, Sheryl flows aimlessly within the frantic meandering crowd, until she spots a concourse seat being vacated. She dives for it, gaining possession against stiff competition. Settling into the plastic shell, she allows herself a breath of relief and then grabs her cell and locates Muhammad's number.

"Hey, Muhammad," Sheryl says loudly, fighting to be heard over the background noise. "Me again."

"Oh, hi, Sheryl."

Barely able to hear him, she uses a finger to plug her free ear.

"I was just thinking of you and was going to give you a call."

She's not sure she believes him, but with hopes elevating, she responds, "What do you have, Muhammad? I'm still at the airport, so I'm ready to go!"

"Actually, Sheryl, I just wanted to let you know it's not good news. I can't find anything anywhere right now. But of course, I will keep trying."

Tears well up as Sheryl sighs. "Oh well. Thanks for trying, Muhammad. Just find me something soon, please, anything."

"Of course, Sheryl. I will do my best."

"Thanks again, Muhammad."

Drying her eyes, Sheryl tries Omar, one of Muhammad's competitors. No answer, no voice mail greeting, no nothing. She stuffs away her cell, totally fatigued. *I must have a bed tonight*, she thinks, barely having slept since the onset of all the protests. Mere thoughts of staying at the pungent airport give her the willies. So once again, it's time to brave the crazed city and go back to her hotel, however dreaded and rightfully feared the trip is. What else to do?

Maybe tonight, she thinks hopefully, having no other options, *with everyone out of my hair, finally, I'll be able to fall asleep.* Even as she vacates her chair, it's swarmed.

Outside, there's no line-jousting at the taxi stand. Few others seem to be leaving the airport. Sheryl spots a security squad parting the sea of troubled people, trigger fingers at high alert. She wastes no more time in flagging a cab.

The cabbie barks, "Let's go, let's go!" in broken English.

A normally twenty-minute taxi trek runs well over an hour. In growing darkness, Sheryl and her cabbie endure several tense checkpoints before reaching her downtown hotel. How sad to see the iconic edifice without welcoming lights ablaze. Scattered torches substitute tonight. A cadre of armed guards protects the hotel from looters.

She silently chides herself for even being here. *Hasn't this been in the air for years?* Many of her other Egyptian tours had dangerous moments with assorted incidents, most of which never were reported. In a tortured, private reaction, she reasons, *Why be surprised that the wheels finally have begun to spin?*

The front desk verifies that her room remains available. *No kidding*, Sheryl quips to herself. To the clerk she gratefully says, "Thank you."

From her too-familiar window above Tahrir Square, she reflects on a career track that has taken her to all corners of the globe. She's handled dicey situations in Moscow, mediated temper flare-ups in Kosovo, dodged hurricanes in Jamaica and Puerto Vallarta, dealt with an exploding volcano in Costa Rica, faced personal affronts as a blonde in the Middle East, challenged mobsters in Acapulco, and even talked down a determined jumper at the Golden Gate Bridge. Nothing, though, in the end has ever surpassed this. She survived everything else. Whether she will survive this remains to be seen.

Below, outside on the plaza, torchlights flicker, creating faint flashes against her dirty window's surface. Riot police maintain their vigil. Sheryl wonders if the oppressed are home asleep; or once pressed into action, are they ever even able to sleep?

Refocusing on her own needs, she prays, *Sleep, please, Lord—tonight let me sleep.* Thoroughly exhausted, Sheryl strays from the window. She flops onto the bed fully clothed, yawns with a hippo's ferocity, and stretches out her drained body. Shortly, she falls into a fitful sleep. Dreams come easily; her imaginary body double drifts safely above events at the plaza. Her dreamland includes kaleidoscopic out-of-body views of the hotel lobby.

In the dream, she has just returned from the airport, and she overhears anxious talk in the lobby about Mubarak's having released ten thousand hard-core prisoners to run amok. "Tourists already have been killed!" shouts someone in the lobby.

"They were taking pictures at dusk!" another person harshly retorts.

"Yeah," chimes in a third, "the idiots. What'd ya expect?"

Sunrise returns Sheryl from overnight misadventures to morning's realities. She drags herself to the window. Scores of disenchanted early-bird Egyptians already fill Tahrir Square. They shout revolt mantras with more oomph than the previous day's dispirited crowd. "Ebbs and flows," she deadpans from her overlooking position, sensing that an optimistic atmosphere appears to be regaining traction.

Suddenly anxious to resume her search for a ticket out of here, Sheryl hurriedly dresses and curls up with her laptop in a window chair. However, Wi-Fi is down. "Big surprise," she mutters aloud.

Sheryl passes several more days eavesdropping on living history being made a block away. She reads her Bible and religious journals she has downloaded to her laptop. Praying incessantly, she also keeps her cell phone busy searching for flights out of Egypt.

Finally, word comes from Muhammad as an answer to her prayers. He has used insider local connections to penetrate a newly available waiting list and has gotten her moved up in line. "Get out there by noon!" he insists. "Your flight leaves at four. Don't cut it close."

Sheryl gasps in elation. "Thank you so much, Muhammad! And thank whoever it was that helped make this happen! Gotta run!" Her mostly ready suitcase takes minutes to pack. "Hallelujah, I'm going home!"

She exits the battered hotel that's been her port in the storm. Time to take up the gauntlet once more and brave the ride to the airport. The shuttle scurries through Cairo's hostile streets, surrounded by chaos. Sheryl's mind brings up iconic images of CIA personnel escaping Saigon via chopper off a rooftop.

Just as the last bastion of soldiers anywhere would fear, she does not want to be among the final tourist casualties here. Turning to prayer, she begs, *Please, Lord, get me out of here.* She knows anything still could happen in an instant.

Relief becomes imaginable as the shuttle reaches Cairo International. Ultimately, Sheryl's jetliner fills fast with its cargo of global refugees. Despite everybody's progress in getting this far, doom still hangs in the cabin's stifling air, unwilling to loosen its grip on the fleeing sightseers.

Throughout a white-knuckle liftoff, nobody seems able to let out a breath. Even once the landing gear retracts and their pilot banks for friendlier skies, silence rules. Finally, passengers begin offering fervent prayers in differing tongues. "Thank you, God!" is heard repeatedly in languages from around the world.

Soon enough, the plane levels off, leaving Cairo behind. Joyous pandemonium breaks out, with a cacophony of various victory cheers. Hands reach across aisles as strapped-down strangers reach for anyone with whom to share their glee. Sheryl, as excited as anybody, belts out a loud "Yes!" accompanied by a fist pump, nearly hitting the head of a tall turbaned man sitting in front of her. Raucous chants ring out and spread, despite language barriers. Forms of English dominate early rounds of vocal thanksgiving. In competitive spirit, a few other languages take over one by one.

Everyone feels like comrades-in-arms—appropriately so since most are merely victims of circumstance whose long-sought dream vacations stumbled smack-dab into the middle of hell on earth. For now, at least, all have more in common with each other than they ever could have imagined.

Ultimately, passengers and crew alike begin to laugh a bit—nervous laughter, but laughter nonetheless. Tears of relief follow, and then things begin to quiet down. The realization sinks in that they all still remain far from home. *At least I got my whole group out of there,* Sheryl proudly reminds herself.

As Sheryl leaves her claustrophobic bathroom to rejoin Sterling in her Lincoln Park living room, she carries memories of Cairo with her. She thinks about how she went from her finest working hours into her biggest personal fall. *And it hasn't taken all that long at all.*

Just as he was only months ago, postexodus from Egypt, Sterling again is an unannounced visitor. He is sitting stiffly on the sofa pity perch when she reenters the room. Seeing him there in her hoarder's quarters gives her a sense of helplessness beyond any levels she's ever known. She secretly grieves. *None of this was meant to be.* Sheryl pauses at a dining table chair in what she hopes is an unnoticeable attempt to keep her balance.

Sterling asks, "You all right? I was beginning to worry."

"Sure," she says without conviction, her hand on the back of the chair.

From where she stands amid all the squalor, Sterling almost looks good to her, not to mention he provides ready company, which often has been nice on quick turnarounds between KTC trips. This most redeeming feature of their relationship has spawned continuous growth for them as a couple despite years of tumultuous events and financial pressures. Their many reunions have felt more romantic because they usually have occurred right after travel-induced bouts of absence have made her heart grow fonder; this never seems to fail.

Privately, she ponders, *Who knows? If I hadn't canceled Hawaii and Istanbul, maybe I'd be all starved for him again and susceptible to his baloney.*

"Something on your mind?" asks Sterling.

"Not really. I just kind of blanked out for a few minutes."

"Hey, that's no good. But we've all been there."

"What were we talking about?"

"Before you went to the bathroom, we were talking about mortality."

"Oh yes," she replies, slightly chuckling, "and loved ones in heaven."

"Exactly," affirms Sterling.

With false bravado about their morbid conversation, Sheryl boasts, "Well, I guess I'm way past asking for permission or worrying about a thing. It's a personal choice anyway."

"That's the spirit!" Sterling says.

"Anyhow, what can anybody do about it?"

"Nothing, of course—and the more I think about it, Sheryl," he says very seriously, "the more I believe it's something for us to consider. The two of us, together forever—imagine that."

Light-headed at the thought, Sheryl replies, "Yes, imagine that." Although his words set off warning buzzers in her head, she's powerless to go along with common sense, assuming she still retains any common sense at all. Clearly, the increased dose on those pills is having an effect on her, generally breaking down all senses, common or otherwise. She yawns repeatedly but not in a tired sort of way. Rather, she feels relaxed, so relaxed.

Feeling liberated, she believes she can stave off Sterling's death-wish crusade, quipping, "Keep thinking about it, Sterling—death, life, whatever you choose, for you. Think away. I can't stop that. But count me out."

Sterling shifts gears, asking, "And how goes the shredding, Sheryl? Anything left I could help with? We can work it right into our little party here."

"Never fear, Sterling dear—all done, dumped, and hauled away, today in fact."

In truth, she knows there are unfound things stashed too deeply or in secret places long forgotten and overgrown, things no one ever would want family to find left behind—like that letter, which she can't believe Sterling seems to have forgotten. There are surely other things, too, that his lawyers wouldn't want left lying around, if he even has any lawyers.

If only Sterling knew this, he might not say what he says next. "You always were efficient."

Sheryl's eyes flash at his use of the word "were." Troubled, she remarks, "Well, we're all good at something, right?"

"Yes," he agrees before abruptly declaring, "They say sex is better in heaven."

She unsuccessfully fights off a grin at this claim from nowhere. "Is that right?"

"That's what I hear from reliable sources," he says, smiling.

"Well, how about that?"

Chuckling, he again abruptly changes course. "Hey, we haven't cooked together in ages."

"Huh? Maybe so. What do you have in mind?"

"How about a little kitchen-sink stew?"

Puzzled at first, Sheryl soon recalls his talk of dangerous products stashed around her place. "Very funny," she says without humor.

Sterling snaps his fingers sharply before her eyes, looking deeply into them. "Sheryl, I'm dead serious now. Just listen to me. Are you listening?"

"Yes, I'm listening, Sterling, but I'm not sure I'm liking."

"That's neither here nor there," he says mockingly. "Now, listen and hear me well." In deliberate fashion, he delivers lines Sheryl is sure she's heard from him before. "Your job is done. And you're out of my life." After a beat, he asks, "Do you understand?"

Powerless to think on her own and dizzy to boot, Sheryl mumbles, "Sure."

"Good. And now that you've shred, it's time to make yourself dead. Correct?"

Vacuously, she responds, "Correct," while her brain screams, *What?*

"Good. Now," continues Sterling, lightening his tone, "let's have some fun with this."

"Fun?"

"Absolutely, you'll see. You play sous chef to my diva chef down on hard times."

"How clever," Sheryl replies.

Sterling does a recipe search on his cell again. Finding an abundance of deadly formulas, he directs Sheryl to retrieve various ingredients from either under her sink or inside the pantry. One main element is drain cleaner, a must according to the Web, thickened with scouring powder—and with a little insect spray thrown in for good measure. Right before Sheryl's second visit to the pantry, she notices Sterling quickly stirring in something from a small bottle that she doesn't remember helping him find.

He seems to notice her scrutiny and humorously instructs, "Stay on task now, super sous chef of mine. See what else is in the pantry."

"Right away, sir," she responds, almost without thinking.

Sheryl returns with ammonia as an activator for their foaming fuel. "This is some recipe, all right." She nervously laughs, hovering mentally at the brink as he adds the activator agent.

Sterling quips, "People will come from miles around for a taste of the real thing."

She is totally freaking out and knows it. Losing her sly, sarcastic smile during a dizzy backstep, she staggers but recovers to drift in shock along the narrow passageway through stuff that zigzags around the junction of her kitchen and living room. A bad rush courses up from her ankles to the top of her head, bringing on involuntary arm flapping that tells her just how out of control she is.

Her mother's face floats above her as an apparition. It is an angry face, out of character for Ruth. Sheryl feels outed on many levels and sobs, calling out to her mom in front of Sterling.

"Sheryl, you're here with me," Sterling says, "so be calm." He gently adds, "But if you want to, you can be seeing your mother by dawn, for real. Think about that."

Spacey, sad, and several beats behind in the conversation, Sheryl answers with silence. She takes the ammonia back to the pantry.

"Are we done yet?" she asks from the pantry. "Need anything else?"

"Yes, my dear, we're done," he responds from the kitchen. "So all we need is for the queen to join her king for a toast!"

Returning empty-handed and glum, she mutters, "I can hardly wait."

Sterling is at the sink, carefully filling the second of two glasses with toxic-looking liquid. Once he has finished pouring, he smiles warmly at her and sets down the glasses on what little space serves as open countertop. "And so the time has come," he says ominously.

Speechless, she can't believe that her life, once so promising, has led to this dead end. *It must be a mirage*, she vainly hopes one last time.

He picks up both glasses, offering one to Sheryl. She stares at the frothing glass in her hand and boldly declares, "You go first! When I see that, I'll know you're serious."

Sterling deliberately puts down his glass and takes hers away, carefully placing it near his. He warmly pulls her into an embrace and brushes back tangled hair from her still-pretty face. "How long till you believe in me again?" he asks. "If I have to prove my love with a demonstration, so be it." Sterling checks his watch and concludes, "I can't catch the next bus, but the one after that will be a cinch. So just before I leave, I'll drink mine down in front of you."

Sheryl recoils in anger. "Leave? Where's the romance in a suicide pact if we don't literally go out together? This is sounding pretty sketchy to me."

"Oh, don't misunderstand me, dear—I'd much prefer holding hands as we leave this world, fused together. Only what's the biggest factor in our both being so up against it all? Financial ruination! Foreclosure tyranny! Thanks to banks, lawyers, and politicians. So we should tie our deaths to that, dying in our own homes, in hopes the dual headlines might help others get a break."

"This is all news to me," gripes Sheryl. "I'm not looking to be a martyr."

"It's something good we can do for society. But we have to do our demonstration individually in our own homes."

"I thought this was about us, like Romeo and Juliet?"

"Of course it is. But why not publicly tie our deaths to this foreclosure orgy?"

"Tell me, why?"

"It will be our gift to hundreds, thousands, of poor souls lured into these bad loans."

Grudgingly, with it still rubbing her wrong, she buys into his spiel. Despondent anyway, she feels like she's painted herself into a corner. "Yeah," she sighs. "Sure, I get it. Something good for others. Always first taking care of others."

"Absolutely, darling," he confirms with a kiss.

"What about taking care of me—and us?"

"Once we're reunited on the other side, the devil himself couldn't pry us apart."

"How comforting."

Theatrically, he predicts, "With any luck, the bus driver will catch all green lights, and I'll be home before I start gassing up. I certainly don't want to croak on a bus!"

That gets Sheryl smiling, wishing he would croak in a bus. How perfect. Together, they share disingenuous chuckles. She's mostly back in shock mode, tuning him out as much as possible. Sterling rechecks his watch and then dramatically chugs down his sickening solution.

While hugging and kissing Sheryl, Sterling slips the empty glass into a pocket, further instructing, "Leave your foreclosure and dunning notices on the table."

"Nobody will have to look far to find all that."

He smiles like a wolf, promising, "I'll be looking for you in the next plane."

Sheryl can't think and talk simultaneously yet somehow manages to respond, "I'll be looking for you too," but there is no tenderness behind the words.

At the door, Sterling emphasizes, "Don't forget to lock up tight from inside."

"That's routine."

"Good."

Before edging away further, he adds, "Don't forget to drink your pop, my love. That wouldn't exactly be playing fair since I've already finished mine, now would it?"

"No, dear, it wouldn't," Sheryl says in an obedient monotone. She figures her deadpan face betrays her resignation to suicide. Something beyond her comprehension is compelling her along this crazy path without any brakes. Certainly, there is no enthusiasm for the journey.

Sterling seems to question her sincerity, though. Sternly, he says, "Hey, listen, this is no joke. We have a deal—kissed on it. I'll be bleeding my guts out soon enough for you."

She declares clearly, "You know my word is good." Inwardly, truth be told, Sheryl is horrified at feeling in some way obligated to down her own glass. She's anxious for him to leave. "Go! You don't want to miss that bus."

Contrarily, Sterling removes his hand from the doorknob. "I'll sit and die at your neighbor's door if you don't drink that stuff now, while I'm watching. A deal's a deal. Time for games is over."

She struggles, wondering whether or not to drink. *To hell with him!* she thinks.

However, Sterling stares her down in his well-practiced manner. She looks away, lost. Her meandering gaze takes in a tight panorama symbolizing the overall mess she's made of her life. Nightmarish living conditions conspiring with thoroughly spent emotions succinctly summarize her plight, more clearly than ever.

"Much to regret, little time to wallow," she soberly grumbles.

"Say what?" Sterling barks like an impatient drill sergeant.

"Nothing," squeaks Sheryl. Softly, she adds, "Okay, you're right. A deal's a deal."

Immediately gentler, he says, "I knew your integrity would win out."

"I don't know about that anymore. But I guess this life of mine—ours, whatever—with so many years of lies in the making, won't be too much to miss. I guess."

"You're doing the right thing, dear. We're doing the right thing. And we'll be reunited before you know it, in a better place—with those gone before us, for sure."

"Right, I guess. We'll see."

"Don't worry, Sheryl. You will see."

"If you say so."

With great deliberation, as though coming out of an isometric clench, she slowly raises the foul glass to her lips and drinks it down. Its rancid taste immediately sticks to her taste buds, coating her tongue. The frothy mixture freefalls fast into Sheryl's stomach, churning her innards. *Panic!* screams her entire nervous system.

With a smirk, Sterling simply says, "Good girl," and leaves.

Sheryl locks up behind him using several door bolts she's always been proud about having installed on her own, thanks to a toolbox Dad long ago put together for her. *Got pretty handy, I guess*, she thinks, grievously reflecting on her part in this do-it-yourself project gone wild. "What's done is done," she says quietly, fully terrified over the internal bonfire blowing apart her innards.

Grimly, she forces a faint smile at what she fears will be her last clever thought. *I'm going nowhere fast, forever inconsequential.*

Sheryl coils herself up on the sofa, cradling her belly as though pregnant. She can feel the motion of gut-wrenching roiling substances with her fingertips. It is indescribably awful. "Ow!" she cries against ruthless pain. Suddenly, she thinks, *Water!* It could be her only possible salvation.

She staggers to the kitchen sink. Opening the cold faucet, she sticks her mouth directly on the spigot, sucking down as much water as possible. An instinctive will to survive says maybe she has a chance since she's not been eating much lately. There's nothing in there to slow anything down, so maybe she can push the poison through as fast as possible—speed counts! The body can recover!

"Ginger ale!" she shouts in pain. Taking two quart bottles of ginger ale to the bathroom, she vows to beat Sterling's elixir with a homemade remedy of her own. Her spirits rise to midlevel, about as high as can be expected under these circumstances. Sitting on the toilet, gulping down gaseous pop, she replays the memory of Sterling swallowing his own deadly brew. A pleasant idea crosses her mind—perhaps Sterling was hit like this even before he made it to the bus. *How perfect if he were to die on the street,* she dreams for an instant before segueing into sobbing. "How did this happen?" she cries out. She's at a loss to explain, and ginger ale is not the cure. "My God! What now? Please get me out of this! I swear I'll get it together! Please!"

Soliloquies halt at the sudden onrush of bloody stool. Severe intestinal burning follows, and nerve-rattling pain races through her entire nervous system. Electrical jolts flash ancient memories onto a corner screen of her mind, even while elsewhere, the realization sets in that imminent death approaches; the end, barring a miracle, is forthcoming. Groaning deeply, coarsely, at the edge of disaster, feeling like a self-murderer, Sheryl wonders, *Am I headed for hell or purgatory? Lord knows it won't be heaven.*

Verging on heaving, she jumps up and turns around to face the bowl, and not a second too soon, as a bloody mess erupts, splattering the seat. Contaminated toilet water splashes into her face. Cheeks dripping vilely, she staggers to the tub, shedding her pants in the process. Climbing in, she turns on the shower, using a flexible hose to deliver a powerful enema. *Just gotta dilute this crap!* she thinks desperately.

Competing voices inside her head alternately cheer or jeer. A voice exclaiming, "Go for it!" shouts down one saying, "Forget about it, girl"— for the moment, anyway. However, her lower intestine explodes, splattering around her feet, quickly collecting in the backup of a slow drain. Surely, the ugly stew contains intestinal linings. Blood tints the broth red as it rises up above her ankles. *Blood and guts*, her remaining wit interjects. *Maybe this is how a battlefield looks. My final battlefield.*

Need being the mother of invention, for good measure she shoots the hand-held spray down her throat, chugging away till the volume of water she's absorbed seems surreal. She towels off and pulls on her robe, watching her own movements as though out-of-body, looking down on her last private performance. What a show. Scurrying about her cluttered world cradling her sore gut, she anxiously seeks her misplaced cell phone. Realizing it won't be found, she is shattered at not even being able to dial 911. *It's probably cut off, anyway*, she thinks.

With time at a premium, Sheryl pulls on replacement pants to at least go out with a little dignity. She settles down on the sofa. Thankfully, the puking urge has dissipated. This gives her a peaceful moment to reflect on the reality of the end being near, very near. *Oh my God*, she suddenly thinks, *my family! If I'm found like this, it'll kill them!*

Another rumble in her gut says there will be no surviving this quandary. She thinks again of her family; now it will be plain for them to see, without a doubt, just how foolish she has been over so many years. A veil of shame crashes down upon her. "What have I done, Lord?" she cries out loudly.

A bloody mess sops through her pants. Sheryl knows now for certain that nothing good can come from this, nothing short of death, and she's almost there. It has to be better than this. "I'm doomed," she whispers. "Some legacy I leave." She wants to cry in the worst way but can't. There's no more allowance for tears. Not a drop. Waterworks have gone dry. *Too bad—because maybe one can cry oneself to death*, she hypothesizes. Feeling faint, she guesses, *This is it.*

Sleep comes upon her but brings no REM.

Elsewhere, north on Lake Shore Drive, as Sterling settles into bed, he thinks about how his final performance on Sheryl's stage played out flawlessly—right down to the smuggling in of arsenic for her and a flask of nasty but not deadly brew for him. *Just an old-fashioned shell game.* He laughs to himself and drifts off to sleep like a baby. He needs his beauty rest for a night of dancing at the Drake. Proving indeed that he is an equal-opportunity opportunist, his newest mark is a wealthy widow from Kenwood who's already smitten with good Dr. Jackson.

◦◦◦

Back in Lincoln Park, before long, sunlight glimmers on a watery horizon outside Sheryl's window. As the sun emerges from below the waterline, its powerful beams of light ricochet off Lake Michigan, breaking through Sheryl's dusty windowpanes to awaken her. She can't believe that it's already daybreak or that she's still alive.

Instantly, with the intuitive power gained from having slept on something, it dawns on her that Sterling might have pulled a sleight of hand in their insane toast last night, or that he might have had some antidote to take in the elevator ride to the lobby. "Duped again, maybe," she taunts herself. "The final insult. That asshole!" The more this thought sinks in, the more she gets beyond "might have."

She is fully awake fast, with the nonstop pain tossing Sterling from her mind. "This is unbearable, Lord," she whispers. "What's taking so long? I just want it to end!"

Unable to linger longer on the sofa, this being her last daybreak—a thought hard to handle—she flops to the floor and splays out, recalling moments when she wondered, *How does it feel?* Or more to the point, *How would it feel to off oneself?*

After concluding that feeling sorry for oneself is the lone balm that cuts the pain, even if only ever so slightly, she figures offing oneself simply is the ultimate form of self-pity, unless a person is mentally unhinged, drunk, or on drugs. She knows she's not drunk. Diving further into loss of self-respect, she stares straight up from her position on the floor. The ceiling itself now is spinning. Yet her mind multitasks like never before. Rationalizing away the revolving ceiling as a mirage of her hemmed-in world, Sheryl feels everything grind down to slow, so slow.

It's the homestretch, ready or not. The ceiling rotations pick up speed. Stars dance like fireworks on the periphery of her vision, as if real. Hinting that death's sharp edge draws near, these brightly popping constellations steady the spinning ceiling somehow, seeming to bring a sense of calm. Equilibrium returns.

She gets to her feet, thinking about a speech for St. Peter, as if she will have a chance of meeting him. *He and the Lord above must be furious with me,* she tells herself. A surge of stinging tears drains any remaining spine from her backbone. Limp, she falls back to the floor. "Throwing away life like this," she murmurs. The ceiling spins ever faster. "When do actual flashbacks begin?"

Sheryl sobs upon remembering she already has had some. In reality, they've been coming for months, leaving her to wonder how long she has really been trekking along this death march. Her busy bowels interrupt her thoughts. Though near death, she still can't allow herself to unload where she's flopped, if avoidable, and she senses she can make it to the bathroom. "Let this be the last toilet run," she says as she stands up and stumbles down the hall.

In her cramped but familiar bathroom, sitting for the last time upon her trusty toilet, Sheryl decides one final shower is appropriate. Climbing into the tub is a struggle, and she shortens the process by cleaning up only below the waist, but by the time she's toweling down, she is glad for having made the effort. She opts for a sweatshirt and jeans, trying again to look not so bad while speculating about who will find her. Maybe days from now, her odor will attract attention.

Hold on! an inner voice calls out. *I can't just sit here and die! This is too much!* She fears both eternal punishment and an agonizingly slow death while trapped in her own home, and even higher levels of panic kick in than before. Waiting it out in itself could be a fate worse than death. At warp speed she develops another theory: what if the poison worked just well enough to almost kill her, and she'll be found alive? However, surviving with the damage done would be devastatingly tragic. *No quality of life left, that's for sure*, she rationalizes.

Beyond treatment, rehabilitation, and expenses, it would take great dedication, a huge effort. And all the while, she would be depressed about how it had come to be. Then there would be the humiliation. That never would end. *And how would I eat? What could I eat?* she wonders.

Sheryl wonders if her thoughts are profound or pathetic. Regardless, thoughts come so fast that she can't keep up with them. The bottom line, though, is that the only escape from this wretched predicament is to jump. Or so she sees it. *Come on, it's not like I haven't ever thought of it before*, she thinks, with her usually living high above the ground whether at home or on the road. Such thoughts have come even more lately, since the now-obvious coaching Sterling gave her coming back from American Cuisine. So as much as the idea of jumping scares her, reeling from excruciating pain, she moans, "Jumping's the only way. Do it! I say do it!"

By this moment, the sun's rising presence is growing stronger through her bedroom window. As her plan develops, that favored window becomes her doorway to the next plane. Its view is among her favorites anywhere around the world. Over the years, how glorious it has been for the globe-trotting traveler to know, upon returning home, that this view awaits.

Zeroing in on the view, Sheryl takes comfort in thinking, *How much more appropriate could it be than to leave this world by stepping through that window into the next? No turning back now*, she decides. *I'm going down for the count taking one last glimpse of the lake.*

That leaves only the writing of her epitaph—which won't take long, she realizes in a bummer rush. Forever after, most everyone will remember her for having gone out a jumper, before anything else comes to mind. She knows so from her own previously held views on jumpers. *How grim*, she thinks, *but I understand. That's the lasting impression.*

Sheryl opens her window, immediately focusing outside on the air conditioner's through-the-wall extension. It provides an extra ledge beyond the small windowsill for her to utilize in doing this deadly deed—a perfect launching pad.

Her hyperactive mind jumps back to that American Cuisine night, when she and Sterling returned home stealthily via the Dumpster door. She looked up at her window from the ground, and eyeballing the distance in the dark, she figured it'd do the job. However, going out in tandem with Sterling on a suicide pact was way off her radar then. "That darn pact," she grouses, knowing it ultimately is what has brought her here. Nevertheless, in a clear moment of honesty, she reasons, "I've maybe been on the brink of this for ages." But who's to say Sterling also didn't have a hand in those previous flirtations with the brink?

She studies the utility room roof below, guessing that to avoid it, she would need to jump out and away from the building about ten feet. *Ten feet? No way!* she concludes. But landing on the utility roof would make this most likely only an eight-story fall, not nine. *Is that enough?* wonders Sheryl. *I don't want to live through this!* After brief reflection, she concludes, *I'll just lead with my head. That should work.*

Suddenly, she considers all the heavy-duty obstacles outside the utility room near the back door. Basically, it's dicey ground, a garbage dump for her entire building. So even if some miracle or updraft were to launch her ten feet out from the window, she could end up in the compactor. She almost chuckles at the thought. *Or, as bad, it could be the Dumpster*, she thinks. *Not funny.*

Sheryl shoves up the window as high as possible. Even still, it's a small opening to duck through for air conditioner access. Seconds later, she can't believe she's crouching outside the brick exterior of her building's walls. Terrified, she has no words, just steady breathing as survival mode self-starts. She wants off this perch, safely.

Way below, fanning out a block or so, early-morning foot traffic, complete with someone happily whistling, foretells a brilliant spring day to come. Sheryl predicts that this day, one way or another, more than her birthday, forever will be her day. Time will tell.

Sharply interrupting from somewhere nearby, a woman's voice urgently shouts out, "Hey! What are you doing, dear girl? Please! Get back inside!"

Her high-pitched plea for sanity makes Sheryl twitch and nearly fall. Catching her balance, she breathes a sigh of relief and then scans the rush of people and vehicles fanning out below to points beyond. Everybody and everything is coming alive for the day, except her in this mad dash to die. Some pedestrians stop in their tracks, looking up at her. One pedestrian hollers out, "Don't jump! Don't do it!"

The first voice again desperately pleads, "Please, my dear, get back inside!"

These ringing voices bring more bystanders to observe this developing drama. Sheryl, not wanting to fall, carefully rises from her crouch to stiffly force herself into a standing position. She leans back against the upper window, looking down across the courtyard to a neighboring high-rise from where the first shouts came.

An elderly woman on a lower balcony frantically waves hello. "Please," she begs of Sheryl, "go back inside! There is help for you. I will find help for you!" The woman pauses before sweetly saying, "Now go back inside, dear. You will be so glad that you did."

Sheryl is numb. Her brain is fumbling over what to do next. Nervously, she kneels down and slowly backs up into her bedroom.

Down below across the courtyard, the elderly woman joyously shouts inside to give someone an update for 911. On the street, a cop car pulls up, attracted by the commotion. Leaving his car double-parked with all lights flashing, he joins the little clot of pedestrians and runners that has formed near Sheryl's window. Word filters around that a crisis has been averted, so most get back on their way to somewhere. The cop, of course, sticks around and calls the precinct for paramedics.

Inside her bedroom, Sheryl thinks, *Okay, I'm back inside, but now what?* Blood and other internal fluids, some of which may once have been solids, continue oozing out of her. Intolerable pain runs rampant. *No getting around it—I have to jump.* Embarrassment alone over this public scene would be icing on an insane cake if she were to survive. She wants no part of it. It's that simple. End of discussion. "I'm out of here," she announces.

Experienced now, she's back outside on top of the air conditioner in a standing position before she knows it. It's a long way down, but maybe not that long. The question remains: Will this even work? Her new mantra: "Lead with the head." Thinking now of rumors—there are so many rumors on this subject—she wonders, will she black out just before the end, escaping pain as some claim? From where Sheryl stands, certainly there will be pain.

Interrupting her thoughts from below, the cop hollers at the top of his lungs, "Don't do it! It's not worth it!" From the crowd someone adds, "Please don't jump!" The balcony lady returns outside, horror-struck, but refrains from shouting, probably in fear of overloading her nervous neighbor.

Suddenly, the air conditioner shifts under its heavy load. Sheryl's balance swings beyond control. Reflexive instincts kick in, and she uses her last millisecond of contact with the AC unit to fool herself into thinking she's retained footing on something, anything.

But no, this is the end; she knows it within the next millisecond. The springing liftoff has sent her plummeting headfirst toward earth. Leading with her head is a wish fulfillment.

For all to hear, she shrieks, "Oh my God!" A territorial warble from a red-winged blackbird echoes her shriek, sparking a flashback to bungee jumping at New Zealand's Kawarau Bridge. Talk about total déjà vu. Her mind frees itself from fear, knowing only exhilaration from this dark tie to happier days down under.

But somehow in slow motion the utility room roof looms ever closer for Sheryl. *Take your time*, she hopes against hope, wishing she could reverse her position, getting her legs into play for the landing. Maybe then she'd stave off death, giving medical science a shot at building some sort of gastrointestinal tract for her. It's a fleeting thought pinched for time. The flashback spell is broken.

Sheryl utters a sorrowful "Oh boy," followed by a last inner quip—*Bummer, no tether to the rescue here.* She'll take whatever the point of impact gives. No blacking out as per urban legend. It won't be pretty. Well, she'd feared this would be the case.

Her head thuds onto the utility room's flat roof, bouncing up like a ball, and she loses the ability to think. The weight of her lower body flips her over for the last stage of descent, and she lands at the foot of the compactor one floor down, splat on the ground, no rebound, only nothingness. That fast, over and done.

"Oh no!" someone screams from the sidewalk. Other onlookers also scream in horror or choke up at a loss for words. The balcony lady faints. Her husband appears outside to attend to her needs. Sirens approach fast in the background. They'll be way late and unable to put Sheryl back together again.

Witnesses stand stunned from what's just happened before their morning eyes. One grizzled cop who thought he'd seen it all knows that neither the images nor the spine-tingling soundtrack ever will vanish from his mind. He shakes in his shoes as he calls the precinct with surface details. Detectives soon will conclude unassisted suicide, despite lack of a note. Her door having been locked from inside is all they will need to see—an open-and-shut case. The event is heartbreaking, but no bold headlines will be found in back pages.

Meanwhile, out over Lake Michigan, the heavens' brilliant metronome continues its rapturous ascent, its rising glory reflecting off mirror-still waters. Sadly, few in the big city even see it. Whether they see it or not, for many Chicagoans a promising day to come still hangs hopefully in hallowed air.

Sheryl, however, who knew sunrises here better than anyone, has no clue about this one, no admiring input about its amazing visuals. She has no place in this world anymore, evermore. The world, however, survives without her.

But that is not to say it will be quite the same.

Printed in the United States
By Bookmasters